I0781490

The Library of Second Chances

Praise for Savannah Carlisle

"Carlisle's novel is thoughtful, with well-developed characters who move beyond common small-town girl and big-city boy tropes. Instead, she pulls together two characters who turn out to have far more in common than they think."—*Kirkus Reviews*

"I was completely enchanted by this charmingly sweet beach read and just adored the letters exchanged in the Little Free Library."—**Teri Wilson, *USA Today* bestselling author**

"Fans of 'You've Got Mail' will swoon over Lucy and Logan in this charming romance that celebrates the splendor of small-town living."—**KJ Micciche, author of *The Book Proposal***

"After reading *The Library of Second Chances*, Savannah Carlisle is now one of my go-to authors for heartwarming, Kleenex-clutching, feel-good romance!"—**Annie Rains, *USA Today* bestselling author**

"...Savannah Carlisle's debut is sure to delight . The author's vivid descriptions put me right in Heron Isle along with the characters and had this city girl longing for the cozy and picturesque small-town life she masterfully depicted."—**Meredith Schorr, author of *As Seen on TV* and *Someone Just Like You***

The Library of Second Chances

SAVANNAH CARLISLE

HARPETH ROAD
PRESS®
Nashville

HARPETH ROAD PRESS

Published by Harpeth Road Press (USA)
P.O. Box 158184
Nashville, TN 37215

Paperback: 979-8-9887744-1-9
eBook: 979-8-9887744-0-2

The Library of Second Chances: A Heartwarming Summer Romance

Copyright © Savannah Carlisle, 2024

All rights reserved. Except for the use of brief quotations in review of this novel, the reproduction of this work in whole or in part in any format by any electronic, mechanical, or other means, now known or hereinafter invented, including photocopying, recording, scanning, and all other formats, or in any information storage or retrieval or distribution system, is forbidden without the written permission of the publisher, Harpeth Road Press, P.O. Box 158184, Nashville, Tennessee 37215, USA.

Quotations from pages 49, 132, 260 of *The 5 Second Rule: Transform your Life, Work, and Confidence with Everyday Courage* reproduced by permission of Post Hill Press, publishers and Mel Robbins, author. Further reproduction, distribution, or transmission is prohibited, except as otherwise permitted by law.

Little Free Library® is a registered trademark of Little Free Library, a 501(c)(3) nonprofit organization, and is used with its permission. Little Free Library is not affiliated with Harpeth Road Press.

This is a work of fiction. Names, characters, places, and incidents are the product of the author's imagination or were used fictitiously, and any resemblance to actual persons, living or dead, business establishments, events, or locales is entirely coincidental.

Cover Design by Kristen Ingebretson
Cover images © Shutterstock

First printing: May, 2024

To my mom, who's been taking a red pen to my writing since kindergarten. And to my dad, who loves Hallmark movies as much as me. Thank you both for teaching me I could be anything I want to be!

ONE

Lucy

"Spill! You got another one, didn't you?" Lucy Sullivan's best friend, Taylor Donovan, screeched so loudly she scared off three seagulls roosting on the beach a few steps from them.

Lucy tried to suppress a bubbling feeling of excitement, instead taking particular interest in a pelican diving for its breakfast out over the water.

"They're just book recommendations." Looking down, she flipped over the pointed top of a conch shell with her toe, hoping to find the rest still intact, but it was only a fragment of the original shell.

Taylor grabbed the book Lucy was holding and skipped ahead, her long brunette ponytail swishing behind her. "They're not just book recommendations." She turned around to face Lucy and began walking backward. "No one else leaves notes in the library addressed to specific people."

Taylor was referring to the Little Free Library Lucy had installed downtown after the town's original library was forced to close due to lack of funding. It was for people to trade used books with others in the community. Lucy had the idea to leave index cards and pencils inside for those who left a book to write a note telling others why they might enjoy it.

Readers rarely signed their notes with their real name, instead making up fun monikers like "Hopeless Romantic" à la *Sleepless in Seattle*. In a small town where everyone knew everyone, it had become a fun game to try to guess people's monikers. Was Bob Newhouse, the carpenter and hardware store owner, secretly a fan of romance novels? She'd noticed the same male handwriting on notes left in Nora Roberts's and Nicholas Sparks's books, so it had to be a local.

As Lucy reached out to take the book back from Taylor, something fluttered from inside the novel and fell onto the sand. She managed to snag it as Taylor turned the book upside down and shook it to see if anything else would dislodge from between the pages. Lucy had already hidden the index card with its personalized note in her pocket before meeting up with Taylor, so she was surprised something else had been tucked inside.

"Ooh, what's that?" Taylor returned to Lucy's side, giving her a conspiratorial shoulder bump.

"It's a map of Paris," Lucy said, fighting the sea breeze to straighten out the map so they could both see. She tucked her shoulder-length blonde hair behind an ear to keep it out of her face.

"Not just any map of Paris." Taylor jabbed a finger at one of the handwritten notes on the map, which said: *Brasserie Flottes—best onion soup in Paris.* "It's a *personalized* map of Paris." She raised an eyebrow at Lucy.

Taylor was right. The map was filled with little arrows and notes pointing out restaurants, bookstores, galleries, and there were even a few spots marked: *Take a book here for the afternoon*.

Lucy had been exchanging notes with a mystery user of the Little Free Library for a couple weeks. It had started after she'd left a copy of *Gatsby's Girl*, a novel about F. Scott Fitzgerald's first love, who was thought to be the inspiration for Daisy Buchanan in *The Great Gatsby*. The next time she visited the library, Lucy was surprised to find someone had attached a sticky note to a book addressed to her moniker: Island Girl.

Inside the book, there was an index card with a note referencing *Gatsby's Girl* and a suggestion that she might like the novel they'd left, *West of Sunset*, which focused on F. Scott and Zelda Fitzgerald. The person thanked her for opening his eyes with the book she'd left, commenting that he knew what it was like to lose himself in a relationship the way Zelda had. He'd signed his note, Gatsby's Ghost.

Lucy loved historical novels, so it had been easy to pick out another suggestion for her fellow reader, and she'd left *The Paris Wife*, a novel about Ernest and Hadley Hemingway. They'd been going back and forth like that for weeks now, plowing through books focused on the 1920s. Lucy had never met anyone who read as quickly as she did. One of the advantages to owning a bookstore was having plenty of downtime for reading.

"What did the note say?" Taylor asked as she turned the book over to look at the back cover description. It was a guide to the most beautiful walks in Paris.

Lucy reluctantly pulled the index card from the pocket of her shorts. Something about showing it to Taylor felt like sharing a secret she held with its author, but she reasoned that Gatsby's Ghost had left it in a public place where anyone could have read it. She unfolded it and read out loud, "'Island Girl, I don't believe in bucket lists. If you want to do something, you should just do it. Until you can get to Paris, however—and you *must* go to Paris—enjoy this tour. Gatsby's Ghost.'"

"Sounds like he wants to be your tour guide," Taylor said, grinning as she nodded at the map in Lucy's hand. "How'd he know you've never been to Paris?"

Lucy shrugged. "It was in the note I put in the first book he read."

"A man who listens. I like this guy already."

"We don't actually know it's a guy."

"I saw the handwriting on that last note. And 'Gatsby's Ghost'? Definitely a guy." Taylor nodded. "It's just so romantic. It's like *You've Got Mail* but in a Little Free Library."

Lucy laughed. "Yeah, well hopefully he's not here to open a chain bookstore and drive me out of business." As soon as the words were out of her mouth, Lucy's mind began racing. What if it was some guy in town scouting a spot for his chain bookstore in the new development that had been proposed? Construction had been halted for now, but she knew the town council was still trying to push their agenda of adding retail space on the downtown waterfront. If the last plans she'd seen were any indication, the only types of businesses that would be able to afford the leases would be luxury stores or big chains that survived on volume.

She shivered at the thought despite the warm June sun rising over the ocean to her left. "You don't think that's going to happen, do you?" Lucy's eyes were wide when she turned to Taylor.

"Of course not." Taylor reached over to rub Lucy's arm as they continued their walk. "We fought the big bad developers and we won." Taylor punched and jabbed at the air as if she were a champion fighter.

Enjoying her friend's banter, Lucy looked out over the water. The sun had transformed from a fiery blur creeping up from the horizon into a giant yellow ball in the sky in the short time it had taken them to walk down the beach. The best friends loved walking the beach when they could find time, starting from the marina at the edge of historic downtown Heron Isle and finishing at Lucy's cottage, but lately they'd been too busy to do it often.

They continued walking along the tide line, the foamy edge of approaching waves nipping at their bare feet. The gentle lapping of low tide was a different tone altogether from that of high tide, which would come in a mere six hours, the sound of the waves reverberating off the dunes to create a noise that could drown out even the high-pitched shrieks of small children running into the water with abandon while their parents watched from nearby towels.

Thumbing through the book, Taylor stopped in a place where Gatsby's Ghost had underlined a passage and written a note in the margin. At first, Lucy had been horrified someone would defile a book in such a way, but she found she loved feeling as if she was reading along with a friend.

Next to her Taylor read out loud, "'I learned you can love a city in much the same way you love a person. For me, Paris was love at first sight. I stood on the Pont Alexandre III spanning the Seine, and time stood still even though my heart was racing.'"

Taylor closed the book and held it to her heart in her trademark dramatic fashion. "He sounds so romantic. I wish Jack still wrote me notes."

Taylor and Jack had been dating for the past two years. As Taylor told Lucy about the notes Jack used to leave hidden around the house for her to find anytime he traveled, a familiar Great Dane appeared running toward the water from the dunes. The figure that emerged next was Pam Beasley, a fellow downtown business storekeeper and Ava the Great Dane's owner. Pam was holding her sandals and wearing a wide-brimmed straw hat and a blue linen coverup dress.

Lucy waved and she and Taylor began to angle up the beach in Pam's direction. Lucy and Taylor always wore athletic shorts and tank tops for their summer morning walks, but twenty years their senior, Pam was always meticulously dressed. Her love of clothes had led her to open the island's only consignment store, which was a thriving business on their little island.

Ava returned from the surf with a tennis ball in her mouth and dropped it at Pam's bare feet to initiate a game of catch. Pam threw the ball toward the water and Ava took off, scaring birds hunting for their breakfast along the shoreline.

"Mornin' ladies—"

"He left her another one!" Taylor waved the book she was still holding as if it was a winning lottery ticket.

"A letter in the Little Free Library?" Pam's eyes grew wide, a smile spreading across her face as she looked to Lucy for confirmation.

"Yes! That makes, what—half a dozen or more now?" Taylor turned to Lucy.

Lucy rolled her eyes to show she wasn't taking it nearly as seriously as Taylor. "We just have the same taste in books." Lucy shrugged. "He could be ninety. Or maybe it's not even a *he*."

"What if *he* is handsome and available?" Taylor was smiling like the Cheshire cat.

Lucy frowned. "Then he's just passing through." In a tiny town like this, more than an hour away from a major metropolitan area, it was unlikely he was a single man her age. Men like that were usually only there on vacation or working a brief stint at one of the resorts located outside of the historic district until a promotion took them somewhere else.

It was both a blessing and a curse that she loved her sleepy little town. Its relaxed vibe and slow growth meant it was only a stepping stone for men like Taylor's boyfriend, Jack, who was the general manager of the biggest resort on the island, and Lucy's ex, Carter, who had been the assistant GM at the other resort on the island until he moved to Chicago at the first opportunity, taking with him her heart and the diamond ring she'd returned on his last night on the island.

"Oh, come on." Taylor's eyes were begging. "Give it a chance."

"There's nothing to give a chance. We're just book buddies."

"Book buddies? What are you, kindergartners?" Taylor shook her head.

"Speaking of kindergartners, I need to get home and change. We have story hour this morning at the store." Lucy turned her attention back to Pam, who'd been observing their conversation while continuing to play fetch with Ava. "See you tonight?"

"Yeah. You heard the rumors, right?" Pam whistled for Ava to come back from where she was playing in the surf.

A cloud moved over the sun, cloaking the beach in shadow. Lucy shifted her weight, stuffing her hands in the pockets of her shorts.

"No. What rumors?"

That evening was the monthly town council meeting, which for the past six months had been the scene of vigorous debate over the future of the waterfront. Although the agenda tonight had an item related to all that, Lucy had assumed it would be a postmortem of the development plans that had failed to garner enough votes to pass. Pam's talk of rumors had her worried.

"Bob heard they're bringing in some guy who specializes in helping cities redevelop their waterfronts. Says he's some kind of—oh, what did he call it—a 'fixer.'" Pam nodded as if that explained everything she'd heard from the hardware store owner.

"What's a fixer and what is he here to fix?" Taylor bent to pet Ava, who was now lying in the sand with her chin on her tennis ball.

Pam shrugged. "The waterfront, I guess."

"Maybe this guy is just an accountant or something to help them reconfigure the budget now that the waterfront development is a no-go." Lucy was certain there had to be a reasonable explanation. All three of the previous proposals had been voted down by the council following the petitions and pleas of the Downtown Business Owners Council and the Heron Isle Conservancy, among others.

"Mm, maybe," Pam said. "I hope so. Save me a seat if y'all beat me there."

"What rotten timing. You'll have to fill me in later." Taylor turned to Pam. "Jack and I are leaving later this morning to go to North Carolina and hike for a few days."

"Hope the weather is cooler up there." Pam wiped away the sweat forming on her brow. "Can't believe it's already this hot in June. Bring some of that mountain air back with you."

Taylor laughed. "I'll try."

They both said goodbye to Pam, then turned to walk back toward the beach cottage where Lucy had grown up. As they approached her home, Lucy thought about the four generations of Sullivans who'd lived on Heron Isle, Florida. What had her father and his ancestors thought as the resorts were built on the north end of the island and houses started going up closer and closer together on the beach? At least then the developers had been kept away from the historic downtown area, the heart of the island. Did each generation always feel as if the peace and serenity of the island was under attack? She wished her dad was still around to ask. He'd know what to do.

Luckily, the bookstore had been busy all day, which had kept Lucy from fretting over the council meeting that evening. Customers had trickled in at regular intervals, and every inch of the rug in the children's section was filled during story time. She didn't really have a set amount she hoped to sell each day, but she knew it had been a good day when she'd spent as much time behind the register as she had away from it making suggestions for customers as they browsed the shelves.

Lucy hummed along with a song playing over the ancient sound system as she reshelved the books she'd pulled out for story hour. She loved the way the children's eyes lit up in wonder as she read about magic flying carpets and the way they smiled so sweetly when the princess found her Prince Charming. She wasn't silly enough to believe life was a fairy tale; she'd learned that lesson when she wasn't much older than the kids who'd stared back at her cross-legged that morning. But she did know that a good book could transport its reader to a different place and time, allowing them to escape to a place where their parents never fought, mothers never voluntarily left their children, and good always prevailed over evil.

She gathered a couple novels that had been left by the big blue armchairs up front and moved the rolling ladder back into its position along the bookshelves. She didn't let customers climb the ladder because her insurance agent had warned her it was a potential fall hazard, but she loved to get up on it herself when the store was empty. It was one of her favorite things about the bookstore when she was a kid. When no one was around, Annie, the former owner, would let her get on it and push her down the wall just like Belle from *Beauty and the Beast*.

Lucy sighed. She missed Annie. Something in the bookstore reminded her of Annie every day, which was both comforting and heartbreaking. From the smell of the coconut-vanilla candle she lit at the register just like Annie had, to the whimsical playlist that reminded her of a fairy tale, she'd chosen to keep most things exactly as Annie had left them.

Annie and the bookstore had been like a port in the storm of Lucy's parents' failing marriage when she was younger. Annie had never married or had children, and now that Lucy was older, she realized Annie had needed Lucy as much as Lucy had needed her.

The bookstore was Annie's final gift to Lucy, bringing her back home to the island when she'd needed it most. Her publishing dreams had gone up in smoke, but she always knew her life was destined to be about books. She'd just imagined it was going to be as a librarian who wrote books on the side, not as a bookstore owner. But life—and Annie—had other plans. Lucy had made it home after Annie's death in time to have several good years with her dad before he passed away, and being part of the community fabric as a business owner had given her a renewed sense of pride in her hometown.

Lucy grabbed two books she'd left by the cash register, turned off the lights, and flipped the antique wooden sign on the door to "Closed" before locking it behind her. She had forty-five minutes before the council meeting began just a couple blocks away, and she wanted to stop by the Little Free Library in the town square to leave her latest recommendation for someone else to enjoy. She'd also thought of a book she wanted to leave for Gatsby's Ghost.

As Lucy started walking toward the square, a man stopped to read the historical marker on the building that held her shop. Tourists usually breezed past things like that, pausing only to look at the latest resort wear in the shop windows or to watch as the fudge store spread its hot, sugary mixture onto the marble slab table to cool. Lucy had always been proud of Heron Isle's history and loved hearing stories of its founders who had planned Main Street and what each building had originally held.

"See that bay window up there?" Lucy said, pointing to the end of the adjacent building as she stepped up beside the man.

When he turned and smiled at her, the first thing she noticed were his green eyes. They were the same shade of bright green as the grass across the street in the park. Then, just as quickly as he'd turned to her, he was looking up at the window where she was pointing.

"Yeah." He looked back at her, an interested smile on his face as he waited for an explanation.

Staring into his eyes again, she had to catch her breath before she spoke. Was he wearing contacts? She'd never seen eyes that green. They were set against tan skin, his jawline and dark-brown hair forming perfect angles as if he'd been chiseled out of something very intentionally. He was one of the most handsome men she'd ever seen in real life. Definitely not a local. His wasn't a face she'd forget.

Feeling as if she were falling under a spell while his emerald eyes studied hers with amusement, Lucy forced herself to look back up at the bay window.

"It used to be a dentist office in the 1870s. Back before lighting was what it is today, the dentist that worked out of that office found a clever way to get more light for his procedures by installing the bay window and using a series of mirrors hung around the room to reflect the light into the patient's mouth so he could see what he was doing. Pretty genius, huh?" She smiled at the man, glad she'd been able to pass along a little bit of the town's history to a visitor.

"Wow. Now that's something else."

When he smiled this time, she looked away from his eyes long enough to notice the dimple in his right cheek. There wasn't a matching one on the left, and although she was usually a stickler for symmetry, it worked to make him even more attractive. As if he were more approachable because he wasn't perfect.

"You must live here," he said.

"I do." She nodded proudly. "My entire life. Well, most of it anyway."

"Charming town," he said, looking across the street at the town square. "I can see why it was voted 'Happiest Seaside Town' in *Vacations Today* last month."

"Yes, it tends to have that effect on people. It's a great place to slow down and unwind. How long are you here?"

He seemed to take a moment to decide how much he wanted to share. "My return date is open-ended at the moment."

She wanted to know more but didn't want to pry. "Well, as we say here, 'Put a chair in the sand and stay awhile.'"

"I might just do that." His smile was a little lopsided, but it was enough to make his dimple pop like an exclamation point that said, *Look how handsome I am!* He'd taken a step away from the building into the sun and he looked like a Greek god with his lean, muscular build, and those other-worldly green eyes.

Was he flirting with her? The way he was staring at Lucy made her heart pound, and she fiddled with the tassel hanging from the zipper of her purse, willing herself to look away. Her mind was a jumble of thoughts, none of which were appropriate to say out loud. She wasn't normally at a loss for words, especially when it came to her beloved island, but she'd also never met a man who was so undeniably gorgeous. Finally, she decided it was best to extricate herself from the situation before she said something stupid.

"Well, I hope you enjoy learning more about our little town." She backed away to give him his privacy, but just as she did, something collided into her, pushing her forward into the green-eyed man. Her first thought wasn't what had shoved her from behind, but of her face pressed against the man's rock-hard chest. If he hadn't grabbed her shoulders and pulled her away to ask if she was okay, she might have just stayed put, breathing in his dreamy aroma.

Lucy was still catching her breath, so she simply nodded her answer.

"I think the lady deserves an apology," the man said, making her aware of the person who'd run into her. He hadn't said it gruffly or in an intimidating way. His tone was gentle with none of the false machismo so many men injected to make themselves seem more manly.

"Sorry, ma'am," a sheepish voice behind her said as she turned.

It was a young tourist, probably no older than twelve or thirteen, who avoided her eyes as he bent down to pick up his skateboard.

She assured him she was fine.

"Maybe don't ride that on the sidewalk anymore," the man said. Again, his voice was calm and easy. The way he handled the boy made her wonder if he had kids of his own.

"No sir, I won't. I'm sorry," the boy said as he glanced up at Lucy for a quick second before turning and walking back up the sidewalk, head bowed, skateboard tucked under his arm.

"Who knew the sidewalks of Heron Isle were so danger-ous?" The man smiled wide, revealing what seemed like an endless string of gleaming white teeth.

Lucy hadn't realized she'd dropped her bag in the chaos until the man reached down and scooped up the young adult book that had fallen out. He studied it as he handed over her purse.

"Advanced reader copy, huh? Are you an editor or book reviewer or something?"

She laughed nervously. "No. I own the bookstore right

over there." She pointed behind her. "Thank you," she said quietly as he handed her the book.

"You're welcome." He tipped an imaginary cap. "Maybe I'll see you around."

Smiling and giving a little half wave, she turned just in time to avoid tripping over the curb, although she did manage to lose her slide-on sandal in the process. Shoving her foot back into it, she nearly darted across the street to get away from him, willing herself not to look back to see if he'd noticed. She had always been a tad on the klutzy side, but did she have to do it right in front of the most attractive man she'd ever seen in her life? She shook her head as she crossed into the park that bisected Main Street, pausing moments later when a crazy thought popped into her mind, a small smile tugging at the corners of her lips. Slipping right out of her shoe. Wasn't that what happened when Cinderella met her prince?

Two

Lucy

With a safe distance now between her and the green-eyed man, Lucy walked down the path that ran through the town square, the towering branches of live oaks that were more than one hundred years old creating a canopy that shaded her from the late-afternoon sun. Spanish moss dripped from the branches and danced in the breeze coming off the ocean at the end of the square.

Tourist season had begun, and the sidewalks were crawling with families, small children running ahead to get closer to the fountain in the middle of the town square. The park extended north and south from the fountain, creating more of a rectangle that ran nearly the length of Main Street. Despite its shape, everyone still referred to it as the town square. Town *rectangle* just didn't have the same ring to it.

Reaching down to pick up a piece of crumpled paper on the sidewalk, she saw just enough of the image on it to know it was one of the pro-development posters the last developer had put up around town. Never mind that town ordinances didn't allow them to be plastered on light poles. The developer had disregarded that rule just like they'd completely ignored the valid concerns the locals had expressed about the plans. Lucy balled up the paper in her fist and threw it in the next trash can she passed.

Lucy and some of her fellow business owners had been accused by those who'd presented previous plans of being anti-tourism because of their objections to the waterfront develop-ment, which was ridiculous given that they all depended on locals and tourists alike to stay in business. But that was what developers liked to do—pretend everything was black and white. Either the town wanted progress and supported tourism, or it wanted to remain stuck in the past.

The planning board had reviewed three plans submitted for the waterfront development meant to replace the docks and restaurant that currently sat at the north end of Main Street and add additional commercial space in new buildings on either side of the marina. Lucy, who had been nominated president of the Downtown Business Owners Council when she missed the annual meeting earlier in the year, had attended every town council meeting and combed over every plan. Not only were they all aesthetic nightmares, but they were also completely devoid of any concern for their impact on the envi-ronment or the people who lived and worked downtown. From building a seawall that would disrupt native fish and plant life to shutting down the thirty-year-old family restau-rant that currently anchored the marina space, the develop-ment plans were all a disaster from start to finish. She was so glad they had all failed to get through.

The sight of the Little Free Library standing just north of the fountain eased the tension in Lucy's shoulders as she approached it. She marveled once again at the perfect miniature replica of an old Victorian mansion that used to sit at the end of Main Street. When Lucy first had the idea to add a Little Free Library to the town square, Bob had volunteered to construct it, and done a wonderful job, producing a dollhouse-size replica of the mansion on top of a post, like most Little Free Libraries were. With the town library then closing, however, it quickly became clear that dollhouse version wasn't big enough to meet the demand. So Lucy and Bob got the proper town permits and constructed a small walk-in library. Shaped like a miniature Victorian house on the outside, the interior was a six-by-eight-feet room lined with shelves and just big enough for two or three people to enter at a time.

Lucy opened the door and was glad to see she was alone. A small ledge in the back was marked for people to leave their books so she, as the steward, could shelve them in the correct section. She'd tried to fit a used-book exchange into her bookstore, but people liked being able to use the Little Free Library at any time, day or night. She visited it almost daily to organize the new books.

She grabbed one of the index cards and a pencil from the wooden box on the ledge. Leaving the notes always reminded her of when Annie would walk her around the store, pulling books from the shelves and telling Lucy why she loved each one. Lucy never had enough allowance money to buy more than one book, but Annie often slipped a second one into her bag with a wink. She'd say, *"Let this book take you away, and when you come back, you'll be someone new."*

As a child, Lucy hadn't really understood what she'd meant, but by the time she was a teenager she longed for the escape and tore through books so quickly that sometimes she'd take one back to the library the day after she'd borrowed it. Little Free Libraries had become popular around the country in the past several years, but Lucy liked the unique touch of leaving notes with the books. It was her ode to Annie, her way of passing along the wisdom Annie had given her.

Lucy's latest read about two best friends who grew apart in middle school, told in alternating viewpoints from each girl, was perfect for tweens inevitably going through all the awkwardness and adjustment of those middle-school years. Lucy penned her note and signed it Once a Teenage Girl.

Next, she pulled out the book she wanted to leave for her new reading friend. It was a little-known account of Zelda Fitzgerald she thought he might enjoy. She'd long since gotten rid of the copy she'd read, so she'd ordered this new one from her distributor. She didn't want Gatsby's Ghost to know that though. It felt a little weird to buy a book for a stranger. As she'd left notes in the margin for him the evening before, she'd flicked through the pages and cracked the spine to make it look used.

As she riffled through it now, one of the passages she'd underlined caught her eye.

"To reinvent oneself demands an embrace of metamorphosis, a wistful longing for a world in flux, rather than a self in constant alteration."

The passage had spoken to her because she knew firsthand how difficult it was to reinvent yourself. Gatsby's Ghost had marked something in a previous book about how failure can sometimes be so big it liberates a person to reclaim their individuality. She'd been trying to figure out what that meant for days now. It certainly wasn't what failure had felt like to her. When she'd failed at publishing her novel, she'd just felt like a big fat failure.

Gatsby's Ghost had her wondering what it would be like for failure to be liberating. How did that work exactly?

With a sigh, she closed the book she was leaving for him

and set it on the ledge where he'd hopefully see his name on the sticky note she'd affixed to the front. She looked through the other books that had been left recently and put them in alphabetical order by the author's last name on the appropriate shelves, which were labeled for a dozen or so categories such as Biographies/Memoirs, Romance/Women's Fiction, Thrillers/Mysteries. A few titles caught her eye, and she stopped to read the notes before organizing them.

Imagine if every store in our town catered to the wedding industry and the whole island was dedicated solely to destination weddings. Wouldn't that be dreamy? That's what this book is all about!

Enjoy,
Wedding Bells Are Ringing

Lucy shook her head and smiled. Only Caroline Cassidy, the town's resident wedding planner, would think an island that exists solely to make bridal dreams come true would be paradise.

The next book Lucy chose was a beach read. She loved all books and read across virtually every genre so she could make recommendations to her customers, but kicking back in an Adirondack chair on her back porch looking out at the ocean reading about summer romances was one of her favorite pastimes. Lucy pulled out the index card to read.

After Hallie's aunt passes, she finds out she has to complete a bucket list she made as a child in order to get her inheritance. She returns to her aunt's beach house to complete the tasks and finds something that means even more than any inheritance. Loved it!

Signed,
Sucker for Summer Love

Lucy didn't know who had left this one, but she had a feeling they could definitely be friends. The book was by one of her favorite authors, but she hadn't gotten the chance to read this latest release yet because it had flown off the shelf at her store. She dropped the book into her purse and checked her watch. Time to get over to the town council building so she could get a good seat.

When she entered the council chamber it was already half full. The waterfront development had become a contentious issue, prompting crowds to appear at council meetings to ensure their voices were heard. As of yet, they hadn't found a plan a majority of locals could get behind. Some, like the Heron Isle Conservancy, whose president and several members were already seated on the right side of the room, wanted the parking lots that currently served the docks to become green space instead, an extension of the park that formed the town square. They were directly opposed by the charter fishermen who needed the parking lots so tourists had easy access to their deep-sea fishing charters. Then there were the general contractors and tradesmen from the larger nearby city of Jacksonville who wanted in on building the multi-use complex proposed by two of the developers. As Lucy looked around the room, the groups looked like rival cliques from high school taking to their own corners of the lunchroom.

Even though she found the seating amusing, Lucy

followed suit and went to sit with the other downtown business owners. She was, after all, their leader and they'd look to her to make a statement during the public input portion of the meeting if anything concerning was addressed. Lucy scanned the crowd for anyone she didn't recognize, trying to get an idea of who her newest adversary might be, but she didn't notice anyone out of place.

Bob was seated in front of her, so she leaned forward to whisper to him, "Pam said you heard they brought in someone. A fixer?"

He turned around to face her, his deep wrinkles giving away his age. Bob had owned the hardware store Lucy's entire life. She'd always loved going there with her father to find the bits and pieces they needed to repair a railing or build another bookshelf for her always-expanding collection.

"Yeah, Pete said he overheard them talking about it when he was here yesterday getting a permit for his new front door."

Pete owned the menswear store in town. His was another familiar face that had been around since she was a kid.

"What's a fixer do?" Lucy asked.

Bob shrugged, stroking his beard. Lucy had always thought he looked a lot like a Black Santa Claus when she was growing up, and he'd only grown to look more like Saint Nick as he'd aged.

"Sounds like he's supposed to get us all onboard *another* waterfront development."

Lucy's pulse quickened. She thought this meeting would be about tabling the waterfront development until they could explore the possibilities a little more thoughtfully.

"A different one?"

Shaking his head, Bob shrugged again. Just as he was opening his mouth to say more, the mayor banged his gavel to bring the meeting to order. The room was full to its seventy-five-person capacity with a few people standing along the dark-paneled wood walls.

As the mayor opened the meeting, led the pledge of allegiance, and went through some general housekeeping, Pam slid into the seat next to Lucy, who had been keeping her head on a swivel, watching the stragglers as they came in, trying to spot anyone she didn't recognize who might be the "fixer," but all she saw were familiar faces. She fidgeted as the council went through the other agenda items, ranging from designating a day to honor a former fire chief who'd recently passed to listening to a presentation by the local humane society on its new "Dog of the Month" program. Pam nudged her and smiled during the last one, mouthing Ava's name, whom she'd no doubt enter every month until she won.

When it was time for the final item on the agenda, everyone seemed to straighten a little in their seats. It was time to get down to the real business.

"Up next on the agenda is the potential development of the Heron Isle downtown waterfront." The mayor cleared his throat, looking up from his notes to scan the crowd. "We'd like to open with a presentation from Mr. Logan Lancaster, a consultant the town has hired to help us come up with a solution that increases the town's revenue while also addressing the concerns so many of you here tonight have previously voiced."

Hushed whispers erupted across the crowd, but the mayor banged his gavel quickly. Once the room quieted, he held up his hands in surrender.

"Look, I know the waterfront development has become a hot-button issue. I live here too, and I want what's best for our community. But the budget is hurting. We lost the library almost two years ago now, and the elementary school needs some serious work on its plumbing and air-conditioning, not to mention upgraded technology in the classrooms. That money has to come from somewhere. I implore you all to listen to what Mr. Lancaster has to say. There will be plenty of time afterward for public comment."

The crowd began whispering again, but Lucy was too busy looking around the room to see who she was up against. Then she spotted him. The green-eyed man from earlier was striding confidently toward the podium. Her heart sank. He wasn't Prince Charming to her Cinderella.

He was Logan Lancaster.

THREE

Logan

Logan took his place at the podium, aware that every eye in the room was on him and every hushed voice was talking about him. He didn't mind. People always acted this way when he came to a new town. Change wasn't something people readily accepted, but he'd seen first-hand what happened when someone refused to adapt.

"Mr. Mayor, council members, thank you for inviting me to speak tonight," Logan said as he faced the crowd. He'd learned it was important to address the townspeople, not just the elected officials. He had to make people feel they were part of the process, that their opinions would be heard. And they would be, but he might also have to try to change a few of them along the way. Often they couldn't see the forest for the trees because they were too close to the situation.

He'd seen city after city thrive after his plans were implemented. Municipal revenue went up, which meant better roads, improved schools, and infrastructure upgrades, and he always tried to accomplish his goals without disrupting anything with history or character. Preservation and progress didn't have to be mutually exclusive, a fact he'd successfully convinced a dozen other towns to believe.

"Ladies and gentlemen," he continued, "my name is Logan Lancaster, and I'm here as a consultant with the town of Heron Isle to find a plan for the waterfront that benefits each and every one of you." He paused to make eye contact with several people in the crowd. He wanted them to feel he saw them and understood them. "I know you've already seen three plans and that none of them fit your needs." He paused as the crowd mumbled its disapproval of the previous plans. He then held up his hand.

"And that's okay. I'm here to help you find one that does fit the unique attributes of your beautiful island. I've only been here for a few weeks—mostly holed up in my cottage reviewing your past meetings and proposed plans—but I'm already taken by what I've seen of your pristine sandy beaches and your beautiful historic architecture. I can see why you all love it so much and want to protect it. I promise you, I'm not here to destroy that. I simply want to find a way to enhance what you already have in a way that benefits the city financially so your island can continue to thrive."

And so I can get the heck out of here as fast as possible, he thought, but didn't say.

This job hadn't been his first choice or even his third choice. It had been his only choice after he blew his last job in San Diego. None of the other big cities would touch him in the immediate aftermath, and he'd had to practically beg for this job since he didn't have any small-town experience. He'd played up his small-town upbringing, which had done the trick only because his favorite professor called in a favor to an old friend, Mayor Jenkins. It was his sister Carly's idea, urging him to put his ego aside and use the connections he had to help him get back on track. It had been humiliating to ask for the favor, but she had been right, as usual. If he could just put an impressive win here between him and his failure, he could land the next big job.

Logan started picking out additional faces in the crowd to make eye contact with—his goal was to reach at least half the people in the room by the end of his presentation. Since the chamber only held about seventy-five people, that shouldn't be a problem. The redhead in the front row to his left was scowling when he first locked eyes with her, but he saw her face and shoulders relax when he flashed a smile her way.

Reaching down in his bag next to the podium, he brought out a stack of large folded-up renderings and began to unfold them.

"I've looked at the three plans that were submitted, and I agree with you all. They're not right for Heron Isle." He made a big show of ripping the plans in half and then in half again. "Do we have a trash can?"

As if on cue, the bailiff standing next to the platform where the councilmen sat lumbered over with a waste bin. Logan dramatically tossed the papers. The redhead was so excited she began to clap. Score one for the eye contact, but he could see the rest of the room remained skeptical.

"We're starting over. Sure, there are some elements we might take from each of those plans, but the slate is wiped clean. We can do anything *we* want." He emphasized the "we" to further cement the notion that they were part of a team here, the council, the townspeople, and himself. "I get it, though. You don't trust me yet. So let me tell you a little bit about myself so we can all start to get to know one another. I'm a local-government consultant with nearly fifteen years of experience. I have a law degree with a certificate in land use, and my undergraduate degree is in urban planning. I've helped cities far worse off than yours find ways to boost their budget and create spaces to be enjoyed for generations to come."

He made eye contact with a well-dressed man to his right, noting he was the only person in the room in a full suit. Logan was glad he'd ditched his usual suit for a more casual look of khaki slacks and a checkered button-down he knew brought out his best feature, his green eyes.

Next, he walked them through his successful redevelopment projects in Baltimore, Phoenix, and St. Louis. He left out San Diego. No one needed to be reminded of what happened there, least of all him. He moved his gaze past the man in the suit a couple rows back, and saw familiar brown eyes framed by blonde curls. The charming bookstore owner who'd told him about the dentist office. Sure, she'd been talking about the history of dentistry, but she'd been downright adorable doing it. Then she'd nearly been tackled by the skateboarder, and the memory of the coconut aroma of her hair as she'd clung to his chest might have mesmerized him had the notification on his phone not gone off to remind him of this meeting. He was here for business, not pleasure. He'd learned the hard way the two should never be mixed.

It certainly wasn't pleasure he was feeling now, though, as the warm brown eyes he'd studied earlier were replaced by a gaze so cold it felt as if the air-conditioner had just come on above him. Her arms were crossed stiffly across her chest, her mouth pulled into a tight line. He flashed her a smile, nodding to acknowledge her, but her expression remained unchanged. Forcing himself to look at the other faces around her, he noticed they were all equally cold.

He'd miscalculated. This wasn't a crowd that would be impressed with his work in cities. The kind of people who lived here were here specifically because they didn't want a big-city life. He should have known better, given his hometown was even smaller than Heron Isle, but it had been a long time since he'd actually spent any time in a small community.

Yet he was nothing if not adept at reading the room and making adjustments.

"Heron Isle is different though." He extended his arms as if to encompass the whole room. "This isn't some major metropolis where we're going to throw up new apartments downtown and try to attract Fortune 500 companies. I'm here to figure out what *your* vision is for the waterfront and then bring it to life." A few faces in the crowd relaxed. They weren't exactly hanging on his every word, but at least they no longer looked as if they wished they had rotten tomatoes to throw at him.

"I've already had the chance to meet some of you, and in the coming weeks I hope to meet many more of you." He looked right at the woman he'd met earlier, willing her smile to brighten her features, but her face remained unmoved. He carried on. "I'll start by visiting the downtown businesses and dropping in on the Rotary club, the Lions club, and any other club that will have me." He laughed, trying to lighten the mood, scanning the crowd, trying to gauge if there was anything else he could add to ensure he got off on the right foot with the townspeople.

His eyes kept returning to the woman who'd found such joy in telling him about the history of the bay window earlier, who'd been so flustered after the encounter with the skateboarder that she'd lost her shoe as she stepped off the curb. He'd felt a spark in the brief moment he'd touched her, pulling her away from his chest so he could see if she was all right. Had she felt it too? Even if she had, his charm was clearly lost on her now. She sat like a statue, arms still crossed, and her cute little mouth still pulled in that tight line. It was time to wrap it up.

"That's it for now. I look forward to speaking more with

you all soon." He turned back to the commissioners, giving them a smile that was far more confident than the looks they were returning. He reminded himself not to sweat it. Every project started out like this, and he always managed to turn the tide of sentiment before he was packing his bags to move on to the next one.

As they opened for public comment, Logan moved to the back of the room to listen as the townspeople got up one by one and gave a range of opinions. It became clear there was a contingent of folks who built houses and commercial buildings outside of the island's historic district who were salivating at the idea of working on a new project, but they were outnumbered by the two groups Mayor Jenkins had warned him opposed all three of the previous plans: the conservancy group and the downtown business owners.

When the woman he'd met earlier rose to make her way to the podium, he stood taller and waited impatiently to hear her name as she read herself into the record.

"Lucy Sullivan, owner of Beachside Books and president of the Downtown Business Owners Council."

His heart sank. She wasn't just any business owner; she was the leader of the opposition.

"I think I speak for all my fellow downtown business owners when I say I'm amazed that instead of taking the time to consider why the first proposals failed, you all have decided to bring in yet another outsider"—she gestured in his direction, her narrowed brown eyes cutting through him even though her voice was shaky—"to tell us what we should do here. I respect Mr. Lancaster's experience, but haven't we all learned that no one understands what Heron Isle needs if they haven't lived and worked here?" It was a rhetorical question she didn't pause for anyone to answer. "I don't know about the rest of you, but I feel misled."

She turned to the crowd, acknowledging those who were

nodding at her. She turned back to the commission. "We thought tonight was about tabling this whole waterfront discussion until the proper research was done on the impact any development would have on the environment and the existing downtown businesses."

The mayor began in a soothing tone, like a father talking to his daughter. "We appreciate your concern, Lucy, and that of everyone else here tonight. Mr. Lancaster is here for exactly that, to help us facilitate the needed research and discussion. His job is to balance that against the city's need to generate more revenue. Our waterfront is one of our greatest resources, and the councils that have come before us have admittedly done a poor job of maximizing it."

Lucy crossed her arms, a disapproving frown taking over her features. He could hardly suppress the part of him that felt compelled to find a way to put the cheerful smile he'd seen earlier back on her face. He was the white knight for the town in this story, not the villain.

"Lucy, I would think you'd understand more than most," the mayor continued. "You fought so hard to save the library, organizing all those fundraisers when the city couldn't afford the maintenance on the building. You know what our budget looks like. What would you have us do?"

The exchange reminded Logan of his hometown in Wisconsin. It was as if they were discussing the matter over coffee, not on record in the commission chambers. He'd worked in big cities for so long he'd forgotten how small towns were more like navigating a family squabble than a commercial negotiation. He'd get his feet under him, though. And this time he'd be more successful than he had been with his father, who'd resisted Logan's "adapt or die" warnings to his detriment.

Lucy's delicate features had relaxed, although her shoulders still looked tense as she shifted from one foot to the other before dropping her arms by her sides. Her voice was quieter when she answered.

"I'm not trying to be unreasonable. None of us are. But this isn't a decision that can be made lightly. It could impact us all for a very long time. I just hope he knows what he's doing." She flicked her head in his direction, but didn't turn to meet his eyes.

Logan knew it wasn't a good sign when someone couldn't even look at him. He made a note to look further into the whole library story. He would learn as much about Lucy Sullivan as he could before they met again and be ready to show her how the influx of tourists his plan would bring would benefit her bookstore, not harm it. He'd turn on the charm and win her over. For business purposes only, he reminded himself. He couldn't let his interest in a woman derail his work again. He'd had enough heartbreak to last a lifetime, both personally and professionally.

Several others got up to speak after Lucy, most echoing the same sentiments. As the meeting ended, he moved to the back of the room and positioned himself by the door so everyone would be forced to walk past him on the way out. He'd smile and shake hands, looking for the ones who seemed most receptive. He hoped no one would hear his stomach growling. He'd been in so many meetings with commissioners and other town personnel today he'd missed lunch.

David Stallings, as he'd introduced himself, made a beeline to Logan as soon as the meeting adjourned.

"My family has been building on this island for three generations. Let me know if you want to sit down and work on some plans," he said, practically salivating at the idea of building something new.

David was the first and last friendly face Logan would see. Lucy's speech had flipped the scales in her favor. Others passed by him scowling, shaking their heads.

"Outsider," one elderly woman muttered as she passed him, spitting it out like a curse word. It was clear the town didn't like outsiders meddling in their business, but it had been expected. It would just require a more personal approach.

Helen Bowman, head of the local tree conservancy, stopped next to introduce herself.

"Do let me know when you have time to meet. We have a few concerns I'd like to share with you."

She was nice enough, but Logan wasn't sure why the tree conservancy even had a dog in this fight. There weren't really any trees in the area, just a few scattered palms in the parking lots that flanked either side of the marina. In his experience, tree conservancies were worried about things like live oaks and cypress. He'd never worked in Florida before. Maybe palm trees warranted some protection here, although he knew they weren't that difficult to relocate.

Helen was in the middle of a lengthy explanation about the difference between a sabal palm and a sago palm when Lucy headed toward the door. She was surrounded by the same people he'd seen her sitting with, several of whom had gotten up to speak and introduced themselves as downtown business owners. He tried to catch her eye without being rude to the tree conservancy woman, but Lucy seemed to be making a concerted effort not to look at him. Before he could break free from Helen, the business owners group had slipped out the door.

Logan went outside as soon as he finished with Helen, hoping Lucy had stopped outside to talk to someone. He was disappointed to find the sidewalk empty in both directions and none of her group in sight. His shoulders slumped, but his stomach reminded him he didn't have time to hang around. Besides, he needed more time to research Lucy Sullivan and find out what made her tick. Then he could figure out how to get her—and the other downtown business owners—on his side.

So what if that meant he had to spend a little extra time with this particular resident? It was just business. Sure, it was business with a woman he hadn't stopped thinking about since she'd tripped off the sidewalk and scurried across the street earlier, but it wasn't like he could avoid working with the president of the Downtown Business Owners Council just because she had a cute smile and smelled like a sunny afternoon. He was a professional. A professional who had this one final shot to salvage his career. Nothing—and no one—was going to get in the way of that.

FOUR

Lucy

Lucy trailed behind Pam, Bob, and Pete as they walked down to the Waterway Café for dinner after the meeting. She still couldn't believe the handsome man with the dazzling emerald eyes—whom she'd let herself believe, if only for a moment, resembled Prince Charming—was actually the man the town had brought in to shove a new development down their throats. But it was just her luck.

"Yeah, that's exactly what we need," Bob was saying ahead of her. "Some big-city lawyer or planner or whatever he is coming in to tell us how our town should be."

"Clearly the entire council is dead set on development, not just Councilman Turner," Pam said, referring to the lone developer on the council. "This guy is just like all the others they've brought in to do presentations."

"He's at least better looking though, right?" Pete turned

back to the ladies and patted his right hand over his heart. "Did you see those eyes? Be still my heart."

Pam laughed. "Don't let Frank hear you say that." Frank was Pete's longtime partner.

"What?" Pete shrugged. "I'm allowed to look."

Pam nudged Lucy. "I caught him looking at you more than once. Maybe you can charm him onto our side."

Lucy grimaced, a bitter taste filling her mouth. Before she could answer, Mildred Banks, who owned the Waterway Café with her husband Marty, opened the door to the restaurant to greet them. "Come on in, y'all."

"Hi, Mildred," Lucy said, stopping to hug the older lady.

"I heard about the meeting," Mildred said. "Marty's in back filleting fish. That's what he does when he's really upset."

"Tell him to make enough for me too." Bob chuckled. "I tend to bang nails into a board when I'm mad. At least Marty's doing something productive."

"I'll tell him y'all are here in case he wants to come out and commiserate." Mildred took them to a table in the far-right corner where they'd have some privacy. A few tourist couples and one family were sitting in the opposite corner where they could overlook the water. The views at the Waterway Café were nearly as good as the food.

A weathered blue-gray building perched atop tall stilts that extended out of the marina's docks, the restaurant looked a bit like their island's namesake, the great blue heron. Eating there after a meeting that could lead to the restaurant's destruction was bittersweet. All three of the previous plans had included demolishing the current docks and restaurant in favor of all new builds. The Waterway Café was welcome to lease one of the new spaces, but it wouldn't be the same—not in atmosphere or price.

Steve, one of the servers who'd been at the restaurant for at least the past decade, came to take their drink orders. Sweet teas for Bob and Pam, lemonade for Lucy, and champagne for Pete. Lucy raised an eyebrow at Pete's order, but he was too busy chatting with Steve to notice.

"I've been thinking about what we should do," Lucy said. "Clearly they're going to move forward with something with or without us, so we need to make sure our voices are heard this time."

"What did you have in mind?" Bob asked.

"I think we all have to get on the same page about what we want. Best-case scenario, what goes into this new development? How big is it? How do we make sure it's environmentally friendly? What kind of aesthetic do we want?"

"Getting all the downtown owners on the same page is a bit like herding cats," Pam said.

"Yeah, the kind that wail outside your window at night in heat." Pete laughed as he picked up the glass of champagne Steve had sat in front of him.

"What are you celebrating anyway?" Bob asked Pete, pointing at the champagne glass.

"Life, my dear man. Cheers to being on this earth one more day." Pete held up his glass to the others and they begrudgingly followed suit.

"It wasn't exactly the day I had in mind," Pam grumbled.

Steve soon returned to take their orders, and they all got their usuals: a fried fish sandwich for Bob, crab bisque and a house salad with grilled shrimp for Pete, shrimp and grits for Pam, and a burger and fries for Lucy.

"I know this building isn't historic," Lucy said, looking around, "but it's been here for thirty years. I'd hate to see it go." She lowered her voice to a whisper. "And what will Marty and Mildred do? They're so close to retirement, I doubt they'll want to start over in the new development."

The group continued discussing Marty and Mildred's dilemma until Steve reappeared with Pete's crab bisque.

"Oh, crab bisque, I'll miss you the most." Pete dramatically dragged his spoon through his soup, lifting it high before letting the contents pour back into the bowl.

Lucy's shoulders slumped as she took another sip of her drink. This was depressing.

"Pardon the interruption," came a deep voice that had been foreign to her until today.

Now it seemed she couldn't escape it. It was him.

Logan Lancaster had appeared out of seemingly nowhere. "I couldn't help but overhear. I know you probably all see me as the enemy, but I assure you I'm here to help. I want to find a plan that works for all of you."

Logan focused on Lucy, the green of his eyes deeper in the dim light of the restaurant. She noticed gold flecks she hadn't seen before glimmering in the candlelight. Unable to hold his gaze any longer, her eyes fell to his lips, and she found herself imagining what they would feel like on hers.

Pam's voice interrupted her thoughts just in time, and she forced her mind back to the business at hand.

"You do realize you're saying that as you stand in a building that will almost certainly be torn down?"

"If you'd tried this crab bisque, you'd understand what a tragedy that would be," Pete said as he lifted the spoon to his mouth and sighed with contentment as he swallowed the creamy liquid.

Logan looked around the room as if really seeing it for the first time before turning his gaze back to them. "Have you all seen the engineering report the city commissioned after the last hurricane? As charming as it is—and that crab bisque does look divine"—he looked at Pete's bowl appreciatively—"this building is on borrowed time. Instead of wasting money on a legal battle over whose responsibility it is to fix the damage, the Waterway Café could have a state-of-the-art restaurant in the new development."

Lucy hadn't read the full report, but the *Heron Isle Observer* had summarized it. So much of the substructure of the restaurant had been damaged that it would only take one more strong storm to wipe it out. The building had been deemed safe for now, but it needed substantial repairs to withstand the next severe weather event. The Bankses had been embroiled in a legal battle with the city for months over who would fund the repairs, each claiming the poorly written lease agreement from decades prior put the burden on the other.

The table had fallen silent; they'd all seen the newspaper article and knew about the ongoing legal fight. They also knew the Bankses couldn't afford the structural repairs on a building they didn't own, especially not so late in their lives.

"And what are the Bankses supposed to do for the next two years while they're closed down and waiting on a new building?" Lucy didn't give him a chance to answer. "And what about the competition from the other waterfront restaurants that will go in? Right now, they basically own the waterfront, so how is this plan what's best for them?"

"See, those are the kind of things we all need to sit down and discuss. They are valid concerns that should be taken into consideration when the city makes them an offer to end their lease a few years early."

He wasn't hearing her. The Bankses didn't want someone to write them a check and send them on their merry way. They wanted to keep running the restaurant they'd spent the past thirty years here building. She'd heard Marty say it himself at a previous planning meeting.

Suddenly, Lucy had an idea. "You know what? Stay here. I'll be right back."

Logan gave her a curious look but said, "Sure."

Lucy got up and approached the host stand where the owner was waving goodbye to a family shuffling out the front door. "Mildred, I need you to come with me for a minute."

Mildred's eyebrows knitted together, deepening the wrinkles in her forehead. Lucy wasn't sure exactly how old Mildred was, but she had to be in her mid- to late sixties.

"Is something wrong?" she asked as she began to follow Lucy back to the table.

"No, nothing like that. I want you to meet someone."

When they arrived at the table, Lucy noticed Logan rocking back and forth on his feet. He was uncomfortable standing there waiting for her return. Good.

"Logan Lancaster, I want you to meet Mildred Banks. She and her husband Marty own the Waterway Café. I'd introduce you to Marty, but I think it's best you let him take out his frustration on the fish in back instead of on you."

Logan raised an eyebrow as if trying to guess where she was going with this. Turning to smile at Mildred, he reached out to shake her hand. "Nice to meet you, ma'am."

Logan's friendly smile had engaged his lopsided dimple. If Lucy didn't hate him so much right now, she might find that look even more attractive than the full one-hundred-watt smile he'd weaponized during the meeting to try to win everyone over. This smile was the one he'd given her earlier on the sidewalk. As if she'd just done something irresistibly cute, and he wanted to grab her and kiss her.

Good grief. She had to stop thinking about kissing this man. What was with her? Nothing about Logan Lancaster was cute. Nothing. He was a money-grabbing outsider who'd come to turn their island into some over-commercialized strip mall on the water.

Lucy jumped in before he could try his charm on Mildred. "Mildred, this is the man who's come to help the town take away your restaurant."

Pete gasped from his seat at the table, and Mildred's mouth fell open as she looked from Logan to Lucy and back again, but no words came out.

Logan was unfazed as he turned to Lucy. "Now, I think that's an over-generalization. Don't you?"

He was looking at her as if he genuinely didn't know what she was talking about. What was it about those eyes that made it so hard for her to think straight? She concentrated on imagining all the evil characters in children's books who had hypnotic eyes. He was a villain, not Prince Charming.

Turning his attention back to the older woman in front of him, Logan spoke in a soothing tone. "Mildred—can I call you Mildred?—it's true the town brought me in to see if I could help turn around their financial predicament, and a big piece of the puzzle is better management of this amazing waterfront real estate. If I remember correctly from the complaint you all filed against the city, you have had to repair some of the decking structure on your own in the past. Am I right?"

Mildred nodded, still obviously a little shell-shocked from the unexpected encounter. Her eyes flitted from Logan's to Lucy's and finally around the table, but they were all as caught off guard as she was.

"Well, I think that's just nonsense, Mildred. You and your husband shouldn't be putting out your own money to get this kind of work done. The city owns this property, and they should be doing those things. But they haven't been—and I've already said this to them—because they're a terrible landlord. They don't have the first idea how to manage property, maintain it, or maximize its value. That's what I'm here for. I'm not just going to come up with a plan to address the immediate need for a better structure here; I'm also going to help them hire someone to manage the new development so we never run into these issues again in the future." He gave her another full smile, dimple and all.

Lucy could see Mildred was falling under his spell, nodding as he rattled off his speech. She wanted to break in and tell Mildred that they were all prepared to help her and

Marty save the restaurant—and get the city to foot the tab for the repairs—but she actually didn't know exactly how to do those things.

Logan took the restaurant owner's hand in his. "Mildred, I promise you that I'll work to find a compromise you and Marty can be happy with, and you won't ever have to worry about your safety or pay for your own repairs ever again."

Mildred nodded, clearly mesmerized by his charm.

Lucy's plan was backfiring. She'd hoped that by humanizing the restaurant and introducing Logan to sweet Mildred, he'd start to see that this wasn't just another big-city project where major corporations moved their pieces around on a chess board, each jockeying for their slice of a fancy new development. That these were people's livelihoods, their life's work at stake.

"See?" Logan looked first to Lucy and then at the rest of the table, grinning as if he'd just solved world hunger. "For every problem there's a solution. That is, if we all work together."

Mildred excused herself quickly as she saw another table headed for the door. Seven days a week, she was always there by the front door acknowledging everyone as they came and went. She knew the locals by name and which tables or servers they preferred. You just didn't get that kind of customer service from a chain restaurant, which Lucy was sure Logan would love to court as anchors in his new building. Just what they needed, a Joe's Jumbo Shrimp Shack with its gaudy cartoon jumbo shrimp emblazoned on the side of the building greeting people as they walked out on the docks or wandered up from the beach that flanked the marina to their left.

"You've just got an answer for everything, don't you?" Lucy mumbled under her breath, crossing her arms.

Logan turned to her, the space between them closing to only a few inches. He was so close she could smell his cologne.

She hadn't noticed it earlier, probably because she'd let him hypnotize her with those darn eyes. He smelled like Christmas, notes of pine and vanilla reminding her of eating cookies by the tree with her dad.

"Well, I certainly hope I do. When I leave here, I want to know both the city and its residents are going to be thriving for years to come. You'll see, Lucy. I'm not so bad."

And then he winked at her. The nerve.

She stared at him as he nodded to the others and then walked away. Those green eyes, that lopsided smile with the one dimple, the dizzying cologne she couldn't seem to breathe in enough of. Logan Lancaster was bad news. For her and for Heron Isle.

FIVE

Logan

At sunrise, Logan had given up on sleep and gone for a run on the beach. Even at such an early time it was almost too warm to enjoy the run, so he left his T-shirt at home and hit the sand barefoot wearing nothing but his running shorts. He was hoping the sun would tan his arms and chest that were normally hidden underneath button-up shirts.

He'd tried to outrun the look Lucy had given him last night. The one where she seemed disappointed in him. He knew he shouldn't care. People always viewed him as the villain when he came to town, and it wasn't as if she really knew him. And yet, he couldn't get her out of his mind.

After returning to his cottage, he grabbed the last book Island Girl had left him off his counter and took it out on the porch with a cold glass of water. In response to the book he'd left on Fitzgerald's time in Hollywood in the later years of his life, she'd given him a fictional tale about all the American writers and artists in Jazz Age Paris.

He slipped the index card out of the front pages and read it again.

Gatsby's Ghost,

Since you seem to be interested in the Fitzger-alds, I wonder if you might also be interested in a fictional account of that period. I'll admit a bit of a fascination with 1920s Paris. Okay, a bit of a fascination with Paris in general, although I've never been. It's on my bucket list!

Enjoy,
Island Girl

He'd been in town for a few weeks now, but he'd mostly been hiding out in his cottage poring over the boxes of old budgets, leases, meeting minutes, and other paperwork the town had sent over. Then at night when he couldn't stop running through potential redevelopment scenarios in his head, he'd read the latest book he'd found from Island Girl. He'd soon found himself ordering books he'd read previously online just so he could pass them along to her.

He'd enjoyed the books she'd left for him so far, but it wasn't the authors' prose that had kept his attention. It was the loopy handwritten notes in the margins. Whoever Island Girl was, the passages she'd marked, along with her notes to the side, revealed seemingly opposed personality traits. She was at times both a dreamer and a cynic. The combination of the mystery of her identity and her completely opposed outlooks was quickly becoming a drug he couldn't get enough of. He instinctively felt as if Island Girl understood him.

The first passage she'd marked in the latest book showed her dreamer side.

"In that precious interval betwixt night and day, a space of enchantment unfolded, defying the constraints of mere hours—a mystical lavender expanse, suspended between worlds, where time dared to linger."

In the margin she'd written:

This is how I feel every time I watch the sunrise.

He wiped sweat from his forehead with the back of his hand as he looked out at the water, the sun now well above the horizon. He'd never experienced hot like this before. Sure, it had been hot on some of his runs the past two years he'd been living and working in San Diego, but there hadn't been this kind of humidity. It was as if someone had put a wet towel over his head and told him to try to breathe through it. Maybe the sunrise here felt more magical in the fall. He hoped he wouldn't be here long enough to find out. The city couldn't afford to hire him to stay on and manage the development—although they would need someone—so he was only here for however many weeks or months it took to come up with a profitable plan they could implement on their own.

He flipped to the next passage she'd underlined, this one markedly darker than the last:

"They went on, living their lives, forging ahead through blunders and missteps. Meanwhile, I found myself stalled in some indistinct moment, a prisoner of my own uncertainties, with no clear knowledge of the escape route."

There was no note in the margin this time, which only made him more curious about her. Why did she feel stuck? Was she stuck in a marriage? A dead-end job?

He flipped to another underlined passage.

"Happiness, it seemed, might resemble an hourglass with its sands steadily dwindling, particles sliding and intermingling, much like thoughts in one's mind."

Her note in the margin asked a simple question:

Is happiness a state of mind?

For the next underlined passage, she'd simply drawn a heart with a jagged line down the middle.

"Regret's sting lies in the halting of affection for that initial love, a sentiment once as unbridled as the open sea, now confined to the quiet depths of memory."

Did it confirm his suspicion she was stuck in a loveless marriage? He knew all too well what it was like to realize your relationship was over. To admit you'd failed. It had been doubly hard for him since he'd demolished both his love life and his career at the same time.

After Logan had spent two years putting together the North Port project in San Diego, it had all fallen apart in the eleventh hour because he'd had the audacity to break up with

Catherine Albright, the daughter of one of the wealthiest and most well-connected men in San Diego, Jack Albright. Jack had never even bothered to find out what had caused the breakup, but in less than forty-eight hours he'd convinced every anchor tenant in the North Port project to abandon it and with that the bond issue had failed. With no funding and no anchor tenants, the city decided to hit pause while it searched for a new consultant. One that could get the job done.

It was the second time in his career that his love life had gotten in the way of him closing a deal. He'd vowed it would be the last. The first had been early in his career, when he'd gotten so wrapped up in his budding relationship he'd missed the signs the deal was collapsing, but the second had been more egregious. A career-ending kind of failure. Business and pleasure should never be mixed.

The Heron Isle job hadn't only been appealing because it was the first—and only—offer he'd finally landed after San Diego, but also because the mayor had joked with him about his romantic prospects here. He'd apologized for it being a terrible place for a single man like Logan because the local population was so small and most of those of marrying age were already coupled off and settled down. It had sounded perfect to Logan.

But now here he was, only a few weeks on the island, and not one, but two women were distracting him. First, what had started as a friendly note to a fellow Fitzgerald lover had turned into some sort of book-pen pal situation that was becoming increasingly personal and vulnerable. And then he'd met Lucy with her big brown puppy-dog eyes and her boundless enthusiasm for the historic building that had once been home to what were surely some traumatic dental procedures before the days of Novocain.

Maybe they were both married anyway. Except he hadn't seen a ring on Lucy's finger. He'd checked before his brain registered what he was doing. But she was the opposition, so that would keep her at arm's length. And the woman in the Little Free Library? Well, he didn't even know her name, and he certainly didn't plan to be in town long enough to find out. She had good taste in books, but that was it. Okay, so she was also the embodiment of some bizarre dichotomy that made his brain work in overdrive, and he loved trying to put the puzzle together. But mostly he was reading to keep from wallowing at night and drinking more bourbon than he should. That was all.

Closing the book and standing to go back inside, Logan looked up the beach to the north and marveled at the wide, sandy expanse that seemed to go on forever. The other side of the dunes were dotted by one- and two-story beach houses that looked as if they'd been there for decades. Boardwalks snaked from nearly every house through extensive dune systems that separated the homes from the sand by a good fifty yards in most places.

Unlike many of the towns up and down Florida's east coast, the incorporated portion of Heron Isle had restricted development to no more than twenty-five feet high, which had kept the island's two resorts relegated to the small unincorporated north end of the island. Here they'd retained the quaint feel of a Florida beach town of yesteryear. He had to admit he'd never seen anything like it.

While there was a certain appeal to the nostalgia of it all, his practical side knew the town couldn't go on like it had been. They had some serious infrastructure needs—from the boardwalk he'd walked down this morning that shifted under his weight to the failing air-conditioning at the elementary school he'd read about in the paper.

None of these problems were insurmountable. In fact,

they could easily be solved if the town had some new revenue streams. That was why the job had appealed to him—it was exactly the quick win he needed. He'd find the new revenue streams, help the town hire someone to manage it all, and then he'd be off to somewhere bigger and better.

After showering and dressing, Logan headed straight for the coffee shop downtown to fuel up for a big day ahead. When he parked at the marina, he marveled again at the premium land the city owned—land that could easily be better monetized. In addition to the marina and the building on it that housed the Waterway Café, the town also owned all the land that extended one hundred yards in each direction from the marina along the water. It was a thin strip of land because of the port that had historically been run by the city, but it was still prime real estate.

Walking east from the marina into the historic downtown, he stopped to read more of the plaques attached to nearly every building, which reflected a surprisingly wide variety of architectural styles from Classic Revival to beaux arts with Italian and Spanish influences that made the town unique even among historic towns. He stopped to read the marker for the oldest surviving hotel in Florida, a two-story boarding-house-style accommodation that still operated on Main Street.

The Heron House was originally built as the first boarding house on Heron Isle. It has housed a variety of guests since it was built in 1855, including Union soldiers during the Civil War, famous visitors such as the Vanderbilts and Carnegies, three Presidential candidates and one sitting president, Ulysses S. Grant. It remains the oldest surviving hotel in Florida.

Aside from the quick win, the incredible history of Heron Isle had also attracted him to this job. Historic preservation had been his minor in college, and he'd always taken great care to preserve what he could in each city where he'd worked. He'd been delighted to learn the project wouldn't involve the demolition or relocation of any historic buildings.

The Waterway Café was the only building on the chopping block, and it had no historic value. It was built by the city in the early nineties in an attempt to generate more revenue, but between the below-market lease the restaurant enjoyed as a result of a poorly written contract decades prior—that kept automatically renewing—and the upkeep required for a wooden building that sat right on the water, the entire venture had become a burden on the city.

Logan scowled as he thought again of how Lucy Sullivan had tried to demonize him in front of Mildred Banks and the others. He was used to locals who opposed his plans, but they didn't usually look like Lucy. When he first met her, he'd loved how excited she got talking about the history of the old dentist's building, her shoulder-length blonde curls bouncing with her movements. She'd been bubbly and cheerful, the kind of person who seemed to never have a bad day.

As it turned out, she had an entirely different side, and he imagined that was all he'd get to see now—the Lucy who thought he was a soulless outsider looking to destroy their precious town.

The coffee shop was empty when he arrived except for the woman behind the counter and Mayor Jenkins, who sat at a table by the window eating a pastry while he read the paper.

"Mayor." Logan nodded as he entered. "You're up and about early."

"Please, you can call me George when we're not on the clock." He motioned for Logan to join him. "I sit here every morning to drink my coffee and catch up on the latest news. The residents all know they can find me here if they need to talk." He folded his paper, giving Logan his attention. "Reminds them that I'm one of them, a local who's lived here most of my life and drinks coffee and reads the paper just like they do."

The waitress took Logan's order for an iced coffee and hurried back behind the counter to get it.

"Did we make the headlines?" Logan asked. No doubt the top news in a small town like this would have to be the surprise announcement of his presence at the meeting last night.

The mayor chuckled. "Not yet. Our paper only comes out on Wednesdays and Fridays. Not enough news around here to support a daily." He tapped a finger on the paper he'd folded neatly on the table. "This one's the Jacksonville paper. They don't really cover us, but it keeps me up to speed on what's going on in northeast Florida."

That gave Logan one more day before he could read what some local reporter would say about him and his intentions for Heron Isle.

"So how do you think it went?" Logan tested the waters, curious if the reception from the locals was what he'd expected.

"Well, I'm not sure you made any friends." The mayor smiled as he rocked back in his chair and folded his hands over his robust middle. "But I didn't think you would. Not yet anyway. You're a charming fellow, though. I think you'll have no problem winning them over in the end."

Logan nodded, but wasn't convinced charm would be enough. It had worked on Mildred, but Lucy certainly seemed immune.

"I ran into Lucy Sullivan—a couple times yesterday, actually," he said. Her big brown eyes flashed before him. Clearing his throat to bring himself back to the present, he asked, "What's her story?" Not that he cared. He was only asking for business reasons so he would know how best to get her on his side.

"Ahh, Lucy." The mayor shook his head. "Means well, but she can be overly passionate sometimes. She's a bona-fide local, born and raised here. Her daddy was from here too. I think she's third or fourth generation. Poor thing. Her mother left when she was young. Just packed her bags one day and was gone."

The mayor frowned. "Lucy always had her nose in a book after that. Annie over at the bookstore took her under her wing, and Lucy inherited the store when Annie passed. She fought like heck to save the public library, but the building was in such a state of disrepair it was a lost cause. There wasn't any other space downtown big enough, so we had to shut it down. Lucy was devastated. She's also fought this waterfront development tooth and nail."

So she was a champion of lost causes? She probably had a house full of abandoned animals. Logan sipped his iced coffee as he pictured what Lucy's house might look like. He imagined it was full of antiques, and she probably had a story that went along with each one. He saw himself walking through with her, watching the excitement in her eyes as she told him about each one. He was just picturing her curling up in a window seat surrounded by her knickknacks, a book in hand and her blonde hair falling in her face, when the mayor interrupted his thoughts.

"Have you seen the little library?" The mayor flicked his head toward the park across the street.

Logan nodded, not admitting just how well he'd been getting to know it.

"It was Lucy's idea." The mayor laughed. "The first one was small, like a dollhouse, but it was so popular she and Bob —he owns the hardware store—got permission to build the walk-in structure. They modeled it after a house that used to sit at the end of the town square. It burned down decades ago, but it's the house we use for the town logo."

Mayor Jenkins continued with a history lesson on some of the most notable Victorian-era homes in town. Logan decided he should sign up for one of the history tours at the small three-room museum over on 3rd Street. After all, the historic buildings were half the reason he'd convinced himself he could make the best of this job on Heron Isle.

When he'd finished his coffee with the mayor, Logan headed toward the fountain in the square. He'd admired the craftsmanship of the Little Free Library the first time he visited, but he wanted a closer look now that he knew more about its story.

After he rounded the fountain and continued on the sidewalk north, he spotted the cream-colored miniature Victorian house on the right of the path near a bench. A giant live oak draped its long arms over the sidewalk, Spanish moss hanging over the sides and swaying in the breeze. He stopped to admire the intricate gingerbread detailing outlining every door and window of the library. It really was remarkable craftsmanship.

He opened the door and stepped inside and immediately went to look through the books on the ledge on the back wall. Whoever maintained the library—Lucy or Bob maybe?—had been skipping shelving the books he and Island Girl had left addressed to each other. His heart began pounding as he realized there was a new book addressed to him about Zelda Fitzgerald. He opened it to read her note.

Dear Gatsby's Ghost,

You've read Scott's version of events, so I thought you might enjoy what one writer imagined Zelda's story might have been. She was so glamorous, but at the same time so sad. She always wanted something more, but she never found happiness.

She has been overlooked in death in much the same way she was in life, and that is perhaps the saddest thing of all.

I see a bit of myself in Zelda. I know what it is to feel unheard, overlooked, and even unloved. To want things beyond my reach.

And even though I knew the ending, I couldn't help but hope that somehow the story ended differently.

To Les Années Folles,

Island Girl

To Les Années Folles—to the crazy years, as the French called the time period in the 1920s when the Hemingways, Scott and Zelda, Gertrude Stein, and the others of the Lost Generation lived, worked, and played in Paris.

Island Girl had him more curious than ever now. He tried to piece together what he knew about her so far. She enjoyed historical novels about the Lost Generation. She'd never been to Paris, but wanted to go, which was why Logan had ordered the memoir by the literary walking tour guide he'd enjoyed.

And now he knew more about her. But this note was sadder than the ones that came before it. She said she could relate to feeling unheard, overlooked, and unloved. He was more convinced than ever she was in a difficult marriage. He felt a sense of protectiveness, even if he didn't know her. You could learn a lot about a person from the books they read—who they admired, what piqued their interest, even how they viewed the world. Heck, he felt he knew more about Island Girl from her notes than he'd ever learn on a first date. Not that it was like that. He wasn't interested in a relationship, and it sounded like that was the last thing this woman needed right now.

He was intrigued, though, and he didn't want this discourse to stop. It reminded him of the pen pal he'd had as a kid. Their little classroom in Wisconsin had been paired with one in New York. Their teachers thought it would be good for kids growing up on farms to learn what it was like to grow up in a big city, and vice versa. They'd exchanged letters all school year.

He'd learned that his pen pal Dominic lived on the fifth floor of a building in Manhattan and had to walk three blocks to catch a glimpse of grass, a stark contrast from the acres of farmland that surrounded his childhood home. Virtually everything about their lives had been opposite, and it was fun to imagine what it would have been like to ride the subway to school and take field trips to Broadway shows. Those letters from Dominic had inspired Logan to go away to school, to experience big-city life firsthand. He occasionally thought of Dominic and wondered what he was doing now. Maybe he'd been as taken with small towns and farm life as Logan had been with Dominic's city life and was off in the Midwest somewhere milking cows. Nah, probably not.

Moving from city to city so frequently could be lonely, and Logan blamed his poor relationship choices on the nature of his job. Having a book pen pal was perfect. It would give him the friendship that was so difficult for him to form when he arrived in a new town, without any of the romantic entanglement. Besides, it seemed Island Girl needed someone to talk with as well.

Taking the book with him, he headed to his temporary office at city hall. He had to focus on the job at hand. If he couldn't pull out a win on Heron Isle, he might be the one who wound up back in the Midwest milking cows.

Six

Lucy

Lucy stared down at the same blank page in her journal that she'd been looking at for the past hour. On the mornings she didn't meet Taylor to walk, she'd go out on her back porch overlooking the ocean and write in her journal while she drank her coffee and watched the sunrise. Spending time at the beach was the perfect start to every day.

Unfortunately, her peace and tranquility had been interrupted this morning when she spotted a man she was pretty sure was Logan Lancaster running on the beach. He'd been heading south toward town. Even from a distance, she could see the well-defined muscles that sculpted his chest and arms. That image of him had occupied her every thought since, and instead of journaling, she'd wasted a half hour chastising herself for thinking about Logan's physique and those piercing green eyes. Her morning time was hers alone—until he'd barged in and taken over even that. Later today she needed to think about how to get him out of town and out of their business.

Pulling in a deep breath, Lucy closed her eyes and concentrated on the sound of the waves crashing on the shore beyond her porch. A laughing gull flew overhead, its unique call the only other sound this early. Later in the morning, families would set up umbrellas and scatter sand toys for kids to build castles, and the gentle breeze that blew in off the water virtually year-round would carry the sounds of the children shrieking with excitement as waves crashed over their legs. Lucy loved the soundtrack of living by the sea in the summer.

As the tension in her shoulders eased, she began to write.

> *I am grateful for this view.*
> *I am grateful for—*

She paused; her pen suspended above her journal. What? That there was still time to stop Logan Lancaster and the rest of the council pushing for the development?

No. Her gratitude journal was for things she was truly thankful for, like her little cottage on the beach or the bookstore. Other days it was the Waterway Café having had her favorite soup on special or the peonies she'd brought home from the flower shop to sit on her counter. Lucy looked toward the edge of her porch for the dune sunflowers that sprang from the sand, but even they looked wilted this morning, and it wasn't even that hot yet, at least not by Florida summer standards.

Frustrated, Lucy slammed the journal shut. She couldn't remember the last time she'd been unable to find something to write in it.

Annie had taught her to keep a gratitude journal back in high school when she was at that age when girls needed their moms the most. It had been hard to find anything to be grateful for when her mother had just walked out one day, telling Lucy and her father she was moving to Los Angeles because she needed "something more."

Why wasn't Heron Isle ever good enough for people as it was? First her mother, then Carter, her ex-fiancé. He'd left two summers ago for a job in Chicago saying the offer was "too good to pass up." Now, even the people she thought cared about the island more than anyone else—the mayor and the town council—had decided what they had wasn't good enough. They called it progress, but it mostly felt like a sucker punch. Why did everyone want something more? Bigger, better, more exciting, more growth.

People came to Heron Isle year after year because they loved the long stretch of beach that felt uncrowded even during high season, the freshly caught seafood that came in on boats every day, and the chance to slow down. Didn't the council see that they could lose everything that made Heron Isle special? People came here for something different. Every major tourist destination from Myrtle Beach to Daytona Beach and beyond had chain restaurants serving frozen seafood, go-cart tracks, waterparks, and fancy stores lining their shores. And that was exactly what the last set of proposals had looked like—the first step to becoming what every other beach town had become over the past three decades.

Newly motivated, Lucy decided to hit some of the downtown businesses that opened early before it was time to open the bookstore for the day. She'd meant what she'd said last night: it was important for the business owners to get on the same page. She didn't have time to wait for their meeting later in the week. Logan might stop by any one of them before then. She had to get there first.

She stopped by the bookstore to put her lunch in the

fridge in back and quickly go over her notes from their previous Downtown Business Owners Council meetings to refresh her memory. She pulled the file from a cabinet beneath the front counter and turned on her computer to check for any new emails in the chain the group kept going.

While she waited for it to boot up, she checked the one message blinking on the answering machine. She hadn't been able to bear throwing away the machine because it still had Annie's outgoing message on it, and Lucy called to listen to it every once in a while, just to hear her voice. She knew eventually she'd have to figure out how to move the recording over to digital voice mail, but for now the system still worked. The message was from a literary agent asking if she'd received the details for an author's signing the following month, so she went back to her computer to check her spam folder for the email since she hadn't seen anything come in.

But before she could, her hand froze on the mouse when she saw Leona Lord's name at the top of her inbox. She hadn't heard from *her* literary agent in months. Leona had landed Lucy her first book deal, but the publisher went belly up before it was released. Her agent had tried to shop the book around, but after a string of rejections she advised Lucy to start working on her next book. Lucy had written another, but it, too, was passed on by every publisher her agent had pitched.

Lucy was too dejected after that to write a third. The first deal had obviously been a fluke because the other publishers passed quickly, saying things like "cute idea but missing that special something." She wasn't even sure Leona actually was her literary agent anymore. The last time they'd spoken, Leona had implored her to write another book. When Lucy hadn't, she assumed Leona had finally given up on her.

Taking a deep breath, Lucy clicked to open the email.

Lucy,

I heard from Sarah today. She's still free-
lancing, but she thinks she might be
landing somewhere soon. She asked if you're
working on anything new, and I told her I
would check in with you. I know you needed
time to get over the shock of what happened
with your first book, but it's been nearly
two years. Have you been working on
anything? Do you still want to pursue being
an author? It would be a shame to see a
talent like yours wasted.
Leona

Lucy read the final question again, her heart thumping. Did she still want to be an author? Of course she wanted to be an author. But wanting to be an author and becoming one didn't always go together. She didn't think she could survive spending months pouring her heart and soul into another book only to be told it wasn't good enough. Again.

As she pondered how to reply to Leona, one of the bookstore's resident cats, a gray-and-white tuxedo cat named Lizzy, brushed up against Lucy's leg, arching her back as she begged for pets. Much like her literary name-sake, Elizabeth Bennett, Lizzy was headstrong and impos-sible to ignore. Along with Alice, a muted tortoiseshell cat, Lizzy lived in the bookstore, much to the delight of customers both young and old. Lucy headed to the back room to see if the cats needed feeding, Lizzy following so closely at her heels she nearly tripped over her. As Lucy was pouring a fresh bowl of food, she heard the bells on the front door jingle.

"I'm sorry, we're not open yet—" Lucy rounded a book-shelf toward the back of the store and spotted her best friend. "Taylor! Why are you here?" Lucy practically jogged across the store to hug her. "I thought you didn't get back until the weekend."

Taylor flopped down in the nearest armchair, letting out a huge sigh. "Never left. Jack twisted his knee walking up my stairs yesterday." She rolled her eyes. "I've been telling him to see someone about his knee for months, but you know how he is. Thinks he's Superman."

"Oh, no, I'm sorry you didn't get your vacation," Lucy said, dropping into the chair next to Taylor. "But, boy, am I glad you're here."

"Yeah, I got your text. Sorry I didn't text back; we were in the ER in Jacksonville all afternoon and evening. So they really did bring in some new consultant?"

"He's the worst. Slick, arrogant. Thinks he knows what's best for us when he hasn't even taken the time to get to know us." *Handsome. The most gorgeous green eyes you've ever seen.* An image of Logan's lopsided smile, his lone dimple punctuating his chiseled features, flashed through her mind and she shook her head to try to dislodge it.

"Why do they always want to bring in someone from the outside?" Taylor said.

"New perspectives and all that." Lucy waved her hand in the air dismissively.

"Yeah, Jack was complaining after he got back from his last business trip that we still don't have DoorDash or Uber Eats. What do we need that for anyway? You can get anywhere on the island in fifteen minutes or less."

Lucy sighed. Ever since Taylor had met Jack, when his company relocated him to Heron Isle to become the general manager of the resort on the north end, Lucy worried he would grow tired of small-town life and take Taylor away from her too. Taylor was a phenomenal hair stylist and makeup artist who made a nice living for herself with all the destination weddings that took place on the island, but Lucy was sure she could do that in any other town where she followed Jack. Taylor had moved to Heron Isle as a teenager, so although she liked it here, Lucy wasn't sure she'd always want to stay. Jack could probably make a compelling case for somewhere else where Taylor could make a bigger name for herself.

"So what's this guy's deal? What's he wanna build down by the water?" Taylor asked.

"Who knows?" Lucy threw up her hands. "He only spoke at the meeting for a few minutes. Babbled about big projects he'd done in Phoenix and St. Louis, like that's supposed to impress us. Why would they even bring in someone from a big city? And why would someone who's *so fabulous* want to work here anyway? Smells fishy to me."

"Well, I'm sure he's no match for my best friend, Miss Downtown Business Owners Council President." Taylor bowed from her chair, her brunette hair tumbling over the shoulders of her yellow sundress that highlighted her summer tan.

"Yeah, pretty sure they're going to regret appointing me. They thought it was funny to nominate me when I wasn't at the meeting, but the joke's on them now." Lucy tried to muster a laugh, but she was genuinely worried her fellow business owners had made a major mistake when they appointed her their leader.

"Nonsense." Taylor rolled her eyes. "You're young and you're smart. You went off and got that fancy degree."

"In Library Sciences." Lucy shook her head. "I don't know anything about city government or real estate development."

"You're good with people, though. No one's ever met you who didn't like you, and you'd talk to a brick wall. Have a conversation with this guy. Figure out what he's all about."

"Oh, we've had a conversation." Lucy rolled her eyes. "I actually met him before the meeting. He probably thought I was flirting with him." Lucy buried her head in her hands. "But it was before I knew who he was."

"Wait." Taylor sat up in her chair, turning to the side to lean toward Lucy with a smile, waiting for more details. "He's cute? Is he single?"

"I don't know, and I definitely don't care." Okay, the thought had crossed her mind, but she wasn't going to let it go there again. "He's the enemy, remember?" She was reminding Taylor as much as herself.

"Yes, absolutely." Taylor wiped the smile from her face and did her best to look serious, her brow furrowed. "But how handsome of an enemy are we talking?"

"He could be cast in a Hollywood movie kind of handsome." Lucy sighed. "And I think he knows it. Seems like the type who uses his good looks and charm to get what he wants. You should have seen Missy Goodwin at the meeting. She was practically drooling over him. He made this big show of tearing up the previous proposals, and she actually clapped." Lucy shook her head. Missy owned the flower shop in town and was a hopeless optimist. She gave everyone the benefit of the doubt, even when they didn't deserve it.

"What are you going to do?"

"I actually came in early so I could hit some of the other businesses that open before me. I think we all need to get on the same page. He said he's going to start visiting all the big groups in town, and I want us to strategize before he gets to us."

"Well, you were successful last time. They did abandon the other proposals."

"Did they? Or did they just bring in reinforcements?"

"Did you just read a war novel or something? This whole conversation is starting to sound like a plan for battle."

Lucy walked over to the counter, grabbed a book, and tossed it to Taylor.

When Taylor read the title, she laughed. It was a book about how to think like a military leader by a marine general. "You're like the mad hatter."

Lucy narrowed her eyes, her brows knitting together. "The mad hatter?" *Alice's Adventures in Wonderland* was one of her favorite books—it was why the other store cat was called Alice —but she didn't understand the comparison.

"Yeah, the mad hatter had all those hats and he'd put one on and transform into a character that matched the hat. That's how you are when you read." Taylor stood and handed the book back to Lucy. "I can always tell what kind of mood you're in by what you're reading." She winked at Lucy.

"You know what they say, a book a day keeps your problems at bay."

Taylor laughed. "Who says that?"

"I do."

"Of course you do. You should get that printed on a bookmark or something. It's cute. Just don't read a book on archery or marksmanship or something next. I'm confident you can take him in a war of words." Taylor smiled and gave Lucy a quick hug. "I've gotta run. Poor Jack can't even drive himself to physical therapy this morning his knee is so swollen. I'll call you later."

As she watched her best friend walk out the door, Lucy picked up the book by the marine general and took it back to the counter. The email from Leona was still open on her desktop. She closed the window and wondered how to tell her agent she wasn't going to write another book and put herself through being rejected all over again. She also wasn't sure she could bring herself to tell Leona she didn't really need a literary agent anymore. It was the one part of the journey where she'd been successful—only a small percentage of authors made it out of the slush pile and were offered representation—and she'd clung to that small success.

She'd read the terms of her contract with Leona over and over, and it said either of them could terminate the relationship with thirty days' notice, otherwise it would continue renewing annually. For now, at least, she could tell people she had a literary agent when they asked about her writing. She didn't have to tell them she didn't think she had another book in her.

Seven

Lucy

When Lucy exited the bookstore to try to catch Bob before she had to open for the day, she nearly ran into Logan. She smelled his dreamy cologne even before she looked up to register who it was.

"You're here early." He gave a small smile as he backed away to put some distance between them. With his leather messenger bag slung across his body, he looked more like a bike courier than a slick salesman today. "You were on my list for later today, but there's no time like the present. I think we got off on the wrong foot."

Lucy frowned, backing up another step to try to avoid his intoxicating scent clouding her thoughts. "Are you just going to be everywhere I go from now on?"

"Well, it is a small town." He held out his hands and shrugged, looking around as if to say there was nowhere else for him to be.

"Yeah, what do you know about small towns?" Lucy crossed her arms. "Isn't this a big step down for you? We're not exactly Phoenix or St. Louis."

"Ever heard of Berlin, Wisconsin?"

"No."

"It's never heard of you either." He laughed.

Lucy stared back at him.

"Just something funny my friends and I used to say. Basically, it's in the middle of Wisconsin. Population of about five and a half thousand. It also happens to be my hometown."

Lucy was surprised. She'd imagined Logan had grown up in a high-rise in Manhattan or Chicago or some other big city. She could hear Annie reminding her not to judge a book by its cover.

"Interesting. Why'd you leave?" She already knew the answer. Greener pastures and all. That was what everyone who left Heron Isle said.

"I wanted to get out and see the world." He shrugged. "I went to undergrad at USC and then law school at NYU."

Lucy huffed. Of course, Los Angeles and New York. Figured.

"What about you?" His eyes were fixed on hers. "Did you ever leave Heron Isle?"

"Yes, of course I left Heron Isle." Lucy rolled her eyes. She might not have traveled the world, but she hadn't remained on the twelve-square-mile island her entire life. "I went to the University of Florida over in Gainesville and then I worked in Ocala just south of there for a few years."

She'd never been ashamed of living in Florida her entire life—she loved her state—but she figured he must think her life was small compared to his. He'd lived in virtually every region of the country by the sound of it.

"A Floridian through and through." He smiled, his single dimple in full display.

"What can I say? I like it here." Plus she'd wanted to stay close to home because she didn't want to leave her dad alone for too long and she liked being able to go see him on weekends when she could.

"I like a woman who knows what she likes," he said, his green eyes locked on hers.

Was he flirting with her? His gaze was so intense, she worried he might actually be able to read her mind. She tried to telepath to him how much she wanted him to go away and leave her and her town alone, but if he got the message he didn't react.

Lucy stuffed her hands inside the pockets of her floral maxi dress, ready to be done with this conversation. "Well, I also like my island the way it is. Does that mean you'll leave it alone?" A woman could dream.

"I do have to earn my paycheck," he said, laughing.

"Which means you're just here to tell us how everything we've been doing is wrong and that there's a better way."

"Well, that's not exactly how I'd put it."

"Really?" She forced herself to look him in the eyes again. "How would you describe what you're here to do?"

"I'm here to find a compromise. We could work together, you know."

The way he said it felt like flirting again. No, this was just what someone like him did. He charmed his way into new towns until he got what he wanted, then he was off again to go terrorize another city. She nearly said something about how his good looks and impossibly green eyes weren't going to change her mind, but thought better of it. He might think she was flirting back.

Lucy remembered one of Annie's sayings that was a common refrain throughout the South: *You catch more flies with honey than vinegar.* Maybe she'd try a different tack. "So tell me. What would a compromise look like in this situation?"

"How about I tell you over a cup of coffee?" He motioned in the direction of the coffee shop. He was all dimple and green eyes again, the dull shade of his army-green polo making his eyes even brighter, if that was possible. His chiseled jawline softened when he smiled.

Lucy hesitated. She had to keep her wits about her. It would be too easy to let Logan's charm convince her of something that wasn't true, like those magicians who draw your attention in one direction to distract you from what they're doing in the other.

Keep your friends close and your enemies closer. That wasn't one of Annie's sayings. She trusted everyone until they gave her a reason not to, but Lucy had learned the hard way what it was like when she trusted too much. No, it was important to watch people for clues. Then you could be prepared when they blindsided you. She needed to figure out what kind of plans Logan was already considering.

"On one condition. We take our coffee down by the water. It's too beautiful to sit inside." Plus, the fresh air might dilute his intoxicating scent that made her want to lean in closer as he spoke.

"Deal." Logan reached out his hand to shake on it.

When Lucy reluctantly slipped her hand into his, she felt the tingle all the way up her arm and across her chest. His hand was strong, but soft. She let him hold hers for a beat longer than she should have, and when she pulled away and took a step back to put some distance between them, she nearly tripped on a portion of the sidewalk that was being uprooted by a nearby oak tree. Logan grabbed her arm, saving her from a fall. She could still feel the warmth of his hand even after he'd taken it away.

"Let me guess. That's another great example of something that's unsafe here and needs to be removed." Lucy motioned toward the sidewalk as she started walking toward the coffee shop two blocks south.

"It does present a tripping hazard, but it's an easy fix. They just need to cut out a little of the concrete to enlarge the pit around the tree. It would make the sidewalk a little narrower, but it's not like anyone's going to take out a live oak."

Lucy nodded, surprised by his answer, but she didn't want him to know that.

"My minor was in historic preservation." He pointed toward a marker on the building they were passing. "That's why I was reading the plaque the other day. It's also why I was interested in this job, because it doesn't involve the demolition of anything historic."

Lucy wasn't sure how to respond to that. She definitely hadn't pegged Logan as a preservationist. So far, he'd seemed like everyone else the town had brought in on the waterfront project, someone who just wanted to throw up a new development that boosted the bottom line.

"Surprised?" He turned to smile at her, clearly knowing he'd caught her off guard.

"I am. Why historic preservation?"

"Berlin—where I'm from—still has a number of its original buildings. My high school was built in 1918. They moved to a new building after I graduated, but the old high school was restored and turned into affordable housing apartments for our aging population that had moved off their farms. Berlin also happens to have some of the finest Victorian houses in the Midwest, including the one I grew up in. My great-grandfather built it in 1864."

"Interesting." Lucy tried to imagine Logan living in a historic home instead of the high-rise she'd previously pictured. Maybe she'd been too quick to judge after all.

"See, I'm not so different from you." He winked as he opened the door to the coffee shop for her.

Given his clear preference for living in big cities previously and his penchant for progress, she doubted they had anything in common beyond historic architecture. Plenty of people appreciated that; it was part of why tourists loved Heron Isle. Visitors had their choice of historic tours through downtown on foot or by horse-drawn carriage, and tickets sold out nearly every day in the summer months. Lucy loved hearing the clip-clop of the horses as they took people past her store and guides told stories about the people who founded the town.

After they'd grabbed iced coffees to go, they cut through the town square toward the marina.

"These are the original cobblestones." Lucy pointed down as they walked. "They paved Main Street back in the late seventies but left the cobblestones in the street crossings and here in the square."

"A town that respects its history." Logan nodded. "That's part of what makes this place special."

They both grew quiet as they passed under the shade of the towering oaks. Spanish moss danced in the wind, giving the square an ethereal quality with light filtering through in tiny beams across the square. Maybe if Lucy could show Logan what she loved about Heron Isle, he'd be more empathetic to the concerns she and most of the other locals shared. She understood why the town felt something had to change on the waterfront, but it didn't have to be a massive shopping and entertainment complex. The problem was, neither she nor anyone else opposed to the last round of development plans had been able to come up with anything else that would be profitable enough to help bolster the town's budget.

They sat on a bench at the marina overlooking the docks, a light breeze blowing the salty scent of the sea in their direction. Gulls swirled overhead and brown pelicans waddled at the edges of the boat slips hoping for scraps from the fishermen who were loading their boats to head out for the day. The serious commercial fishermen would already be on the water, but the charter-boat captains were just preparing to welcome their guests. Fishing was better at sunrise, but tourists could rarely be bothered to get up so early on vacation.

"What do you envision for the waterfront when you sit here?" Logan's voice was low and even as he looked over at Lucy. He had the deep tenor of a deejay on a slow jazz station.

Just one more sexy quality she had to work to ignore.

Lucy focused on stirring her iced coffee with her straw to avoid his gaze. "A fixed-up version of what's already here? We all love the restaurant, and someone suggested we could add an open-air seafood market where the local fishermen could sell their catches. I like that idea because aside from the two hotel resorts, most of our accommodations are beach cottages that families come to stay in for a week at a time, so they like being able to cook with local ingredients. Plus, if we had something open-air, we'd be able to see through it to the water instead of blocking the view with a giant building."

Logan lifted one leg to prop his ankle on his opposite knee, his expression thoughtful. "Hmm, I like that. Something that would benefit both the locals and the tourists, and preserves the visual connection between the water and down-town. But how do you bring in more tourists?"

"Who said we wanted to bring in more?" Lucy laughed. "There are plenty of folks here who want to find a way to help the town bring in more revenue without compounding our infrastructure problems by increasing tourism. All the accommodations we have maintain high occupancy rates. If you start bringing in more visitors, then you start needing more hotels, more parking, more lanes on the roads."

"What if they came in on cruise ships? Then they wouldn't be staying in hotels or driving cars. They'd pull up to dock here and spill into town to shop and eat. That would be good for everyone, right?"

"Cruise ships?" Lucy shook her head vehemently. "Absolutely not. You'd have to routinely dredge the channel, which disturbs the marine life. Then there's the waste and oil that pollutes the water. There go the fish the fishermen and restaurants depend on that draw so many of the tourists in the first place." She paused to take a breath of the warm salty air, steadying the frantic pace of her speech, before continuing. "Then there are all the boat strikes to manatees, right whales, you name it."

"Lucy, I'm not talking the kind of cruise ships that shuttle thousands of people to the Bahamas," he said, shaking his head. "I'm talking about small ships that ferry one hundred people or less along the Eastern Seaboard. They go into places like Charleston, Beaufort, and Savannah. We could get them to come a little farther south and add Heron Isle."

"That might solve the dredging issue, but it doesn't change the other environmental issues any size cruise brings with it." Lucy narrowed her eyes at Logan. "We changed our code years ago to prohibit pretty much anything bigger than a shrimping boat. I don't think anyone here wants to be a cruise ship destination."

"But you could be." Logan flashed his full watt, sunblinding smile that showed off every gleaming tooth. "Those cruise ships pay a per-guest tax plus docking fees, not to mention what the people who disembark spend in town while they're here. I bet they'd love to grab a book or two from your store to read while they're cruising." He raised an eyebrow in her direction, but went on when she continued to scowl. "What if we just brought in someone from the cruise line to make a presentation? Then we could all weigh the risks and benefits together."

Lucy frowned. "What else do you have?"

"Well, I heard you used to have one of those casino boats here—"

Lucy cut him off. "And where are all those people going to park to board the boat?" She gestured around her. "And it didn't do squat for the business owners downtown. People just came in, parked, went out on the boat for dinner, got back around midnight and left again. There's a reason we don't have one anymore."

"I heard the reason was that the company running the boat went under. Poor management. If you can get a proven company to come in, they can provide jobs for locals and you'll generate revenue from the docking fee and taxes. I worked with a great one up in Baltimore." He sounded genuinely proud of his solution.

"And you have the stats to prove they contributed to the local economy in a way ours didn't before?" Lucy motioned toward the waves crashing on the nearby beach. "There's plenty to do here. We don't need more entertainment. If you can't find something to do here, that's more of a reflection on you than on our town." She raised an eyebrow.

Logan held up his hands in surrender, his tone softening. "Okay, let's hear what else you have. Open-air seafood market. That's a solid start. What else?"

"It was suggested that a few kiosks could be added along the seawall overlooking the docks to serve food. Kind of like food trucks but more stationary. People would rent them out. Maybe it would attract some creative new chefs who just don't have the money for a full-size restaurant yet."

Logan nodded. "That's not a bad one either. What about the restaurants downtown? Would they support it?"

He sounded more hopeful than she felt.

"Hard to say. They're all pretty supportive of one another, and during the busy season they're all so full we could use another option or two. I know we can't make everyone happy, but we can at least try to help people more than we hurt."

"I really like that one if we can get the buy-in from the

restaurants. Let's keep that on the list." He gave her a smile before looking out over the marina and taking a long drink of his coffee.

What did he see when he looked around the waterfront with fresh eyes free from nostalgia? She was surprised by how receptive he had been to her ideas, but she knew an open-air seafood market and a few food kiosks weren't going to bring in the same money as a new retail complex with cruise ships and casino boats pulling into the marina. One good conversation wasn't going to change the fact that Logan had been hired to focus on the bottom line, but at least she knew now what he planned to pitch. She let herself take in one final breath of Logan's warm pine-scented cologne. It was intoxicating. She hoped the gulls calling out overhead kept him from hearing the sigh that escaped her lips. Absolutely nothing about this man's presence was fair.

EIGHT

Logan

Logan pinched his nose between his eyes. He'd been poring over the town's financial statements and contracts since he'd finished his conversation with Lucy. He understood where she was coming from, he really did. But he couldn't get caught up in nostalgia and emotion. He had a job to do, and they hadn't come up with any ideas they could both agree on that would produce the kind of money Heron Isle needed. Besides, three of the seven commissioners had already made it clear they expected a new development on the waterfront. They'd assured him they could get the fourth vote if Logan could come up with the right proposal.

The sound of his cell finally pulled his eyes away from his spreadsheets, which were all beginning to blur together.

"Hey, man," he said to his best friend from college, Cameron Fuller.

"What's up? Just calling to check in. Wanted to see how it's going down there."

Logan groaned as he leaned back in the desk chair. "Remember that summer when you interned in Idaho Springs?"

"Yeah, I got stuck in the sticks when you beat me out for the fellowship in Philly."

Logan remembered how excited he'd been to land the most coveted fellowship of their city planning program. Boy, had his career taken an unexpected detour. He knew Fuller wasn't trying to rub his face in it, but he felt it all the same.

"Remember how those community groups showed up to picket every meeting and hated the idea of absolutely anything new?"

Now Fuller was the one groaning. "That bad, huh?"

Logan filled in Fuller on his first town council meeting and some of the opposition he was facing. When he told him about Lucy, he intentionally left out that she was so attractive he'd almost asked her out for coffee when he ran into her the first time.

"Professor Parlow knows the mayor, right? So you must at least have that guy on your side." Fuller was the only person Logan had confided in that he'd needed their old professor to call in a favor after he was passed over for jobs in almost a dozen other cities. And he was right. Logan needed to spend more time with the mayor and check the pulse of the council. After all, they were the ones who would ultimately vote for the plan, not Lucy and her friends. Sure, it was nice to have the support of the locals, but that wasn't always the deciding factor in a vote like this.

"You really think closing the deal here will erase what happened in San Diego?" he asked Fuller, who was currently the Boston mayor's chief of staff. "Man, I really want to be up there with you when this is all said and done."

Fuller assured him that his word carried weight with the Boston mayor and that all he needed was a victory in Heron Isle to put a little distance between him and the one blip on his resume.

He said goodbye to Fuller and ripped his notes off the legal pad in front of him, starting over on a fresh sheet. Boston wasn't going to be impressed by a few food carts and an open-air market. There had to be a bigger win here on Heron Isle.

"Mayor?" Logan knocked on the open door. "Do you have a minute?"

"Of course." The mayor motioned for him to come in to his office. "Pull up a chair. What can I do for ya?"

"I thought it might be helpful to talk through the different interest groups that came forward to oppose the previous proposals. I'd like to know what I'm dealing with before I meet with people, that way I don't get thrown a curve ball." He'd read through all the minutes from the council meetings over the past few weeks, before he was formally introduced at the recent meeting, but he knew that only told part of the story. "I was hoping you could tell me more about who the power brokers are and what they really want out of this. Deal-breakers are always good to know too."

The mayor leaned back in his chair and clasped his hands over his middle. "Smart. That's why we hired you. Small-town politics can be tough to navigate."

Logan nodded. "I ran into Lucy Sullivan again."

"I see you're getting the real Heron Isle experience. Can't hide out around here." The mayor shook his head, chuckling to himself. "How'd that go? I imagine she's gearing up to go to war with us again."

"She actually had some interesting ideas. Of course,

they're not going to generate the kind of revenue you're looking for, but maybe there's a way to work them into our master plan."

"Lucy's a little bit like a dog with a bone. I'm sure that's not the last you'll hear from her." The mayor chuckled. "She means well, but she's not exactly looking at this like the business proposition it is. I heard she's been trying to negotiate to buy the building where her shop is. I doubt she ever imagined she'd own a business. She was planning to be a librarian, but then Annie surprised her by leaving her the bookstore. She took over the lease and owns the inventory, but it's not like she's getting rich off owning the store. She'd probably have to mortgage the beach cottage her dad left her to get the down payment, and even then, I'm not sure she understands what it means to own a historic building like that and suddenly be a landlord dealing with the tenants in the other spaces in the building and the repairs." The mayor shook his head.

Logan was a little taken aback by the amount of personal information the mayor had just shared about Lucy. It was exactly why he'd gladly left his hometown in his rearview. Small towns were prone to gossip and people always being in each other's business. He remembered how embarrassed his mother had been when she'd overheard two of her supposed friends in town talking about their farm falling on hard times. She'd come home crying and refused to go anywhere in town for weeks. Although his failure in San Diego had made the papers there, people had already moved on to another scandal before he could even pack his bags and get out of town. He could have stayed there the rest of his life and never had anyone bring it up again apart from those in real estate development circles.

Logan found himself jumping to Lucy's defense. "You might be selling her short."

The mayor raised an eyebrow in interest.

"You're probably right that the bookstore alone isn't ever going to be a cash cow, but being a landlord in the highest rent district on the island is a pretty smart move, if you ask me." He had a sudden urge to stop by the bookstore later and find out more about her plans to buy the building, see if maybe he could help. Did she know about the substantial tax credits that would be available to her to update a historic building like that?

He cleared his throat to push down those thoughts and get back to the task at hand. He had enough work to do with the waterfront project, he couldn't be taking on pet projects on the side. Not even for a beautiful woman whose smile was so tender and sweet it physically pained him when it disappeared and was replaced by her disapproving scowl.

Especially not for that reason.

"So other than the downtown business owners, who are we dealing with?" Logan was ready to change the subject and get back to the work at hand.

"Well, there's the tree conservancy. They put together email campaigns like you've never seen. They flood our inboxes anytime there's any development project on the agenda."

"But what's their play here?" Logan furrowed his brow. "There aren't any protected trees in that area, just some palm trees that we can easily relocate."

The mayor shrugged. "They're more of a general conservation group. They started with trees, but when there weren't groups organized to save the turtles or battle beach erosion, they took on those things too. They'd rather see the land on the waterfront be turned into green space."

"Ok, so generally environmental. Got it."

The mayor went on to describe the key players in the organization, and Logan scribbled notes on his pad. The mayor suggested he start with Helen Bowman, the organization's president, but he warned that Helen was a bit eccentric. She rehabbed injured reptiles, from gopher tortoises to garden snakes, and the mayor also told him not to be surprised if he ran into an alligator should he go to Helen's house to meet her. His name was Sidney and he'd lived at Helen's since he was injured by a boat motor as a baby and abandoned by his mother. He couldn't be released back into the wild. Helen had spent nearly three decades as a zoologist dedicated to reptile research and rehabilitation, and she often kept younger alligators to use for educational experiences in classrooms. When they got too big, she sent them to live at the reptile research center an hour south where she'd spent her career, and then she'd take in another young one for a while.

An alligator as a pet? Only in Florida. "It's not an attack alligator, is it?" Logan laughed, but the look on the mayor's face stopped him.

The mayor looked as if he was about to tell Logan that he should indeed beware of Sidney, but then he burst into a hearty laugh of his own.

"Nah, Sidney is harmless. He's basically the town mascot. He visits every first-grade classroom and has been known to be Santa's assistant when the kids come downtown for photos in December."

"Okay, friendly pet alligator. Noted." Logan shook his head as he made the note on this pad, although he couldn't imagine this was a detail he'd forget. "Who's next?"

"Well, then you've got the local fishermen, both the commercial guys and the charters. Both groups want low-cost dock space and for our fueling pumps to be repaired, but the charter guys are concerned about parking too. They need to keep convenient parking nearby for their guests, so they'd rather see a parking lot than more green space."

"Lucy mentioned there was some support for an open-air

seafood market on the waterfront. I assume both those groups would be in favor?"

The mayor removed his glasses and set them on his desk, deep wrinkles forming between his eyes. "Yes, we've been down that road. It's one of the ideas that got pretty universal support. The fishermen are all in support, and the restaurants like the idea of sending their chefs down to grab the latest catch right off the docks. But here are the drawbacks as I see them. Have you ever been in an open-air seafood market?"

"Sure, the one in San Francisco is pretty popular."

"They stink." The mayor scrunched up his nose. "And they attract birds and other critters looking for handouts. Would our tourists value grabbing fresh seafood over the stench it would bring downtown? And the rats? I hear the rats are terrible in those markets."

"It's one of the few things that benefits both tourists and locals though. I'm sure there are ways to deter pests." Plus, it was a small win he could try to get for Lucy. He could picture her smile when he told her the good news, feel her arms wrap around his neck as she hugged him in gratitude. "Did you run the financials? Could you charge enough for the stalls to make it worth giving up that kind of space on the waterfront?"

"Nah, we never got that far. Feel free to look into it if you want. At least it's something that actually got support from more than one group."

Logan made a note to reach out to a friend from grad school who worked in the San Francisco mayor's office.

"There were also some people who supported the previous proposals, right? I'm assuming local developers, general contractors, those sorts of people?"

"Yeah, the ones who thought they stood to profit. There are also some people here and there who understand the financial predicament the town's found itself in and figured the new development was a better fix than raising their taxes."

"Okay." Logan twisted his pen closed and slipped it back into his bag. "I think I've got what I need. I'm off to the Masonic lodge."

"Good old boys' club," the mayor said, slipping his glasses on as he scooted back up to his desk. "They can be convinced to go pro-development if they think they'll get something out of it. That group is full of all the bigwigs in town—lawyers, bankers, surveyors, you name it."

"Noted." Logan stood and started to make his way to the door before turning back to the mayor. "Hey, how big is that alligator? Sidney?"

"Haha, let's just say you can't miss him."

Logan shook his head as he left the mayor's office. He'd gone from black-tie dinners on yachts in San Diego where they discussed business over cigars and fifty-year-old scotch to dodging alligators to get meetings. Surely one day he'd look back and think it was a funny story to tell, but today was not that day.

As it turned out, the meeting at the Masonic lodge on the north end of the island wasn't as far from his dealmaking in San Diego as he would have thought. The attire was more casual, and the scotch was replaced by bourbon, but the rest was pretty much the same. Power brokers acted like power brokers no matter where they were. Logan was pretty sure one developer from the north end had even offered him a bribe, although something could have been lost in translation. He couldn't follow all the southern sayings, and there had been a lot of bourbon.

His brain was too fuzzy to concentrate on spreadsheets after lunch with the Masons, so he headed back home to take a cold shower and sober up. Luckily, one of the men who hadn't partaken in the bourbon offered him a ride home. He'd get his car downtown later.

He thought of the book he'd taken from the Little Free Library and fallen asleep reading the night before. Island Girl had been right. He'd never seen anyone tackle Zelda's side of the story. He'd once heard something described as "hauntingly beautiful," and it was a description that perfectly fit this book.

Settling in one of the tan leather armchairs by the back windows that overlooked the beach, he picked up where he'd left off. It only took a few pages before he came across a passage Island Girl had marked.

"In life's tapestry, catastrophe and triumph alike appear as threads predestined. Neither love's devotion nor wealth's embrace can divert the course already woven. We journey through, subject to the patterns predetermined, vulnerable to the hands of fate that can uplift or unravel us."

He read it again, fighting the bourbon fog in his brain to concentrate on each word. It was true, although depressing. The words made it sound like everything was predestined and no one could actively do anything to change the outcome. He simply didn't believe that.

Glancing up from the book to look at the ocean just beyond the dunes, he thought about why she'd chosen to mark this passage. There was no note in the margin, and he was curious what the words meant to her. Based on the marks and notes she'd left in the other books, she was going through some sort of struggle. Although he didn't know anything about her—aside from her taste in books—his gut told him it wasn't a situation of her making. He was curious, of course, but he also had a strong desire to figure out her problem and solve it. After all, he was a "fixer," as he'd overheard someone call him at the town council meeting.

He couldn't concentrate on reading anymore as his thoughts were too consumed with questions about Island Girl, so he decided to take a shower. Often it was where he got some of his best ideas, and immediately after toweling off and dressing, he went to his box of books. Island Girl sounded as if she needed a little confidence boost, and he had just the book. It was one he'd read on his plane ride out of San Diego to psych himself up for the new job. He located the book on mental resilience and dropped it into his leather messenger bag. He'd walk back to town on the beach, leave the book, and grab dinner. By then he would have sobered up enough to drive his car back to the house.

The sun was hitting the beach at a descending angle from the west side of the island, but it was still unbearably hot. Logan took off his shoes and carried them as he walked toward the shoreline. The water was warm enough for a bath, offering little reprieve from the early June heat.

The sound of the waves crashing less than twenty yards from where he walked on the edge of the waterline was soothing, nearly drowning out the shrieks of the children around him. They ran into the water until waves splashed them in the face, nearly knocking over the smaller ones.

He snapped a photo of the uncrowded beach for his sister, Carly, who had messaged him earlier to see how he was settling in.

"Much quieter here than in San Diego," he typed, before sending the photo.

A giant splash sounded behind him and he felt water spray across his back. He turned to see a Great Dane with a tennis ball dripping with water hanging from its enormous jowls.

"I'm so sorry!" a woman called from a few yards away. As she approached and slipped her sunglasses on top of her head, he recognized her from Lucy's table at dinner the previous evening. She stopped when she'd identified him.

"It's okay. I was hot anyway." Logan laughed as he pulled the wet polo shirt away from his back. "Logan Lancaster," he said, extending his hand. "I don't think we were properly introduced."

"Pam Beasley." Her reply was curt, but she shook his hand quickly.

"And who's this?" Logan petted the dog on its head, which came up to his chest.

"This is Ava. We're just out getting some exercise. She loves the water." Pam took the tennis ball from Ava's mouth and stepped back to lure the dog just out of the sea, then she threw the ball down the beach, where it bounced a couple times on the wet sand before Ava caught up to it. She began trotting back triumphantly with the ball in her mouth.

"Are you a downtown business owner too?" Logan asked. The mayor had warned him before the meeting that the various groups tended to sit together.

Pam nodded, her lips pressed into a thin line. "Cool Change, the consignment boutique on Main Street."

"Little River Band." Logan hummed a couple bars of the song by the same name.

"Exactly." Pam's taught features relaxed into a smile. "It was the name of my dad's fishing boat." She took the ball from Ava again and threw it farther down the beach toward downtown. Ava took off after it as Pam fell in step beside Logan to walk in Ava's direction.

"You grew up here?"

Logan figured Pam to be in her mid- to late fifties. She was petite but very well put together. It was obvious fashion was her thing. Even for a walk with the dog on the beach she wore white linen pants rolled up at the ankles and a matching top with a long, chunky gold chain necklace. Several gold and silver bracelets lined her wrist, jangling when she moved.

"I did. Heron Isle born and raised. I remember when the

Waterway Café was a welcome center that served free orange juice to tourists."

"I didn't know that. What was downtown like back then?"

"Pretty much like it is today. A few businesses have come and gone, but did you know that half a dozen of them are run by direct descendants of the original proprietors?"

"No, I didn't know that either."

"Sounds like you have a lot to learn, Mr. Lancaster." Pam gave him a sly smile that said she knew the task he was facing was bigger than he probably realized.

"Please, call me Logan." He flashed her the smile that had helped him set a record at the date auction held annually for San Diego's humane society. It was how he and Catherine had met. She'd won him, which pretty much set the tone for the rest of their relationship.

Pam nodded, taking the ball from Ava again and throwing it farther toward downtown.

"Logan, what are your intentions here on Heron Isle?"

"Well." He sighed. "I was hired by the commission to find a waterfront development plan that helps fund the budget deficit and keeps the town financially successful for years to come."

"And have you come up with any new ideas for how to get that done?"

"I have a few." He flashed her his winning smile again. "But I'd rather hear your ideas. I'm still trying to get a feel for what Heron Isle needs."

"That would depend on who you ask." Pam looked out over the ocean where a pelican was diving for its dinner. "But I imagine what you'll hear from quite a few is that they like things how they are. They'd rather increase the bed tax and have the tourists foot the bill, but then the tourism board and the two resorts bow up at that idea. Just look around you though." She flung both arms wide, encouraging him to take it all in. "Why fix something that isn't broken?"

Despite the humid air and the sun streaking across the beach, a chill went up his spine at her words. *"Why fix something that isn't broken?"* They were the same words his father had said to him when he'd come home from his freshman year of college with new ideas to modernize the dairy farm. His father had been too stubborn to change his mind, ultimately losing the farm, but Logan wouldn't let Heron Isle make the same mistake. Not on his watch.

NINE

Lucy

Lucy got another early start the following morning, finishing up her journaling on the back porch before eight o'clock. She needed to make the rounds with the downtown business owners before it was time to open the bookstore. Although she thought her conversation with Logan had gone well the day before, there was still something about him she didn't trust. Maybe it was his perfect teeth or his perfect square jawline. Even the dimple that made his face asymmetrical was perfect because it kept him from looking *too* perfect.

And no one was perfect. There was more to his motives than what he was showing, and she was going to figure out what he was hiding.

Her first stop of the day would be the flower shop. Logan already had the power to charm Missy, as they'd all witnessed, so Lucy needed to make sure Missy remembered the downtown business owners needed to stick together. They were closest to the waterfront and would be most impacted by its development, for better or worse.

Lucy followed an unfamiliar woman into the flower shop on the corner of Main and 3rd a block south of the bookstore. The sweet mix of floral scents hit Lucy as soon as she stepped inside. Farmhouse tables were staggered around the space, each piled high with different varieties of roses and lilies and more tropical selections like the giant birds of paradise poking their pointy beak-like buds from tall slender glass vases. Houseplants and succulents lined antique hutches on the left wall, while refrigerated, glass-fronted cases lined the opposite wall to protect the fresh-cut flowers ready for pickup.

Missy was talking to someone up front, so Lucy stopped to look at one of the tables piled high with buckets and arrangements filled with hydrangeas. The varying shades of blue and pink blossoms looked like the cotton candy her dad had bought her at the county fair when she was a kid. The memory made her smile, and she decided she should pick up a bouquet while she was here. She'd remind Missy how the downtown business owners had to support one another.

As Lucy moved around the table selecting several stems to make her own arrangement, she realized the man's voice coming from up front with Missy sounded familiar. She couldn't see over the towering displays of hydrangeas, but when she heard him reference the waterfront, she knew it had to be Logan.

He'd beat her. Of course, he'd gone to Missy first after she'd fallen all over herself to clap for him at the meeting.

Obviously, neither of them had noticed her come in the store. If Lucy just moved a little closer, she'd be able to hear their conversation. From her vantage point, she could see

Logan leaning sideways against the counter, but his head was obscured by a bulbous arrangement of hydrangeas. Missy was on the other side of the counter, and Lucy could only see her from the neck down. At least she was close enough to hear them speaking.

"—it was just so nice of you to come by." Missy leaned across the counter and touched Logan's arm, her voice at least an octave higher than usual.

Lucy flinched at the sight of Missy's hand staying on his arm a beat longer than was necessary. She'd been voted "Biggest Flirt" in their high school class, and some things never changed. But Logan didn't pull his arm away either. Did that mean he enjoyed Missy flirting with him?

Wait. Was she jealous? Missy flirted with everyone from Bob at the hardware store—who was old enough to be her grandfather and whose fifty-year wedding anniversary party she'd designed the centerpieces for—to the postman. And, besides, Logan would only be engaging with her because he needed as many downtown business owners on his side as possible.

"Just doing my part to get out and meet everyone." Logan's voice was slow, almost solicitous. "Obviously, the commissioners and the mayor hired me, but really I'm here to work for the people of Heron Isle."

At that, Lucy got over the temporary insanity of being jealous and rolled her eyes. He was here to work for the people of Heron Isle? Puh-lease. He was here to maximize the bottom line. That was it.

"Well, if there's anything I can do to help, you know where to find me." Missy was practically cooing.

"Yes, I do. It was nice getting to know you better, Missy." Logan's voice was as smooth as the maple syrup they served on the pancakes next door at Harriett's Diner.

"Don't be a stranger," Missy called as Logan headed to the door.

Lucy shifted around the table toward the front of the store to remain unseen as Logan exited. She was so focused on making sure he didn't see her, she bumped right into the other woman who'd entered the store in front of her.

"Excuse me. I'm so sorry."

The woman nodded curtly before going back to examining the calla lilies on the table behind the hydrangeas.

"Lucy, is that you?" Missy rounded the table. "I thought I recognized your voice."

Lucy straightened, tucking her blonde hair behind her ears. She'd left it naturally wavy that morning, but she could tell it was starting to frizz in the humidity.

"Mornin', Missy. Beautiful hydrangeas you have today. I thought I'd get some for the store." She held up the few stems she'd chosen before hearing Logan's voice.

"Well, that's not going to make much of an arrangement." Missy clucked her tongue as she pulled back her long red hair into a ponytail. "Here, let me help you." She moved over to the table of hydrangeas and selected a few more stems. "Let me cut these down for you, and we can do a nice short arrangement you can sit on your front counter."

Lucy followed Missy up to a butcher block table to the right of the register, where Missy began cutting the stems, selecting a short, round glass bowl to place them in.

"I didn't even see you come in. It's been a busy morning. That consultant the city hired, Logan, was just here. You must have seen him on your way in."

"Oh, no, I didn't see him," Lucy played dumb, looking around like he might still be inside. "But he's actually part of the reason I came in to chat," she said, turning back to Missy. "Bob, Pete, Pam, and I went out to dinner after the meeting the other night, and we think all the downtown business owners need to get on the same page about what we want before we have our meeting with Logan. I didn't realize he was going to go door-to-door so quickly."

"I think he's going to be good for Heron Isle," Missy said, looking up from her nearly complete arrangement and smiling. "He had a great idea about bringing cruise ships into the port—"

"Cruise ships?" Lucy hissed across the counter at Missy. "Did he seriously bring up cruise ships again?"

"Again?" Missy looked confused. "That's the first time I remember hearing about the cruise ship idea."

Lucy shook her head. "Never mind. What did he say about cruise ships?" Lucy was gritting her teeth, her fingers turning white as they gripped the edge of the counter. How could he continue to peddle this ridiculous idea after what she'd told him about the environmental impacts? Even the smaller one-hundred-passenger ships had wreaked havoc in other ports.

Unaware of Lucy's growing frustration, Missy began animatedly telling her about Logan's plans. "He said it would bring lots of business to us here downtown as the cruise ships docked for the day. He even said he could work it into the deal that they had to buy certain things from downtown businesses when they pull in. Like, they could buy fresh flowers from me to put on their dining-room tables and in the VIP cabins. Isn't that just the best idea?"

Lucy sighed, pinching her nose between her eyes. "No, Missy. I know it sounds like a great idea, but it's not. Did he mention the noise and air pollution that will impact those of us who have businesses on Main Street, and especially people like you and Pam who live nearby?" Lucy had been reading up on it last night, gathering all the data she could to share at the next council meeting if cruise ships were still on the drawing board.

Missy's bright smile faded into a frown. "No, he didn't mention that."

"Of course he didn't. And did he mention they dump their bilge water that's full of oil and grease and raw sewage?" Lucy scrunched up her nose for effect. "That stuff would pollute the water we swim in, the water our seafood comes from."

"He definitely didn't mention that." Missy slid the flower arrangement across the counter to Lucy, her eyes turned down as she played with the edge of the kraft paper stacked on the butcher block. "I wish I'd known all that. I told him I thought it was a great idea."

"It's okay." Lucy reached across the counter to pat her hand. "It's not like you signed an agreement or anything. He counted on you not knowing anything about the environmental impacts. Heck, I didn't know either until a few months ago. I sat in on one of the conservancy's meetings, and they were talking about the efforts some of the cruise companies have been making to get into towns along the southeastern coast. They figured the companies would come courting us eventually. This consultant has probably worked with them in other cities. He probably even gets a commission for every new port he adds."

"You really think that's how these consultants work?" Missy's eyes were wide.

Lucy shrugged. "Would it surprise you?" For reasons she didn't understand, Lucy didn't actually believe Logan was the kickback type, but she didn't know that for sure and she needed to keep Missy on her side.

"He just seems so nice." Missy glanced at the front door as if he were still there.

Lucy knew what she really meant was that he was handsome and charming. Those things and being nice weren't the same, but Lucy knew it was something she would have to constantly remind herself of too. It was too easy to get mesmerized by those green eyes and the way he smiled so effortlessly.

"Yeah, I preferred the old guy with the big ears they brought in to present that last plan. He wouldn't know charm if it hit him in the head. This guy's a ringer. Even Pete was flirting with him the other night when we ran into him at the Waterway Café."

"He is kind of dreamy," Missy said, staring wistfully at the front door again as if he might walk back in at any moment. "Did you see those eyes? Wowee! We don't get many men who look like him around here. You snapped up the last hunky guy who came to town—" She stopped herself as she realized what she was saying and stared down at the counter. "Sorry, I didn't mean to bring up Carter. Do you still hear from him?"

Although time had dulled the pain from somewhere around a knife in the heart to an annoyingly throbbing paper cut, the reminder of Carter and how he'd left her for the job in Chicago still stung.

"No." Lucy shook her head as she attempted to dislodge the image of him pulling out of her drive for the last time. "No point keeping in touch."

"Well, we're glad you're still here," Missy said, waving Lucy off as she pulled out her wallet. "It's on the house. Just take a few of my business cards and put them out by the flowers. I'll write it off as marketing." Missy smiled as she tucked pieces of her red hair that were too short to stay in her ponytail back behind her ear.

The woman who'd entered the store ahead of Lucy approached the counter holding an assortment of daisies and roses.

"We'll chat more later," Lucy said. "I'm going to stop by all the downtown businesses this week and figure out our plan of attack."

"Okay, just let me know." Missy said as she turned to help the other customer.

Lucy decided she needed to go see Bob to tell him Logan was going door-to-door. He'd know what to do.

The hardware store was unusually busy for that time of day, so Lucy told Bob they could catch up later. He'd suggested she send an email to the group and warn them against discussing anything with Logan before they'd all had a chance to get together.

As she crossed through the town square on her way to open her store, she noticed the door to the Little Free Library had been left open. She detoured up the sidewalk to go close it if no one was inside. As she reached to swing it shut, she saw a few new additions stacked on the ledge at the back and couldn't resist grabbing them to read through the notes.

The first book was a thriller with a recommendation for anyone who loved true-crime podcasts. She read the back cover copy and shivered despite the heat already setting in for the day. She loved a good thriller, but this one sounded terrible enough to give her nightmares.

She thumbed through a few children's books that had been added, her mood lifting when she saw the barely legible crayon handwriting on one of the notes.

I liked the brown bear. I wasn't scared. GRRR!

A drawing of what appeared to be a brown snowman was included. Smiling, she tucked the note back inside the book and placed it on the shelf among the other children's books. A few dog-eared copies of romance novels had been added to the fiction shelf, the creases in the bindings showing they'd been around the block a few times already. Lucy used to read romance novels, but that was before Carter left. Real-life relationships were nothing like the ones she'd read about. The girl didn't always get the guy. Sometimes the guy moved to Chicago.

At this thought, she could almost hear Annie's voice in her head, reminding her that it just meant Carter wasn't *the* guy. He was out there somewhere, and he would choose her and Heron Isle without hesitation. She wouldn't have to compete with a big city or beg him to stay.

Lucy sighed as she moved the last children's book aside. The familiar handwriting of Gatsby's Ghost appeared on a sticky note attached to the next book. She was surprised to see it was a personal development book. *The 5 Second Rule: Transform Your Life, Work, and Confidence with Everyday Courage.* She'd read her share of self-help books, but all they'd done was convince her that some people were born with confidence and others were not. She definitely fell into the latter category.

Pulling out the book, she smiled as she removed the index card inside, eager to see what Gatsby's Ghost had to say today.

Island Girl,

I, too, understand what it's like to strive for something and feel it's always just out of your grasp. But it's like Babe Ruth said: it's hard to beat a person who never gives up.

I'm currently in a bit of a predicament myself. I'm at the plate with two outs, two strikes, and it's the bottom of the ninth. I either win the game or perhaps there will be no more games for me.

I think what I'm trying to say is that we both need to trust our swings when we step up to the plate. This is the book I reread every time I need a boost. Thought maybe you could use it too.

Signed,
Gatsby's Ghost

P. S. I hope you like baseball, haha.

Lucy smiled. Luckily for Gatsby's Ghost, she used to spend nights snuggled in next to her dad in his old recliner watching baseball. He'd loved sport analogies too. She still remembered how he'd yell "batter up!" in the mornings to let her know it was time to come downstairs because her breakfast was ready.

A warmth spread over Lucy as she realized Gatsby's Ghost had seen what she wrote in her last note, and instead of viewing her as weak, he wanted to encourage her to keep trying. She'd have to be mentally tough to take on Logan Lancaster. If he had a confidence issue, it was from being too far on the other end of the spectrum from her. What was it Bob had called him? A fixer. He probably didn't need a book like this to make him feel more confident. He had a natural swagger that was as irritating as it was magnetizing. She needed to focus on the irritating part. She needed to be immune to his charm and those green eyes. She slid the book into her purse, vowing to read it as soon as she had some quiet moments at the store today. She could use all the confidence she could get.

The town had brought Logan in because they meant business, but she wasn't going down that easy. This was her island too. Four generations of Sullivans had lived here. She wasn't going to let some outsider come in and tell her what *her* island needed. That it wasn't good enough the way it was. She wondered if he'd ever gone back to the little town in Wisconsin he was from and tried to push his ideas of so-called progress on *them*.

After Lucy closed up the library and opened her store for the day, she logged on to her computer. Mornings tended to be slow until the tourists headed into town for lunch. As she put out food for Lizzy and Alice, she wondered what Gatsby's Ghost was facing that had him feeling like he was down to his final pitch. Was it work or personal? It had been vulnerable of him to share that he, too, was struggling, and if the dog-eared copy of the book he'd left was any indication, he'd needed a confidence boost now and then also.

Maybe his business was in danger of closing, or he had a big proposal out that he needed to win to make his quarterly sales goal. She tried picturing what a man who loved both literary history and baseball did for a living. Maybe he was a professor in town for summer break who rented a beach house so he could write his novel. Maybe that was his do or die situation—he was on a deadline for his book.

Her stomach flip-flopped as she remembered what that had been like. That feeling, however uncomfortable, had paled in comparison to the gut punch of finding out the book wasn't even being published. She'd given up so many weekends and nights to sit at her computer and write and then edit, letting the rest of her life basically pass her by, only to have nothing to show for it in the end. It was part of why she'd fallen so hard and fast for Carter. She'd been swept away by the idea of settling down with him and having a family of her own where she could find purpose.

Having gone down the Carter rabbit hole once already today with Missy, Lucy decided to take a look at the book from Gatsby's Ghost while the store was quiet. Normally, she would never jump ahead in a book. She knew some of her customers liked to read the end first, but she'd never understood that. She loved letting the story unfold in its own time as she progressed through the pages. Now, however, she found she couldn't resist the urge to flip through until she saw his familiar handwriting in the margins. What nuggets had he highlighted for her?

"Hesitation is the kiss of death. You might hesitate for just a nanosecond, but that's all it takes. That one small hesitation triggers a mental system that's designed to stop you. And it happens in less than—you guessed it—five seconds."

She harumphed out loud to Lizzy, who had crawled into her lap. "So what? We're supposed to make uninformed, impulsive decisions?" she asked the cat, who was now pawing at the book as if she, too, wanted to see what Gatsby's Ghost had written.

"Your feelings don't matter. The only thing that matters is what you DO."

Yikes. Your feelings don't matter? Gatsby's Ghost certainly didn't seem like the kind of robot who would identify with this passage, but there it was—underlined twice.

She flipped ahead, looking for more, finding herself disappointed in his latest suggestion. This was supposed to inspire her to be more confident?

"Yes, you can move mountains. Whatever is happening right now, this is it. This is your life. And it's not going to begin again. You can't change the past, but in five seconds you can change your future."

He'd drawn an arrow in the margin next to the last sentence, tracing over it several times so it was bold and the page was indented from the effort. She read it again. Finally, something she could get behind. She'd add it to her journal later so she could repeat it in the mornings with her mantras.

Wanting to end on a high note, she closed the book and concentrated on petting the cat in her lap until she jumped down at the sound of the bells jingling on the front door, eager to greet their first customer of the day. The mayor poked in his head, as if he hadn't fully committed to entering.

"Mayor, come on in."

"Are you alone?" He looked toward the bookshelves that ran perpendicular to the wall on the right side of the store as if someone were hiding and might jump out at any moment.

Lucy tucked the book between her leg and the arm of the chair. "I am. Is everything okay?" As he shuffled toward her, she pointed to the other armchair. "Have a seat. Can I get you coffee? Tea? Water?"

"I'd take a cup of coffee if it's not too much trouble." He lowered himself into the armchair.

"I was just going to put on a pot." It was a lie, but everyone in the South did it. You never wanted your guest to feel they were putting you out. "Let me get it started. Be right back."

In the little kitchenette, Lucy fished a filter out of the drawer and added a few heaping spoonfuls of coffee inside it, then set the pot to begin. Taylor had given her a Keurig the previous Christmas, touting how quickly it could make coffee or tea on demand for her and her customers, but it still sat in its box on a shelf in the back. She didn't mean to be ungrateful for the gift. It was very thoughtful. Lucy just didn't want to speed up the process. Waiting for coffee to brew gave people time to chat or browse. This wasn't a fast-food joint where she wanted to hustle people in and out the door.

She rejoined the mayor up front. "So is this a social visit or a political one?" She sat in the same chair she'd been reading in, turning slightly to her left to face him.

"Can't it be both?" His friendly smile and easy demeanor had made him a shoo-in for mayor when he'd first run, and now he was a year into his second and final term before the town's term limit would force him to pass the gavel to someone else.

She sighed. "Yes, of course. How are you? How are Mrs. Jenkins and Thomas?" Lucy had known the Jenkins family her entire life. Their son, Thomas, was her age and had often been in her classes growing up.

The mayor was beaming now. "Thomas and his wife are expecting a baby this Christmas. A grandchild! Talk about the best gift under the tree."

"Congratulations." Lucy was sure Thomas would make a wonderful father. He'd always been kind and seemed like someone who would relish being a parent, the same way hers had. "Please tell him I send my best." Thomas had moved away for college and never come back, like many of her classmates. The lure of bigger cities seemed to call to everyone but her.

"I will. He and Jennifer are visiting for Labor Day, so I'm sure you'll see them then."

Lucy heard the beeps indicating the coffee was finished. Standing, she asked the mayor, "Cream? Sugar?"

"A little of both, please."

"You got it. Be right back."

Once she'd returned with their coffees, her curiosity got the best of her. "So what can I do for you, Mayor?"

"I wanted to talk to you about Logan Lancaster."

Remembering how jealous she'd been when Missy placed her hand on his arm that morning at the flower shop, Lucy busied herself with stirring her coffee.

"Mm-hmm." She took a long sip. "What about him?"

"He says you've spoken already. That you had some good ideas he's going to try to incorporate."

"Did he also tell you he wants to bring in cruise ships and gambling boats?"

"Yes, those have been mentioned. They're not the worst ideas I've heard. At least it wouldn't be a giant development on the waterfront, right?"

"They're still not great ideas." She set her coffee on the table between their chairs. "Have you run it by Helen yet?" Lucy was sure Helen would be on her side on this.

The mayor held up his hands in surrender. "That's why I'm here. There are a lot of ideas on the table, and they all have pros and cons. I want to do what we should have done the first time around. I want to hold a series of community forums where we can all discuss these ideas and find the best solution. This isn't just a council decision; it's a community decision."

Lucy crossed one leg over the other and looked out across the bookstore. As much as she wanted everything to remain the same, she knew that now the town had engaged Logan they were going to move forward with some sort of plan for the waterfront. At least this time they wanted to involve everyone in the decision.

"Well, you know I'll be there. I'm sure a lot of people will want to be involved in the process, but with so many opinions, how will we ever reach a consensus?"

"That's why I'm here." The mayor put his mug down on the table. "I want you to lead the community forums"—he glanced away and cleared his throat—"with Logan. The two of you would decide the topics for each meeting, contact any outside experts you want to bring in, that sort of thing. He'll represent the council and you'll represent the community. That way it's fair and balanced."

"I'm not sure I'm the right person." These meetings were too important for her to lead. She'd thrown every argument she had at Logan out on the docks the day before, and if his talk with Missy was any indication, he was still forging ahead with the cruise ship idea. She didn't know how to fight someone like him. "You should ask Helen to do it." Helen was one of the most noted people in her field. She'd probably come up against people like Logan her entire career.

"Helen has to present some kind of groundbreaking research at a conference next month and said she'll be working around the clock until then out in California with another researcher. She promised others from her group will be at the meetings, and she's emailing you info on her experts. She agreed with me that it should be you."

Lucy didn't feel any more confident. "There must be someone else. I don't think I could bear it if I failed. We're talking about the future of our entire town." She racked her brain for someone better suited to the job.

The mayor leaned toward her. "Lucy, I don't think this is a life-or-death situation. Do you really think I would sit by and watch the town be destroyed? We're just talking about a little progress. Look at this building you're in." He motioned around the room. "It wasn't one of the original buildings on Main Street. It came thirty years after the ones closer to the water. And now you can't imagine it not being here, right? Change can feel like the end of something we love just the way it is, but what if it's the start of something even greater?"

She frowned. "You saw the previous plans. Can you seriously compare those monstrosities they wanted to build to this building?" She looked up at the tin ceiling, each tile stamped with delicate designs that looked like flowers growing on vines.

"No." The mayor's voice was gentler now. "But that's why we brought Logan in. Did you know he minored in historic preservation?"

"Yes, he mentioned that. Then just minutes later he suggested trucking giant ships through the channel. Are we just going to overturn the ninety-foot limit we've had on boats coming into the marina and start dredging?" She shook her arm toward the marina on the other end of downtown. She understood why on paper the mayor might think Logan was the right man for the job, but he clearly wasn't. "I did a little research, and even the smallest cruise ships are more than three hundred feet long."

"Clearly you're opposed to that direction. And that's fine. You and everyone else will have your chance to voice those opinions at the community forums. Even more reason for you to lead them with Logan."

She thought then of the last passage from the book.

"This is your life. And it's not going to begin again. You can't change the past, but in five seconds you can change your future."

Lucy felt torn. Of course, she wanted to be part of the discussion and ensure that cruise ships stayed away from Heron Isle. But what if she failed? Then she'd have to spend the rest of her life watching those ships pull into port, knowing it was her fault they were there, because she wasn't strong enough or smart enough to stop them.

She fingered the tiny anchor pendant on the delicate chain around her neck, flipping it back and forth. Her dad had given her the necklace for her eighteenth birthday, shortly before she left for college, to remind her to always have a strong anchor and stand for the things she believed in. Then she remembered the book again.

Five seconds of hesitation. That was all the book said it takes for your brain to stop you. Maybe the author was on to something after all.

"You know what? I'll do it," Lucy said, noting the look of surprise on the mayor's face. Obviously, he'd thought she'd be a tougher sell.

"Wonderful! I'll talk to Logan, and we'll get the first meeting on the books." He reached out to shake her hand.

Smiling, she thought of Gatsby's Ghost and how proud he would be of her.

TEN

Logan

Texting his sister a photo of the beach had led to questions about how Logan's job was going on Heron Isle. He knew she worried about him after what had happened in San Diego.

"It's going well so far," he told her, and it wasn't a lie.

For the first time since he was announced as the consultant Heron Isle had hired to solve their waterfront predicament, Logan really did feel good about the direction it was all headed. His step was a little lighter after he'd visited Missy at the flower shop and then caught Mel, the owner of the general store, as he was opening for the day. They'd both been receptive to his idea of attracting a small line of cruise ships to make Heron Isle one of its ports.

Logan had worked with the cruise line on the Baltimore job. They'd organized a multi-day cruise around Chesapeake Bay with stops in towns like Yorktown, Cambridge, and St.

Michaels to help spread out the tourists. The businesses in those towns had been happy to receive the new visitors, and he thought he could do the same for Heron Isle. The guys at the cruise line had been intrigued, but they didn't have any other stops nearby. He knew that meant all the tourists would descend on Heron Isle, and then Lucy might be right that it would be more of an influx of people than their downtown could bear. Maybe there were ways to trolley them to other parts of the island. He had some time to flesh it out.

The cruise idea had been an easy sell to Missy and Mel. He'd had the idea to bake some incentives into the contract, which he'd already discussed with the cruise line. The ship would purchase floral arrangements from Missy for its dining-room tables and VIP cabins each time it stopped in port, and Mel would get increased foot traffic as passengers disembarked and stocked up on everything from sunscreen to soda and snacks.

Logan caught himself whistling as he walked down Main Street and ran into the mayor. Like a needle to a balloon, their conversation immediately deflated him. The mayor wanted him and Lucy to host community forums. Two words every local-government consultant feared the most. It was impossible to make everyone happy, so the best anyone could hope for was a consensus, and even that was often challenging.

The mayor insisted the downtown business owners and the conservancy were the largest opposition groups, so if he could get them on board he'd be on the right track. Logan had been able to discuss things civilly with Lucy the previous day, and she was far from the worst person he'd ever been forced to spend time with on a project. In fact, she was cute when she wasn't mad at him. Unfortunately, she'd pretty much hated him since the instant she found out why he was on Heron Isle.

Knowing they needed to find some mutually agreeable dates, Logan changed directions and headed over to the bookstore. He spent the short walk trying to find a way to frame their new situation that she wouldn't completely hate.

When he entered the store, he immediately spotted Lucy helping an older woman by the shelves that ran alongside the left wall of the store. She was tucking a blonde curl behind her ear, smiling, and nodding as the customer spoke. Lucy glanced toward the door when the woman paused to look at the book Lucy had handed her. As soon as she saw him, her smile disappeared as if someone had flipped a switch, and his optimism was immediately dashed. Her shoulders stiffened and she politely told the woman she'd be nearby if she needed any other recommendations.

Logan wanted Lucy to understand he wasn't a bad person. That change wasn't bad. This was why he'd always preferred jobs in bigger cities. People in small towns seemed to take change far more personally, like his father and the other farmers in Berlin had. He couldn't let Heron Isle make the same mistakes he'd watched decimate his hometown.

He flashed his best smile at Lucy as she crossed the floor to where he stood near the counter, the heart-pine floorboards moaning and creaking under even her small frame. He imagined how many people must have walked across these same floorboards over the past one hundred and fifty years.

That was it! He loved the history here too. He just needed her to see that side of him.

"This is quite the place you've got here." He looked around the room in a way he hoped showed his appreciation for it. As he glanced toward the back of the store, he noticed the ceiling for the first time. It looked like hand-stamped tin. He pointed up. "Are those original?"

She followed his gaze. "They are. So are the floors."

He couldn't read her even expression, but if her first reaction when she'd noticed him by the door was any indication, she was not happy to see him. He knew they hadn't agreed on everything when they chatted on the docks the day before, but he thought the conversation had gone well overall and they'd broken the ice.

The customer was approaching the counter with her selections.

"I'll just look around for a minute." He nodded to the woman as he excused himself then wandered toward the shelves. He ran a hand over the edge of a shelf. They looked like they were handmade from heart pine too. A ladder hung at the far end of the shelves near the front window with a small sign attached that said: "Please do not climb." He'd always dreamed of having a library in his house one day, and he'd even pictured having shelves that went to the ceiling like this with a ladder to reach the top. Unfortunately, his job didn't lend itself to him having a permanent address, so the library of his dreams would have to remain just that, a dream. It was for the best. When someone stayed in one place too long they got stagnant, stuck in their ways. He would not become his father.

Logan moved to one of the shorter shelves that ran perpendicular to the wall, pretending to be interested in a thriller as he eavesdropped on Lucy's conversation with the customer to distract himself from the memories of his father. The woman was asking if Lucy had a website where she could order books after she left Heron Isle.

"Unfortunately, I'm pretty useless when it comes to technology. But call me anytime. I'd be happy to ship you anything you'd like or make some recommendations." The voice she used with the customer was much warmer than the one he'd been greeted with.

"Thank you, dear. I'm so glad you kept the store open after Annie passed. She was such a remarkable woman. Do you know she always remembered what kinds of books I liked and would have a couple sitting aside for me, ready for my arrival each June?" The woman shook her head. "You just don't get that kind of service from those big corporate stores or ordering online."

"Well, now that I know what you like, I'll be sure to save some of my favorites for you, Mrs. Frances." Lucy patted the woman's hand where it rested on the counter. "Thank you for continuing to visit us every year. Just call me if you need to me to ship you anything in the meantime."

The woman thanked Lucy and left with her bag of books. Lucy busied herself writing in a notebook on the counter, either having forgotten about Logan or purposely avoiding him.

"I didn't mean to eavesdrop, but if you need a website, I know a great guy. I bet a lot of your seasonal customers would buy from you online, especially ones like that who've been coming here for years." He walked up to the counter, curious what she was scribbling.

"I do just fine without a website." She quickly closed the notebook. "If someone wants a book they call and I mail it. It's more personal that way." Gone was the warm tone she'd used with the woman, replaced by something more clipped that felt like standing in front of an open freezer door.

Holding up a hand in mock surrender, he softened his tone. "I'm not saying stop taking phone orders. You could just add online ordering for those who prefer it. What if someone wants to order something late at night or before you open in the morning?"

"Then they leave me a message." She nodded toward a desk phone on the far end of the counter. "I've got an answering machine."

"You don't mean the kind with a tape—" He was joking because she'd called it an answering machine instead of voice mail, but midway through his sentence he spotted something that look suspiciously like an answering machine straight out of the 1990s next to the phone. "Seriously?" He reached across the counter to pick up the antiquated device. "This thing still works?"

"Yes, it works perfectly."

He chuckled. "And what are you doing there? Do you keep track of your sales by hand too?"

"Yes, it's called tracking my inventory."

It was as if he'd stumbled into a time warp. "You have a computer." He motioned toward the monitor on the counter next to her. "I know they make software specifically for book-stores to track their inventory."

"I'm sure they do, but this way works for me." She shrugged. "This shop was here for a long time before computers ever existed, and we've always managed just fine."

"What do you use the computer for then?" He was genuinely curious. He'd never met someone her age—he'd pegged her to be in her early thirties—who was so opposed to modern technology.

"It runs the register. I check my email and place my new orders. Sometimes I use it to help a customer find a book."

"From bookstores who actually have their inventory online for people to purchase?" He kept his tone light so she'd know he was jokingly pointing out that she'd made his point for him.

She scowled at him. "Is there a reason you're here?"

"Mayor Jenkins said he told you about the community forums. I thought we should compare calendars and find some dates that work for both of us." He pulled out his smart phone so he could access his calendar. "Wait. Let me guess. You've got one of those fancy notebook planners in your purse where you write your appointments by hand next to a quote of the day."

She had her purse halfway up to the counter from where she'd been storing it underneath when she shoved it back in its hiding place. She folded her arms against her chest, her mouth a thin line.

"I can make myself available. Just tell me when you want to hold them."

"You do!" He was smiling now as he leaned over the counter, trying to peek underneath. "You have one of those planners, don't you? Let me see."

"Off my counter, please." The corners of her mouth were turning slightly, just enough that he knew she was trying her best not to smile. She pointed to the phone still in his hand. "Tap away on your little device there and just tell me some dates. We should hold them at night when most people are off work and can attend, and maybe at least one on a weekend for people who can't get away during the week."

As he was looking through the town calendar on his phone to make sure they wouldn't conflict with other meetings, something rubbed against his leg, and he jumped.

Lucy giggled as she leaned over the counter. "Don't worry, that's just Lizzy. She doesn't bite." She paused. "At least not people she likes. I haven't told her about you yet, so you should be safe."

He reached down to pet the cat, her sleek gray fur reminding him of a seal. She had a little bit of white on her nose, down her chest, and on her feet, and she purred almost immediately when he began stroking her back.

"She's yours?"

"More or less. I adopted her, but she really belongs to the store."

"A guard cat?" He smiled up at her.

"Sort of. Only she guards against mice, not burglars. Lots of bookstores used to have cats to keep away pests. Plus, the kids love them."

"Them? There's more than one?"

Lizzy rubbed her head against his hand as she walked back and forth in front of where he now kneeled.

"There's one more, but she's a little shyer than this one. Lizzy likes anyone who will pet her. She's not all that discerning."

He knew it was a jab at him, but her voice had been light when she said it. The cat seemed to notice Lucy's voice and leaped up to the counter, nuzzling into her hand as she held it out.

He watched her hand gently caressing the cat, its back arching in pleasure. He caught himself thinking about what her fingers would feel like on his skin and forced himself to look back down at his phone.

"What about next Wednesday for the first one?" His voice came out husky and he cleared his throat. "That gives us a week."

"Sure." She shooed the cat off the counter and grabbed a sticky note to write on as he proposed a few other dates over the coming weeks. "These should work. I'll get the word out on my end. I'm sure you can have someone at the city put out an official announcement."

"You're not going to use a phone tree, are you?" He couldn't help teasing her. It was just too easy.

"Very funny. We have a group email thread for the downtown business owners." The light that had been in her eyes grew dark, all traces of the smile wiped from her face. "I hear you're still pursuing the cruise ship idea. If you insist on doing a presentation from them, I'd appreciate you letting me know so I can bring in an environmental expert to give the other side of the argument." She was all business again, her tone clipped.

"Lucy, I know you don't agree with me on the cruise idea, but I think you might feel differently after you hear from them."

"I doubt it, but obviously it's not up to me. I know you

already charmed your way into getting Missy on board, but not everyone in this town will fold so easily just because you're handsome." As if realizing what she'd just said, her cheeks flushed, and she quickly busied herself straightening a perfectly organized stack of papers on the counter.

Her admission made a warmth spread across his chest, and he couldn't resist acknowledging the comment.

"You think I'm handsome?"

"Oh, stop it with the fake modesty. You know you're good-looking, and I'm sure you use it to your advantage everywhere you go."

He loved the way she pursed her lips and knitted her eyebrows together when she was irritated with him. It made her cupid's bow more pronounced, and then all he could think about was what it would be like to kiss those lips.

Of course, that would never happen. She saw him as the enemy of everything she cared about, and he certainly wasn't going to make the same mistake again and start dating someone involved in his project.

He quickly changed gears. He'd had an idea. "Hey, what are you doing when you close up?"

She glanced at the door, as if willing someone to come in and give her an excuse to be rid of him. Looking back, she searched his eyes as if looking for clues.

"Well, I guess now I have to get the word out about these meetings. Figure out who you've already talked to so I can do some damage control." She crossed her arms.

He looked at the door where her hours were hand-painted onto the glass. "You close at six. Meet me at the corner of Main and West Second when you're done closing up."

She raised an eyebrow. "Why would I go anywhere with you?" The defensiveness was gone from her voice, replaced by what seemed like genuine curiosity.

"You'll like it. I promise. And if you don't, you can leave.

But if you stay, we can grab dinner after, and I'll tell you about some of my ideas that don't involve cruise ships."

Her eyes narrowed. She looked as if she was mentally making a list of pros and cons.

"Come on. What do you have to lose?" He looked directly in her eyes, challenging her.

"Fine." She threw up her hands. "I'll go. You're not going to take me out on a boat and make me disappear or something, are you? Get rid of your opposition?"

He shook his head, laughing. "I think you've read one too many books. Maybe lay off the thrillers. There's no boat involved. Scout's honor." He held up a hand in the scout pledge.

The corners of her mouth were turning up ever so slightly again. He could make her smile if she'd just stop seeing him as the villain in her story. He had to show her they weren't that different if he was ever going to get her on board with his plans, and he thought he knew exactly where to start.

Eleven

Lucy

As Lucy flipped the sign on the front door to "Closed" —the same sign Annie had used for decades—she thought about her friend's other practices she'd simply adopted and never changed. When she'd taken over the store, she hadn't wanted to change anything because it made her feel as if Annie was still there. She hadn't wanted to share such personal details with Logan, so she'd let him tease her and her backward ways. Who cared what he thought of her business anyway?

Approaching the corner of West Second and Main after leaving the store, she spotted Logan ahead speaking to Gladys Holcombe, the director of the local foundation charged with preserving the town's history and administering the preservation program for buildings in the historic district downtown.

"Lucy." Gladys held out her arms to embrace her. "It's

lovely to see you. When Logan told me you were tagging along for our little walk, I was just tickled pink."

Lucy smiled as she hugged the petite older lady, who was decked out as if she was going to high tea instead of on a walk.

"A walk, huh?" She narrowed her eyes at Logan. "And what kind of walk are we going on today? I'm a bit out of the loop I'm afraid." She smiled back at Gladys.

"Why, a historic downtown Heron Isle tour, of course. My favorite." Her eyes sparkled as if she was seeing the historic buildings for the first time instead of being the island's foremost expert on their history.

"I thought perhaps a history lesson might do me some good as I help the town plan for its future." Logan shot Gladys one of his thousand-watt smiles.

Lucy could almost see the older woman swooning. Geez, even Gladys, who had children older than Logan, fell victim to his charm.

"I already know the town's history. Why invite me?" Lucy said.

"I thought a walk around town might give us some new ideas for the waterfront." He shrugged as if he had nothing but innocent intentions.

Gladys nodded, her face growing more serious. "It's such an important project. Did you know the land that runs along the waterfront used to be nothing but giant stacks of lumber? Timber was plentiful here, and it was easy for the early settlers to extract and ship to distant ports."

"The buildings on Main Street were all built from heart pine in the 1820s when the Spanish first took control of the island from the French." Lucy recited what she'd been taught about the town's founding as the three began walking south down the sidewalk back toward her store.

"The only problem was that having all that wood downtown made it like a giant pile of kindling. A lightning strike took out a large portion of the original buildings in the 1850s, and then the Union Army started a fire in the rail depot that used to sit downtown, and it took out many of the remaining buildings in the early 1860s."

"That's right." Gladys nodded, smiling like a teacher who was proud of her star pupil.

Gladys stopped as she approached the corner of Third and Main in front of the Kittredge Building, which housed a small shop on the ground floor that sold homemade candles, soaps, and a variety of decorative goods.

"This is a good shop if you need to buy a gift for your mother or a sister. Or perhaps a sweetheart?" Gladys raised an eyebrow in Logan's direction before cutting her eyes toward Lucy.

"I'll keep that in mind," he said.

His face revealed nothing about his current relationship status, and Lucy couldn't imagine what sort of woman Logan might be interested in. He was hard to read. At first, she'd thought he probably lived in a high-rise with a doorman and a stark modern design. But after hearing he had grown up in a small Midwestern town and minored in historic preservation she was less certain. Possibly even intrigued.

"That brings us to Lucy's building." Gladys stopped as they approached. "It's one of the finest examples we have of the Italianate influences on many of the structures built just after the last big fire. You can see it in the arched doorways and windows and the decorative brickwork up on the cornices." She pointed up.

"It's a beauty, that's for sure." Logan stepped back so he could take in more of the building, and Lucy caught herself studying how his jaw twitched when he was deep in thought and had to force her eyes up to the cornices.

"You really should go in sometime. The hand-carved heart pine is just magnificent going up the staircase. You've got the clothing boutique here on this corner and, of course, Lucy's store sits on the other end. In the middle"—Gladys pointed at a nondescript door—"there's a staircase that goes up to the second-floor offices. The woodwork in this building is simply divine. Have you seen the bookshelves in Lucy's shop?"

"Yes, just today. They looked like heart pine as well."

"They date back to the late 1800s when Annie's—the last owner, bless her, may she rest in peace—grandfather opened the town's first bookstore. The shelves, the floors, the ceiling, it's all original." The pride in Gladys's voice and on her face would make anyone think *her* family was responsible for the preservation.

"It's a really remarkable building." Logan's eyes narrowed as he studied the decorative brickwork on the cornices above them.

"And for sale, apparently." Gladys clucked her tongue. "I always worry when one of the original ones goes up for sale. You never know who might swoop in to buy it or what they'll do with it. As you know, historic protection only extends so far. At the end of the day, it's still private property, and owners do what they will with it."

Lucy bit her lip. She'd tried to look into buying the building, but the whole process had been overwhelming. It wasn't like buying a house. The bank wanted a business plan that accounted for the reserves necessary to keep up a building of this age for decades to come, and they'd wanted her beach cottage as additional collateral since she'd never owned commercial property or been a landlord.

She hadn't officially withdrawn her application, but she couldn't imagine having the time to work on that and the waterfront development and in her store. Part of her still really wanted to get the building back in local hands. The current owner was an out-of-town investor. He'd been interested in the lucrative historic preservation tax credits available when the building needed major renovations in the nineties, but he was ready to move it out of his portfolio before it required more updates.

Lucy felt Logan's eyes on her as if he was waiting for her to say something. He couldn't know she'd been interested in the building herself. Still, she had an odd sense that he knew something. She fidgeted with the anchor charm on her necklace as she turned back to Gladys.

"I'm sure we'll get another great owner."

"Yes, dear. I hope so." Gladys smiled at her sweetly.

Lucy couldn't imagine how much change Gladys must have seen during her lifetime here on Heron Isle. Lucy would ask her later about her thoughts on the waterfront. She didn't want to do it in front of Logan and give him the chance to sway her with his dimpled smile and smooth talking.

They moved on to the post office before walking to the top of the square and crossing to the other side. As they went from building to building, Logan asked thoughtful questions and remarked on tiny details hardly anyone ever noticed. It was clear he'd taken his minor in historic preservation seriously. So why this choice of career? It sounded like he'd been involved in a lot more development than preservation, but maybe she didn't have the whole story. She'd have to do some digging later.

As they crossed over East Fifth Street, Gladys pointed to a two-story Victorian a few doors down. "The Foundation is looking to buy that one to preserve, but we're a long way from our fundraising goal."

Lucy hadn't walked down that way in months, but she knew the place. The Hill House was one of the rare properties downtown that was unkempt. The owner had passed away several years ago and his next of kin had fought over the estate ever since because he hadn't had a will. The city sent someone to mow the yard and pull the weeds every month after sending numerous letters threatening fines for violating ordinances in the historic district and receiving no reply. The man's nieces and nephews were all fighting over who should buy out whose share of the house, but none of them seemed to have any interest in coming to town to take care of it.

"I do hope it falls into the right hands." Lucy followed Gladys and Logan down the sidewalk to get a closer look.

"Do you ever wonder if an old building like this has a soul? Almost like it's a living, breathing being?"

Logan was looking up at the house with such adoration that Lucy couldn't peel her eyes away even to follow his gaze to what had caught his attention. His green eyes were studying the porch carefully, as if it was something he wanted to reach out and touch, but was holding himself back from doing.

He was looking at it with more longing than Carter had ever looked at *her*, and something inside her wished Logan was looking at her that way. Which was, of course, preposterous. Logan was off limits. He was her opposition, and hopefully he'd be heading back to some big city as soon as she convinced the town to do something worthwhile with the waterfront.

"Do you see that gingerbread detailing?" He pointed toward the porch. "Someone had to have not only the patience, but also the artistic skill, to carve it all by hand. They were an artist every bit as much as Monet or Renoir, but no one signs a porch or gets to see it hang in a museum one day. Most people just walk right by and say, 'Oh, what a pretty house,' and keep on walking." He shook his head as if those people were completely dense. "No one makes anything like that by hand anymore. They just throw up some spindles under the railing and call it a day."

Lucy was so surprised by his passion for the subject that she didn't quite know what to say. As much as she appreciated the buildings that made up Heron Isle's historic district, she was guilty of walking by quickly on her way to the post office or bank and not stopping to appreciate the small details. She made a mental note to walk a little slower from now on and take in her surroundings. She knew she was lucky to live in a place like Heron Isle that had preserved so much of its history. That was why the waterfront project was so important to her. Heron Isle had always been here for her, and now she needed to be there for it.

Maybe she and Logan weren't so different. She was glad he'd invited her along on the tour and let her see this side of him. Maybe they could find some common ground after all.

Since she hadn't spent much time on the beach this summer due to being so busy looking into buying her building and fighting the waterfront development, Lucy suggested she and Logan go to dinner at the Sand Dollar. It was a casual restaurant, with outdoor dining behind the building, in a sandy patch separated from the ocean only by a few short dunes. A favorite of locals and tourists alike.

As the hostess showed them to a table near the dunes, their feet sank into the sand with every step. She had on sandals, but Logan was no doubt getting sand in his shoes. They looked like the expensive kind of boat shoes that aren't ever actually worn on a boat, but he didn't seem to mind.

"So what's good here?" He peered over the top of the menu when the hostess left the table.

"Everything. Well, assuming you like seafood. You do like seafood, right?"

"Love it. Point me in the right direction."

"Well, the shrimp is Mayport, caught right here in the waters around the island. You can get it grilled or fried, over pasta or grits. You can't go wrong. Grouper, snapper, mahi," she read down the list of the night's specials. "Everything is caught locally. You'll never find anything frozen here."

When the server came by the table, they each ordered a glass of white wine. Logan set his menu on the table and folded his hands neatly in front of him.

"Was I right? You had a good time on the tour, didn't you?"

"Yes. It definitely beat a one-way boat trip where I ended up sleeping with the fishes." She smiled over her menu at him. She knew what she was going to order, but she kept the menu up so she could pretend to concentrate on something other than him. Every time his eyes met hers, she felt a little tingle creep across her chest, and she worried it was her resolve crumbling. She had to keep her wits about her with someone like him.

He laughed. "Is that what you like to read? Thrillers where someone ends up dead in the water?"

"I just finished *One by One* by Ruth Ware. Sooo good," she said with a satisfied sigh. "If you like thrillers, I highly recommend it. Are you much of a reader?"

The server interrupted to deliver their wine and take their orders. She'd just left when Lucy spotted an osprey flying away from the ocean.

"Look, there's your fresh fish." She giggled when he looked up and his eyes widened at the sight of the fish wriggling in the bird's talons.

"If that's how you people are getting your fish, maybe you were right about needing the open-air market downtown." He smiled and leaned back in his chair after taking a sip of his wine.

"Is that really on the table?" She pushed at her silverware, moving each piece until the bottoms were lined up perfectly.

"Sure, why not?" He shrugged. "As far as I'm concerned, all suggestions are on the table."

"Does that mean the casino boat is still on the table too?"

"It's a harder sell to the downtown restaurant owners since it provides direct competition, but I haven't ruled anything out yet. I think we need all the options on the table so we can make informed decisions."

As she sipped her wine, she looked out past the dunes where the tide was so high she could hear the waves breaking, but couldn't actually see them. Long streaks of clouds swept across the sky like paint strokes, beginning to turn pastel shades of pink and purple as they reflected the sun's descent on the western side of the island.

Lucy remembered how comforting it was when she'd moved home and driven over the bridge in her small moving truck to find everything exactly how she'd left it. Now that she was here, it was up to her to make sure it stayed that way. That the people who came time and again could come back and still find what they loved about it.

When she looked back at him, Logan was swirling his wine, squinting at her like he wanted to say something, but was holding back.

"What? Why are you looking at me like that?" She tucked a curl behind her ear self-consciously.

"I want to ask you something, but I have a feeling I know how you're going to react."

"Is that so? I can't wait to hear how well you think you know me." She let out a nervous laugh because when he looked at her with those emerald-green eyes, she really did feel he could read her every thought.

"Yes. I think you're going to get defensive. You'll probably tell me to mind my own business, but I think that would be a mistake."

"Okay." She dragged out the word as if it had three syllables. "Now I'm really intrigued."

"Just don't jump from intrigued to angry. Deal?" His eyes challenged her, daring her to trust him.

"Sure. Now, out with it." She gripped the arms of her chair, bracing for his next ill-advised plan for the waterfront. What was he going to propose this time? Maybe they could start loading shipping containers at the marina, stacking them all along the waterfront like working ports did in other places.

"I knew your building was for sale before our walk with Gladys. Mayor Jenkins told me yesterday." He paused, searching her face for a reaction.

Her first thought was that somehow, someway he wanted to buy it. Her mind started racing. What would he be like as a building owner? Would he renew her lease next year? Would it mean he was staying in town? Had he somehow fallen in love with the town and truly wanted to stay and make it better?

No, that was ridiculous. She searched his eyes, but he wasn't giving anything away. Her heart was pounding. What was this about?

"Yes... and?"

Logan took a sip of his wine. "He also may have let it slip that you were interested in buying the building yourself."

Her heart slammed against her chest. That wasn't what she'd been expecting. She cleared her throat, grabbing her glass of water for a drink.

"It's more of a dream than an actual effort." She wasn't about to tell him how overwhelmed she'd been at the bank when they peppered her with questions about its renovation history, her proposed schedule for the maintenance a building that age needed, and her knowledge of the tax credits available for the work. She'd known so few of the answers that she'd left feeling embarrassed and overwhelmed. She knew Jerry—the banker she'd known since grade school—hadn't meant anything by it. He was just doing his job. But he'd made her realize how little she knew about owning a historic building versus merely appreciating it.

"Why do you think it's just a dream?" He placed his arms on the table and leaned in, his eyes watching her carefully.

She fingered the anchor on her necklace and glanced at the family at the table to her right. A toddler was on the ground next to the table pushing a tiny dump truck through the sand. She concentrated on him to avoid looking at Logan.

"It was just silly, really. I don't know what made me think I could manage a whole building. I don't know anything about having tenants or maintaining a historic building."

"You do know how you eat an elephant, right?" His tone was playful. "One bite at a time. What scares you about owning the building and being a landlord? Let's go through your objections one by one."

She looked out at the dunes, deliberating on whether she wanted to share her fears with someone she barely knew. Part of her still really wanted the building, and maybe Logan would have some helpful insights. After all, he was a lawyer and consulted with local governments. He seemed like a pretty smart guy.

Remembering the quote Gatsby's Ghost marked in the latest book about how hesitation triggered the brain to stop action, she decided to be brave and share with Logan. Maybe Gatsby's Ghost was on to something. Maybe she was the only thing holding her back.

She told him about the other tenants having leases coming up for renewal in the next year, and how she wasn't sure how much to price their rent in a new lease. The previous owner had mentioned he had reserves for things like replacing the roof and air-conditioning units, but she wouldn't have that kind of money up front and worried she might be getting in over her head. She'd worked up a business plan from a template she and Taylor found online, but the bank wanted her to come back with something far more detailed than the template since it hadn't specifically been for a historic building.

Logan listened to all her concerns respectfully, and then said, "I don't mean to pry, so you can tell me to shut up if you want." He continued when she didn't stop him. "Would you have the kind of cash you'd need to put down on a building like that?"

It was a personal question, but living in a small town, she was used to other people being in her business. Shoving hesitation away, she took a deep breath and dove into the deep end.

"I inherited a little when my dad passed, and the mortgage on my beach cottage is paid off. It's where I grew up." She decided to keep going in case he thought to ask about her mother. That definitely crossed the line into something way too personal. "Annie—the woman who owned the bookstore before me—left me what little she had along with the store. She never had kids and didn't have any other family to speak of." The words tumbled out before she realized how much she was telling him. She fidgeted with one of her earrings, looking back out at where the ocean met the horizon.

Logan let out a whoosh of breath. "Wow, you've had a lot of loss in your life, huh?" He leaned back in his chair, as if he needed a moment to gather his thoughts.

She bit her lip. He had no idea. "It is what it is. Obviously, I'd give up the cottage and the bookstore to have Dad and Annie back in my life again, but I'm incredibly grateful for the legacy they both left behind. They gave me my life here."

"If you don't mind me asking, who was Annie to you?"

"She was family. Not the blood kind, but the family you choose kind. My childhood—" she paused, asking herself again why she was divulging so much to him so easily and coached herself to dial it back. "It was complicated. Although I couldn't always afford to buy a new book, the bookstore was my favorite place to be because of Annie. There was just something about her. She always knew exactly what someone needed to hear, whether it was from her or in a book she suggested. I worked there in high school, and she's the reason I wanted to become a librarian. That's what I did before she passed and left me the bookstore."

Logan was quiet, so she continued, the wine clearly having loosened her tongue. "I like to think she knew what she was doing when she left me the store. She knew it would bring me back home. My dad was still alive then, and it gave me some great years with him before he passed a couple years ago. Heart attack. He was only sixty-four. Annie was like that though. She was intuitive. She always knew exactly what people needed, from something as simple as the right book at the right time or something bigger like bringing me home as an adult."

"Was it a hard decision to give up your job and move back to run the store?" He was leaning forward, his attention fixed squarely on her as if her story was the most interesting one he'd ever heard.

"Nope. It was the easiest decision I've ever made. I'm honored to carry on Annie's legacy and that of her family." She didn't add that Annie's timing couldn't have been better. She'd just found out her publisher was closing its doors, and the weight of the embarrassment when she had to tell her coworkers her book wasn't being published had been nearly too much to bear. She'd happily escaped their looks of pity and their constant questions about whether she'd found a new publisher.

No one on Heron Isle even knew about her failed attempt at becoming an author, except Taylor, and it certainly wasn't ammunition she planned to give Logan. She'd already told him enough embarrassing information for one evening.

TWELVE

Logan

Logan was still absorbing everything Lucy had just told him. Pieced together with what he'd learned from the mayor about her mother leaving town, he was getting a clearer picture of Lucy and her motivations. He was only an armchair psychologist, but if he had to guess, he'd say she clung to familiar things—like the town and her answering machine—because her entire life had been like a hurricane spinning around her, constantly throwing things into disarray. No wonder she had such an aversion to change.

He studied her face, the pain in her eyes as evident as those of a puppy who'd been dropped off at a shelter. She was her own worst enemy. She didn't take risks, trying only to maintain the status quo. But in her attempts to avoid the lows of life, she was missing out on the highs.

She was clearly uncomfortable talking about her experience at the bank, but she shouldn't be embarrassed. It wasn't as if she would have learned this stuff majoring in library sciences. Maybe if he helped her, she'd be a better teammate on the waterfront project.

A voice in his head reminded him that personal relationships and business didn't mix, but he reasoned this wasn't a romantic relationship. Control of the building was good for her business, and a successful project plan was imperative for his career at this point. He needed her to start trusting him and stop seeing him as the enemy. He would show her how well they could work together. Besides, he wouldn't want to see the building fall into the wrong hands.

"Okay," he leaned his arms on the table. "Let's just say you have the down payment and collateral to buy the building. If all you need are more detailed business plans that cover the maintenance and upkeep of a historic building like that, let me help you. I've done tax credit work like that in plenty of towns. And figuring out the landlord side of things isn't that hard either. I can show you how to price future rents." He'd taken several real estate courses in law school, and he'd been involved in dozens of commercial lease negotiations over the years.

"Why would you want to help me? This doesn't have anything to do with the waterfront."

She raised a suspicious eyebrow, but he saw something else in her eyes. Hope? It only fueled his desire to help her.

"What can I say? I'm a sucker for historic buildings and the people who love them." He'd meant to lighten the mood, but he saw a flicker in her eyes when he spoke the final words. The spark of interest was familiar to him, and he felt it every time he was near her. But it wasn't like he could stay away from her. They had to work together on the waterfront project, and it wouldn't be that big of a deal to help her with the building too.

"I don't know." She bit her lip.

He'd caught her doing that a few times when she'd been unsure of herself.

"Do you really think I could manage a whole building full of tenants? You saw what my systems are like."

She smiled at him through her lashes, and he found it hard to focus on what he should say next. He cleared his throat and shifted to sit up straighter in his chair.

"It's only a handful of tenants. We can put systems in place to manage that. I'll help you with that too."

The server appeared then with their meals, which gave him an excuse to look away from her soft brown eyes.

"Don't you already have your hands full with your own project?" She frowned as she picked up her fork.

"Well, you're going to help me with that, and I'll help you with this. It's called teamwork."

"Oh, now you think I'm going to *help* you commercialize the waterfront?" Her eyes twinkled, challenging him.

"To be fair, it's already commercial."

She shrugged in acknowledgment, so he continued.

"I want you to help me find ways to make it more profitable that don't ruin the character of downtown."

"Have you come up with any ideas other than the cruise ships and casino boats?" She popped a shrimp into her mouth.

He held up his hands. "Yes. I know those are no-gos for you. They were just the beginning of my ideas. What about paddle board rentals? Or jet skis? I also saw where another town bought these little two-person crafts you can teach anyone to drive with just a few minutes of instruction."

She looked off toward the ocean as she chewed, as if she was trying to picture it.

"The downtown marina is actually a pretty good spot for that kind of thing, but there's never been a proper ramp to help people load their kayaks into the water. It's more like a river than an ocean on that side. From downtown, you could send people to the right toward the west side of the island and that would keep them out of the path of boaters who mostly come in from the ocean side."

"See? Teamwork." He winked at her and relished the way her smile spread quickly and easily across her face. It made him want to come up with more ideas that would make her look at him like that and remind him that he really was good at his job.

Crisscrossing globe lights over their heads flickered on as the sun dropped behind the west side of the building, giving the sandy yard where they sat a romantic glow. The people around them probably thought they were on a date. Two young, attractive professionals chatting over glasses of wine. Except this was strictly a business dinner.

"It's still not enough money though, is it?" Her voice was barely loud enough to break into his train of thought. She poked at a shrimp on her plate, not meeting his eyes.

He sipped his wine. "If we could do the open-air market, the food kiosks, and implement some new recreational areas, it would get us part of the way there. We don't have to figure it all out tonight. The important thing is that we're adding some good ideas to the list."

She gave a little nod. "Can we agree to a bit of a ceasefire?"

"What did you have in mind?" He leaned forward.

"No more going door-to-door trying to sell your plans. It's not fair without someone there to present the other side. We'll air everything out in the public forums." She reached a hand across the table to shake on it.

He slid his hand into hers and felt the electricity. He searched her eyes to see if she felt it too. Her brown eyes glowed almost amber under the yellow tinge of the lights above. When they locked with his for a split second, he felt warmth wash over his entire body.

His voice was husky when he spoke. "Deal."

She pulled her hand away first and he instantly missed the feel of her skin against his.

"To teamwork." Lucy picked up her glass and raised it in his direction.

He cleared his throat, even as he still worked to clear his head. "To teamwork." He lifted his glass to clink against hers and was pleased to see the easy smile return to her face.

Things were looking up. But even as he pondered how quickly he might be able to tie up the deal here so he could throw his hat in the ring for the big Boston job opening up, he couldn't stop wondering if he and Lucy could have been something more if they'd met in another time, another place.

But they hadn't, and he had to remember Heron Isle and Lucy were just a pit stop on his way back to his career path.

He left Lucy with plans to go by her bookstore after she closed the next evening and look at the paperwork she had on the building. She hadn't agreed to letting him help her yet, but she did relent when he promised he'd look at everything objectively and be honest with her about whether buying the building was a reasonable thing for her to consider. He wasn't sure if it was the wine or her good mood from the waterfront discussion, but by the end of dinner the conversation was flowing easily from quirky pets on the island like Sidney the alligator to where he could find the best seashells. She'd let her guard down, and he'd liked seeing her more carefree, the tension gone from her shoulders and her smile lighting up her features.

He pulled out of the restaurant's sandy lot, but instead of driving the half mile to his cottage, he headed back downtown. He couldn't let himself get attached to Lucy, and the woman he'd been exchanging books with in the Little Free

Library was a safe distraction. He didn't know her name, her age, or what she looked like. No danger of mixing personal and business there.

As he crossed the lawn from his parking spot to the Little Free Library, he found himself hoping there was a new book from Island Girl. He hadn't even finished reading the last one yet, but he enjoyed the exchange. It was like the advent calendar his mom always put out in December—you never knew what might be waiting each day. He also had an irrational fear that he'd miss something from her or that someone else might take a book meant for him. They left sticky notes on the books for each other, but still, anyone could take what they wanted. It was a public repository after all.

Logan passed a young couple holding hands and licking ice-cream cones. He'd sat talking to Lucy at the Sand Dollar long enough that the downtown restaurants were closing for the night, families already back in their rented rooms and houses, putting children with sun-kissed skin to bed. Only a handful of couples and groups of friends lingered downtown, walking the streets, and eating ice cream from the store on the corner that was still open.

When he got to the library, he looked around to see if anyone was watching him. It was silly, but he'd begun to wonder if the woman leaving him the books ever hung out nearby and watched to catch a glimpse of Gatsby's Ghost. He thought this because it had occurred to him to do just that. After all, it was hard not to be curious about who was on the other end of the notes. He needed to remain anonymous though. It was safer that way.

When he opened the door, he had to flip the switch to illuminate the space. There was a small stack on the ledge to be shelved, and he was about to give up when he spotted her handwriting on the final book in the stack titled *The Only Rule Is It Has To Work.*

He pulled out the index card and read.

Gatsby's Ghost,

I'm still reading the last book you left me— thank you for that. It's just the pep talk I need right now.

And, yes, I do like baseball. My dad loved the game and raised me to do the same. Go Braves!

I know we don't know each other, but I find myself wondering how your at-bat went. I'm afraid my problem might be that no one ever taught me how to hit. Is there a book for that? Haha.

Rooting for you,
Island Girl

P.S. Did you read Moneyball? If you liked that, maybe you'll like this fun take.

She was a baseball fan. He turned the book over to read the back. Apparently, it was about two statisticians who had the chance to run an independent league baseball team, making up the rules as they went. The *Moneyball* experiment essentially taken to absurd levels. He was surprised he'd never heard of it, but he was looking forward to reading it.

He'd once tried to convince Catherine to read a book he'd thought she'd like, but she'd been too busy to bother. It sat on her nightstand for months before her maid finally put it on a bookshelf where it likely still sat.

On his drive back to the cottage, he tried to imagine the

kind of woman Island Girl might be. Apparently, she read everything from historical novels to nonfiction sports books. If her dad was a Braves fan, she might be a local. There wasn't a baseball team anywhere near Heron Isle, but then the Braves had been claimed by most of the southeast for decades, so she could be from anywhere.

He pushed thoughts of unmasking his pen pal aside. He and Lucy were finally making headway, and the clock was ticking before the Boston job opened for proposals from consultants. Initiating a successful plan in Heron Isle so that he could then help the town hire a permanent manager to implement it could show Boston that San Diego was a blip. And then a win in Boston would put him back on the map. No one would even remember San Diego then.

Eyes on the prize. All that stood between him and Boston were a few community forums.

THIRTEEN

Lucy

Seagulls cried overhead as Lucy sat on her back porch and wrote in her gratitude journal, the sun crawling up into the sky from where it had emerged over the horizon a half hour earlier. It was high tide and the waves crashed so heavily against the shore that it sounded like they'd lap up onto her porch at any moment. Closing her eyes, she focused on nature's soundtrack as she whispered her daily affirmations.

I create room every day for growth and learning.

I only invest my energy in worthy endeavors.

I have faith that I have all the answers I need inside myself.

Each day, I take one step closer to knowing and accepting myself.

My presence shapes moments and touches lives.

Annie had given her a book on affirmations for her fifteenth birthday. Dozens of statements filled the book, and

Annie had helped her pick out the ones she'd felt comfortable saying. Ever since, she'd made time each morning to focus on positive affirmations. Those she used now felt like the right ones for her; however, it had taken years before she could say the final one she repeated each day: *My presence shapes moments and touches lives.*

Saying it and believing it were two different things, but Annie had assured her that the more she said it, the more she would start living it. So she dutifully repeated the words each day and focused on believing them.

She'd stayed up late the night before reading the book Gatsby's Ghost had left her. After flipping through the pages in her journal, she found the affirmation she'd copied from that book, the one he'd drawn the arrow by: "*Yes, you can move mountains. Whatever is happening right now, this is it. This is your life. And it's not going to begin again. You can't change the past, but in five seconds you can change your future.*"

She looked out to the ocean and said out loud, "You can move mountains." The downtown business owners had entrusted her as their leader, and she wouldn't fail them.

Maybe it was time to add some new affirmations to her daily routine.

Lucy channeled what she'd read in the self-help book as she thumbed through the well-worn volume Annie had given her, its spine broken in numerous places and an edge of the paper cover torn in the bottom right corner. She flipped to a random page, closed her eyes, and ran a finger down the page. Opening her eyes, she frowned at her choice: *I grant forgiveness to those who have caused me harm in my past while honoring my boundaries for the future.*

That sounded like something her therapist would have told her when she was in her twenties, when she'd been trying to make sense of her mother leaving when she was only five. She and Taylor had been drinking cosmos one night while watching *Sex and the City* reruns in their college apartment, when Taylor had the idea to look up Lucy's mom on the internet. Lucy's dad never spoke about his wife after she left, and Lucy knew it was too painful for him to discuss. Her mother had made no attempt to contact them, and her mother's parents had only ever known she was alive and living in California trying to make it as an actress.

In the early years, Lucy had been angry at her mother for leaving. Then somewhere in her late teens or early twenties she'd grown worried. Was her mother okay? Was she healthy? Happy?

Fueled by courage from a good cosmo, she and Taylor grabbed one of their computers and searched for her. If what Taylor found was accurate, the only thing Lucy's mother was acting in was community theater. That was what she'd broken up their family for—community theater in Riverside.

It had taken Lucy another ten years of therapy to get to where she was now, which was indeed detached. She no longer cared where her mother was or what she was doing. Missing all those years with Lucy were her mother's loss. Annie had been twice the mother Lucy's own flesh and blood could have ever been. It was a cruel twist of fate that Annie never married or had children while Lucy's mother had a child she clearly never wanted.

Lucy was in her late twenties before she allowed herself to understand that her mother's problems had nothing to do with her and certainly hadn't been caused by her mere existence. Maybe adding this new affirmation would remind her just how resilient she already was. She wrote it on the inside cover of her gratitude journal before trying it out loud.

"I grant forgiveness to those who have caused me harm in my past while honoring my boundaries for the future."

It wasn't the first time she'd felt as though Annie had guided her to the right words. She wasn't sure if she believed in spirits or their ability to interact with the living world, but she always felt as if Annie was right beside her when she closed her eyes and let her finger find a new affirmation.

And Gatsby's Ghost had helped her find another.

She closed her journal and gave herself one more moment to enjoy the sound of the surf, the harsh tenor of waves crashing mixed with the cries of laughing gulls overhead, and the feel of the sun on her skin as the day heated up.

Satisfied, she smiled. It was time to head into work and see how she could use her talents today.

Lucy decided to stop by the Little Free Library on her way into work. Curiosity had got the better of her, and she wanted to see if Gatsby's Ghost had picked up the latest book she'd left for him. Each time she left a book, she worried he was simply a tourist passing through town and the book would never be picked up because he'd already be gone. The thought brought about a feeling she recognized after years of therapy as "abandonment," but it made her sad just the same, even though she had no idea who he was. It was a nice distraction and the first time she'd really felt a connection with someone since Carter moved to Chicago.

Chickadees were chasing one another from tree to tree as she walked through the park, and Lucy stopped for a moment to admire a hummingbird fluttering around a bright-pink hibiscus bloom. It was hot already, even at nine thirty in the morning. Continuing down the path, she waved at a toddler who was smiling at her from his stroller as a family passed by on the sidewalk.

As she approached the Little Free Library, she reminded herself of the gift she'd given the community with this idea. Everyone loved the library, and it had been so popular they'd had to build a bigger one. She tried to stop and acknowledge how her idea had positively impacted the town and its people, but self-doubt crept in. The little library wouldn't have been necessary if she'd been successful in raising money to save the much larger public library. Would she fail the town again with the waterfront?

The Mel Robbins book from Gatsby's Ghost talked a lot about taking action and how any action, regardless of its outcome, was a step toward success. He'd marked a quote that said something like, "Win or lose, at least I'm doing something." She'd taken action and out of those efforts had come this Little Free Library, which had brought him to her. So maybe it wasn't a total loss. He seemed to bring her the right message at just the right time, much like Annie always had. Perhaps Annie had had a hand in it too, just like with the affirmations.

It cheered her slightly to see that the book she'd left for Gatsby's Ghost was gone. So far, their system seemed to have ensured they'd each received the books left for each other.

After scanning the shelf of children's books, she selected a few new ones and took them off the shelf so she could read the cards. She giggled at the one written in green colored pencil about *Alice the Alligator*.

> Alice is nice. She mite like Sidny. He wint to
>   my skol 1 day.
> Charlie

Lucy always stocked plenty of children's books on alligators in the store. The local kids all knew Sidney and wanted to learn more about alligators, and the tourists were always wide-eyed at the idea of running into a pet alligator on the island. Alligators did hang out along the freshwater creek that ran through the island, but tourists rarely ventured away from the beach or downtown to spot them.

By the time Lucy left the library and walked over to the bookstore, her mood had turned positive again. As much as she loved helping adults find the books they were looking for, nothing was better than helping a young or teenage reader find the right thing to read. From understanding something new to feeling understood, Lucy firmly believed there was a book for everything.

As Lucy was turning on the coffee pot in the back, she heard the jingle of the bells on the door. Walking to the front, she saw a woman who appeared to be in her early forties scanning the shelves of new releases. Lucy didn't recognize her and assumed she was in town visiting.

"Hi, welcome." Lucy smiled when the woman turned. "Can I help you find something?"

The woman blushed and seemed embarrassed that Lucy had caught her looking through the shelf.

"Do you have *Hydrangeas on Hill Street*?"

Lucy nodded. "I do." She moved to the left of the woman and plucked the title off the shelf. "I read it when it first came in. It's a lovely book."

"I feel a little silly." The woman opened the book and turned it so Lucy could see the author photograph on the back flap. "It's my first book. I still get a little thrill every time I find it in a bookstore." Her cheeks still flushed pink, her eyes not meeting Lucy's.

"You're Debra Brannon." Lucy smiled. "That's wonderful. Congratulations!" Walking over to the counter, she said, "Please, I'd love it if you'd sign the two copies we have. It's always a treat when authors stop by and sign their books. We have a few local authors, but it's rare to have anyone who doesn't live here in the store. Where are you visiting from?"

"Raleigh. My family used to vacation here when I was a

kid, so I decided to bring my boys this year. They're teenagers, so they're probably not even out of bed yet. I just came downtown to write in the coffee shop for a little bit and when I saw you were open, I couldn't resist the urge to come in and look for it."

She took the marker Lucy held out for her and signed the book in her hand while Lucy grabbed the second copy off the shelf.

"I'm so embarrassed though. It must seem a little self-aggrandizing to go into bookstores just to see your book on the shelf." She shook her head as she handed the first book back to Lucy.

"Please, don't be embarrassed. As a former aspiring author myself, I can't imagine what it would be like to actually see your book on a shelf. It must be exhilarating."

Debra's eyebrows knitted together as she looked up and handed Lucy the second book. "*Former* aspiring author? Why former?"

Lucy shrugged, forcing a smile. "Getting published just wasn't in the cards for me."

Debra pursed her lips. "Hmm, I bet there's more to that story. Publishing is a tough business." She shook her head.

Lucy turned away to put the books back on the shelf. Debra didn't understand. She'd actually managed to get her book published. Deflecting the attention away from her shortcomings, Lucy asked, "What's the book you're working on about?"

Debra took a step closer. "How many books have you written?" She wasn't going to let the subject go.

"You don't want to hear about my writing. Really, it's nothing." Lucy stepped around Debra to go straighten books on a display table that sat in the middle of the front part of the store.

"I live to talk to other authors," she said, following Lucy. "Writing can be a lonely game sometimes."

Lucy offered her coffee and they moved to sit in the armchairs by the front window since the rest of the store was empty and quiet. Debra talked about how she'd started writing short stories for fun, never even showing them to anyone. Then she participated in a month-long writing challenge that gave her the push to write a full novel. Lucy was familiar with the challenge, as she, too, had participated years ago before completing her first manuscript.

"Let me tell you how many books I wrote before that one over there landed here on your shelf. Five." She held up a hand, each of her fingers spread wide. "The first two were so horrific I've never let anyone see them. The next one got me an agent, but after a year of being out on submission she told me it was dead and to write another one. So I spent a year writing the next one only to have the same thing happen. That one"—she pointed toward her book—"is lucky number five. It took me ten years of writing before I got to hold my book in my hands. And you know what? It was worth every single day."

Lucy stopped her coffee mug halfway to her lips. She couldn't believe the author behind one of the summer's most praised debuts had been writing for ten years—and had kept writing even after two rounds of rejected submissions.

"So fess up." Debra motioned in Lucy's direction. "How many books have you written?"

"Two," Lucy said quietly. In the past, she'd hesitated to admit she'd written two books that had never been published.

"Two?" Debra said as if Lucy might as well have written nothing at all. "Did you ever try to get an agent?"

"Yes. I have an agent. Or at least I think I still do. She actually sold my first book, but the publisher went under before it was finished. Leona—my agent—tried to find another home for it, but when it didn't sell, she told me to write another, so I did. That one didn't sell either."

"Honey, getting an agent is huge. Most agents only accept a handful of new clients a year. If you landed an agent with your very first book, you're basically a prodigy."

Now it was Lucy's turn to blush. "I think it was just a fluke maybe. I mean, no one wanted my book after the first publisher folded. And obviously they had some issues if they had to fold. And then they all passed on my second book. Not everyone is meant to be an author."

Debra shook her head. "There are a million reasons why an editor passes on a book. Maybe they just published something like it. Maybe your main character has the same name as the kid who bullied them in elementary school." Debra shrugged. "Maybe they just ate bad egg salad for lunch and hated everything they read that day. All *you* can control is sitting down and writing a good book."

Lucy sighed. "But how do you know if you wrote a good book? If the publishers are all telling you they're not interested, how do you know it's not because your writing just stinks?"

Debra thought for a moment before answering. "What's your agent like?"

"Leona? She's basically straight out of central casting. Exactly what you think a New York literary agent would be like."

"So she's blunt?"

"Yes, she can be."

"Good, because I'm about to be blunt too. It sounds to me like maybe you're your own worst enemy. You obviously have an agent who's stood by you. Do you really think she'd submit you if she didn't think your work was up to snuff? Agents value their relationships with editors. They don't send them just anything."

Lucy hadn't thought about it like that. She knew Leona had tried to boost her confidence after the first book fell through, but she'd never jeopardize her career by submitting something that wasn't good enough. It occurred to Lucy that maybe the problem was that Leona believed in her as an author more than she'd ever believed in herself.

Debra's phone chimed and she pulled it out to check the notifications. "My teenage zombies have finally dragged themselves out of bed. I have to get back. But, hey, promise me you'll think about what I said. Don't give up when you're already so close. Maybe the next time I come in that'll be your book on the shelf." She pointed to the new releases.

Lucy thanked her for signing the books and for the advice, waving as Debra left the store. She hustled over to the computer and typed a quick email to Leona before she had time to change her mind. No more five-second hesitations around here, she vowed.

She even had an idea for the premise of a new novel.

```
Leona,

Yes, I still want to be an author. In
fact, I have a new idea I want to run
by you.

How do you feel about You've Got Mail?
It's always been one of my favorite movies,
and I'm thinking about a retelling where
the couple falls in love via notes left
inside books in a Little Free Library.

You always say to use real life for
inspiration, right? Although he isn't
trying to bulldoze my bookstore, I have
actually been exchanging notes with someone
in our Little Free Library. There's no love
connection there, but wouldn't it be fun if
there was?
```

Thanks for your continued support. Let
me know if I should start fleshing out a
synopsis.

Lucy

Her finger paused over the mouse for a split second before she sucked in a deep breath and hit Send. Debra was right; she was her own worst enemy. Leona had believed in her enough to submit two different books to publishers. And Annie had believed in her ability to be a business owner when she left Lucy her family's legacy. Maybe it was time she started believing in herself as much as everyone else did.

Fourteen

Logan

When Logan entered the bookstore just before closing time, he could hear Lucy talking somewhere farther back in the store. The high pitch and sing-song cadence of her voice made it sound as if she was speaking to a child, and his hunch was confirmed when he heard a young boy reply.

As Logan wandered over to browse the new releases, Lucy led the boy and his mother from the back of the store toward the counter. He gave Lucy a little wave before turning his attention back to the shelf. Something nudged his ankle and he looked down to see Lizzy, the cat he'd met on his last visit. He reached down to pet her head and the cat began walking back and forth to get a few full body scratches before sauntering off to plop down in a patch of sunshine streaming through the front windows. He'd seen a small signed taped inside the window display toward the bottom as he came in that said: "This space is left empty for cats in repose." It was like Lizzy knew exactly where she was supposed to lay.

Logan returned to scanning the shelves. Maybe he'd find something that was perfect for Island Girl.

"Need a recommendation?"

Logan jumped. Lucy had come up behind him, startling him while he was deep in thought about what his new pen pal might like.

"Sorry, I didn't mean to scare you."

He debated whether he should tell her about his experience with the Little Free Library, but thought better of it. He was here to go through the financials the building's current owner had sent over. Besides, it didn't feel right to admit that instead of buying books from her store he'd been trading books with a stranger.

Turning around, he shrugged. "I mostly read reports and spreadsheets these days. Speaking of which, what do you have for me?"

She sighed and he could tell she was trying to talk herself out of buying the building.

"Here's what he sent." She walked back behind the counter and took out a pile of papers, then dropped them on the counter with a thud. "I tried to read through it, but I got a little lost on the last inspection report, and then I saw the reserve numbers and got completely overwhelmed."

"Investing in real estate is rarely a bad idea. It might be a smart investment for you if you don't have other plans for the money you inherited. It'll grow a lot more here than sitting in a bank. Plus, the tax credits for historic rehab will help keep your costs down. Does the store turn a profit?"

She nodded. "A small one."

"And what do you do with it? Do you take owner distributions or reinvest it?"

"I pay myself a reasonable salary, but the profit at the end of the year is so small, I just leave it in the business."

"Mind if I take a look at your books? Do you have your P&L statements from the last few years?"

She pulled a file from a drawer under the desk and flipped through it, then pulled out a small stack of paper and slid it toward him.

He scanned them quickly. "Are you the only employee?"

"Mostly. There's a high school student who helps me some on the weekends and in the summer, but she only works maybe ten hours a week."

He looked up at her. "What if you want to go on vacation or aren't feeling well?"

"I don't really take vacations, and if I'm sick or there's an emergency or something, I just put a sign on the door explaining why we're closed." She shrugged. "We all do that around here."

"Well, as much as I don't recommend trying to do it all yourself, it does keep your labor costs down. Your books look pretty good for a business this size, but I still think I could help you make it bigger. Better."

She groaned. "Please tell me you're not talking about an online store again."

He put his elbows on the counter and leaned on them. "Why are you so opposed to selling online?"

"It's so impersonal." She paused, frowning as she searched for a word. "It's just transactional. It takes away everything I love about owning this place." She looked up at him. "Do you remember the first book you read that made you feel something?"

It was an intriguing question, but he didn't have an answer off the top of his head. When he didn't respond, she continued, her brown eyes glossing over as she looked into the distance.

"Mine was *Alice's Adventures in Wonderland*. When I was growing up, my parents were"—she looked at him as if gauging how much to tell him—"having problems. Let's just say escaping down a rabbit hole sounded pretty good to me." She smiled, but it didn't quite reach her eyes.

Careful not to reveal what the mayor had shared about her mother leaving, Logan steered the conversation in another direction.

"Did you ever see *The Care Bears Adventures in Wonderland*?"

He was pleased when her smile grew wider, her eyes showing surprise instead of pain.

"No. Is that a movie?" Her eyebrows furrowed as she searched his face, as if she was trying to figure him out.

"It was my sister's favorite movie growing up. Very obscure Care Bears film. In fact, one of the only ones they never put on DVD or digitized. She made me hunt down a VHS copy on eBay a few years back and buy a VCR to go with it so we could introduce my niece and nephew to it."

"Mr. Technology bought a VCR? You must really love your sister." She raised an eyebrow. "Or the Care Bears."

He stood taller and gave her his best serious face. "I'll have you know it's a very educational film. It teaches some very important life lessons."

"Oh, please." She leaned on the other side of the counter. "Do tell."

"Well, white rabbits make terrible companions for little girls, first of all. Mischievous little things."

Lucy giggled. "Yes, I always found cats made far more reliable companions."

"Except maybe Cheshire Cat. Jury's still out on him." Logan laughed. "Then there's Mad Hatter. He teaches us that we should always dress for the job we want."

She pointed at him. "That's actually a good one."

"And then there's Alice. In the Care Bears version, Alice is recruited to go to Wonderland to stand in for the princess, who has been kidnapped by the evil wizard." He held up his hands like he was a scary monster. "Except she doesn't think she can convince everyone she's a princess. She doesn't believe she's special enough."

Lucy's expression changed, but he couldn't quite read it. The pain he'd seen before had resurfaced, but it was more like a kind of knowing. As if she could identify with this version of Alice. He knew there was more to her story than what she or the mayor had told him, but he stopped himself from asking. He couldn't develop any kind of emotional attachment to her. He just needed to develop the kind of relationship that made her easier to work with and led to reaching a faster consensus on the waterfront so he could get everyone to sign off on a plan.

She straightened her expression, and the moment passed.

"Is your sister younger or older?"

"Carly is older by three years, married to her high-school sweetheart, Nick, and they still live in our hometown."

Lucy raised an eyebrow. "Meanwhile, you got out the first chance you got?"

"Couldn't wait. I was counting down the days until I could move away to college. I knew there was this whole big world out there beyond Berlin, but we'd never seen any of it. You don't really take vacations when your parents run a dairy farm."

"Little harder to find cow sitters than someone to watch a dog or cat." Her laughter was like hearing someone hit all the right notes on a piano, light and melodic.

He smiled at her. "Yes, exactly."

"What about your niece and nephew? How old are they?"

"My niece, Alexandria, is seven now and my nephew, Aidan, is nine. They're good kids."

"Do you see them often?"

He thought back. When had he seen them last? Christmas? The previous summer? No, he and Catherine had been so busy with fundraisers and galas and dinner parties that they'd never found a date when his sister and her family could come out to San Diego. It must have been the previous Christmas. He'd flown them to New York to experience a real New York Christmas. He'd offered to fly his parents out, too, but they'd turned him down. He'd been too busy with work to travel back to Wisconsin much the past few years.

Even after his dad had been forced to sell the dairy farm, he still wouldn't take a vacation. He was content to stay where he was, keeping things the way they were, which wasn't so unlike Lucy.

He kept his response vague. "It's been a while. Too long probably."

Her eyes lit up. "You should invite them down," she gushed. "That's the best thing about living in a vacation destination. People want to come to you. I bet the kids would love the beach."

He didn't know Alexandria and Aidan that well, just what he got out of conversations with his sister and the rare video chat every few months. All kids probably loved the beach, though. For a moment, he thought about how nice it would be to see his big sister, Nick, and the kids, but he didn't really have time for a family visit. He had to get things wrapped up here as quickly as possible so he could throw his hat in the ring for the Boston job.

"Yeah, maybe." He looked away from her prying brown eyes and shuffled the stack of papers on the counter.

"I don't mean to get on my soap box, but as someone who doesn't have any family to speak of, I think you should make the most of the time you do have with the people you love."

He looked up to meet her eyes, expecting to find a look

that would incite guilt. Catherine had been a master guilt tripper, although she certainly wouldn't have tried to guilt him into spending time with his family. She'd never even met his family. Anytime he mentioned life on the dairy farm growing up, Catherine would scrunch up her nose in disgust. She was always reminding him how far he'd come, but also how far he still had to go. She'd pushed him to achieve more in his career, which had fed his already ambitious goals for the two years they were together.

Unfortunately, when she fell for the son of her father's arch nemesis, she'd made sure Logan found out so he would be the one to break up with her. Then she could play the victim. He just hadn't counted on her father blaming him too, saying he drove her to Joe because he hadn't fit into their society life better. When the dust had settled, he realized he was more upset about losing the project than losing Catherine. His work had fulfilled him in ways Catherine never had, and he suspected no woman ever would.

But just because the work he did was an important part of his life didn't mean his family wasn't still important too, and Lucy was reminding him of that. She wasn't trying to guilt him into anything—her expression was sweet and sincere, her eyes a little glassy. She simply wanted to keep him from making a mistake, from always believing he'd have another chance and could put off his family until next month or next year. Maybe he'd call Carly to see if they had summer plans. He could probably fit in a long-weekend visit.

"Okay, enough about me. Let's focus on you and this store." He pretended to scan one of the pages as he tried to get his brain back on the issue of Lucy buying the building. "So an online store feels impersonal. I get it. But have you ever considered there are ways to make it personal? Maybe you could have a Facebook group where people post about what books they like or what they're looking for, and then you could make suggestions and provide links to the books you recommend from your store."

Her mouth pulled to one side, and a line appeared between her eyebrows. "I don't really do Facebook anymore. It's just a bunch of people trying to show off their highlights to people they wouldn't even keep in touch with otherwise."

"Fair enough." He wasn't really into Facebook either, but more for privacy reasons.

"But it's a really good idea," she said. "I'll look into it. How much do you think it would cost to set up an online store?"

"They make software specifically for doing that." He caught himself before he volunteered to do it for her. "It's all very plug-and-play. You could earmark a good portion of the other tenants' rents to build up your reserves for the building, but it wouldn't hurt to have another revenue stream that's basically passive income."

"That actually makes sense. I know a couple of other bookstore owners, and I can ask what they use."

She bit her lip as she scribbled a note on the pad next to the computer, and he couldn't stop looking at her mouth and thinking about how his would feel against it. He forced himself to look away and focus on her financials again. Physical attraction was a chemical reaction, and it was one he could control.

"The bank asked you to add some stuff to your business plan too, right?"

"Yes. They wanted more about my plans for the building's upkeep and how I intend to pay for it. They'd like to see a timeline, but I'm not really sure how to figure out what will need to be replaced when." She pressed her lips together and he could see the overwhelm in her eyes again. She looked like a deer who knew it was caught in the crosshairs.

"No biggie. I can help you do all that."

She tucked a strand of hair that had escaped from behind her ear back in place, then started to speak but stopped.

"What is it? What were you going to say?"

Her eyes scanned his face as if sizing up how he might react. "Do you think you'll be here long enough to help me? I don't really know how it works with what you do. Will you leave once the community forums are over and the town decides on a plan?"

"Yeah, that's usually how it works. Sometimes it's a couple months, sometimes it's a couple years. This project is pretty small compared to some of the other work I've done. I should be gone by the end of the summer, but we'll get all this done before then." He motioned to the financial documents in front of him.

She was still studying his face, as if there was something about him she couldn't quite figure out. "So you move around a lot in your line of work?"

"Yeah, that's sort of the nature of consulting with local governments. It means I get to see a lot of different places."

"Don't you ever just feel"—she glanced around the room, as if it would provide her with the word she was looking for—"unsettled?"

He shrugged. "Not really. I love experiencing new places, and there's been something to like about everywhere I've lived."

"What do you like about here so far?"

If he wanted to flirt with her, she'd given him the perfect opportunity to say something vague like, "the people." Then he could look deep in her eyes, and she'd know what he really meant was her. Flirting had become a second language for him —and made him lose sight of his goals on occasion—but Lucy couldn't be charmed into cooperating on the waterfront project anyway. He would have to take another approach with her.

"Probably the history. You all have done a great job preserving so much."

She looked up at the stamped-tin ceiling and then across the room at the wall of handmade heart-pine bookshelves.

"This place really means a lot to me. I promise if I'm able to buy the building I'll do everything I can to make sure it's here for a long time to come."

"I know you will. You love everything here just the way it is." He gave her a knowing smile. "But on this we agree. I wouldn't change a thing either."

She smiled back at him, and for a moment he gave in to the way his heart sped up when their eyes met, the way he instinctively wanted to show her what she could do if she only trusted herself more and dared to try new things.

He'd never met anyone like her, so strong one minute and so unsure the next. With seemingly no family, not even her beloved Annie, he wondered when someone had last told her she was smart or capable. Or beautiful.

A deep tugging in his heart said he could be the one, but his brain said no and reminded him of San Diego. The best he could do was point her in the right direction and hope she found her way. He had his own problems to solve.

After they'd worked out the agenda for the first community forum, Logan fought the urge to invite Lucy to dinner—a working dinner, of course—and instead opted to grab takeout on the way home so he could finally carve out a little time to read the latest book Island Girl had given him.

He called ahead and ordered shrimp salad to go from the Waterway Café. He was hoping Mildred would be there because something she'd said the night he'd dined there after the council meeting had stuck with him. After Lucy had tried to make him out to be a villain in front of everyone, Mildred had stopped by his seat at the bar to confide that she was actually ready to retire. She and Marty had a daughter who lived in North Carolina, and she'd just had their first grandchild. Mildred longed for time to go visit, maybe even stay for a week or two, but they were handcuffed to the restaurant.

"I know I could convince Marty if the math made sense," she'd said. The city had mentioned some preliminary numbers when the other development options were being considered, but they never got far enough along to present her with a real offer.

Logan had reviewed the lease a dozen or more times. The landlord's rights to terminate for breach of contract by the tenant were fairly boilerplate, but no thought had been given to the landlord terminating the lease early for other reasons, meaning Mildred and Marty would have to buy out the remaining few years of the lease.

That was part of why his plan needed to generate substantial revenue. He needed to account for buying out the lease, repairing or demolishing the current structure, hiring someone full-time to oversee the management of the real estate and the businesses on it, while also creating a long-term revenue stream to solve the city's budget concerns. The city was prepared to issue bonds to finance everything in the short term if the long-term payoff was enough.

"Hi, Mildred." Logan greeted her like an old friend as he walked through the front door and found her at the hostess stand. "How are you?"

"I'm doing just fine, Logan. I don't think your shrimp salad is up yet, but it should be ready any minute. Can I get you something to drink while you wait? Tea? Water?"

"No, I'm good. Actually, I'm glad we have a minute to chat. I've been thinking about what you said the other night—"

The door opened behind Logan, and he glanced back to see a couple with a toddler enter. He stepped aside as Mildred acknowledged the family.

"Welcome, y'all. Come on in." She turned back to Logan. "I'll be right back."

"Go ahead." Logan nodded, and the family passed him to follow Mildred to their table. He studied several rows of plaques on the wall to the right of the hostess stand. The Waterway Café had won awards ranging from "Best Local Seafood" to "Best Service" from the local newspaper that dated back nearly ten years, all proudly displayed up front to help persuade anyone who came in to take a quick peek at the menu.

"Thanks for waiting, dear. What were you saying?" Mildred was carrying an extra set of silverware and bent to put it somewhere beneath the stand.

"The other night you said that you and Marty might want to retire if the math was right. I checked your lease, and technically there's no guidance for the city breaking the lease early."

Her face fell. He knew she'd been hoping the city would break the lease. What she'd said the other night hadn't been a passing idea; she wanted out. So he continued with the better news.

"But I met with Mayor Jenkins and he had some informal conversations with a few of the council members, and they're willing to offer you a buyout on the lease. Really, it's something they'd have to do if they wanted to terminate early."

Hope filled Mildred's face, brightening her gray eyes. She looked around, probably worried Marty might overhear the scheming.

"Really? How much would it be?"

A server rounded the corner from the kitchen that was situated just behind the hostess stand and handed a brown paper bag to Mildred. "To-go order."

Mildred checked the tag on the bag and held it out to Logan. "One shrimp salad to go. You sure you can't stay? I can get you set up at the bar."

"No." Logan shook his head. "Thank you, though. I've got a good book waiting for me back at my cottage."

"Do you have a number?" she whispered, looking around again to ensure their conversation was private.

"Not yet. But common practice dictates that we take into account your monthly revenue and how much you'd be losing by not being open those months. Plus, there's usually a little extra incentive for your trouble." He winked at Mildred. "I'll make sure of it."

Mildred clapped a hand over her mouth, trying to contain her excitement. "Oh, Logan. I wasn't sure if I was really ready to walk away, but then I said it out loud to you that night, and I haven't been able to stop thinking about it since. I want to see my daughter and my grandbaby. I want to rent an RV and travel out west. There's so much we could do if we weren't tied to being here every day. Marty says he loves it, but he just doesn't know anything other than working. He's afraid he'll get bored."

"Have you tried talking to him about it?"

"Not yet. It didn't seem worth getting him worked up before I knew if it was even a possibility. I think I'll wait until you get me a number. Math, Marty understands." She nodded. "Let's just hope it's a number he can't refuse."

A couple entered the restaurant and Logan stepped aside to let them approach Mildred, who greeted them before turning back to Logan.

Holding up his bag, he said, "Thanks, Mildred. I'll keep you posted."

Exiting the restaurant, Logan walked a few feet to the railing that overlooked the water toward the beach side of the island. He'd seen the engineering reports, and pretty much every plan they had for the marina involved knocking down the restaurant building because it needed more work than it was worth, even if they shored up the pilings to withstand future storms. The town, along with Mildred and Marty, had been repairing things as they became issues, but the whole place was basically held together with patches at this point.

However, if they took down all the walls and just left the foundation and the roof, it might make a pretty decent open-air seafood market.

FIFTEEN

Lucy

Instead of writing in her gratitude journal, Lucy had spent the last few mornings at the wooden table on her back porch mapping out her new manuscript. Leona had loved her idea for a *You've Got Mail* retelling and asked her to send a synopsis to share with Lucy's former editor, Sarah, who'd recently announced her new acquisitions editor role at one of the biggest publishers in the industry.

Lucy hadn't felt this energized about writing in years, and the ideas were flowing easily. She'd gotten so caught up in her writing, she'd forgotten to stop by the Little Free Library to see if she had a new book from Gatsby's Ghost. She made a mental note to go by before the first community forum that evening.

She looked out at the ocean, appreciating the clouds that dotted the sky and provided relief from the early morning heat. Closing her eyes, she concentrated on the rhythm of the waves crashing and then fizzling out before the next crash followed at perfect intervals. She was mentally running through her list of affirmations when she heard a dog yipping. She opened her eyes to see Pete approaching with Milly, his Pomeranian, from the beach.

Pete waved and Milly ran ahead of him on the boardwalk toward Lucy's cottage. Pete's khakis were rolled up a few inches, but still wet from walking in the surf. He and Frank lived a short distance down the beach. Lucy had run into Pete here and there around town while growing up, but her dad was never interested enough in fashion to shop in Pete and Frank's store. He had been more of a T-shirt and jeans kind of guy. Once Lucy took over the bookstore, however, she'd gotten to know Pete and Frank as fellow downtown business owners, and they often ran into one another on their beach walks. Frank loved to cook and had extended a standing dinner invitation, which she took him up on at least a few times a month.

Milly beat Pete to Lucy and danced around in a circle in front of her barking for attention. Lucy leaned down to pet her.

"Hey there, Milli Vanilli."

"Terrible excuse for music. You know that's not where her name came from." Pete frowned as he approached and sat at the table opposite Lucy.

Milly's full name was Amelia, and she was named after a nearby island where Pete was born and raised. Frank always called her "Milli Vanilli" after the infamous band that got caught up in a lip-syncing scandal in the early nineties. He enjoyed getting a rise out of Pete and had even changed his ringtone to the group's "Girl You Know It's True" on more than one occasion.

"Coffee?" Lucy held up her mug as she stood to go get a refill.

"No, if I have any more my heart might explode. Frank got a new espresso machine, and it has these adorable little cups that look like they came from a children's tea party set. They're so tiny that I drank three, and now Milly and I have been walking up and down the beach trying to work off all this energy I have."

Lucy laughed as she pictured Pete sipping from his tiny espresso cups, no doubt with his pinky out to emulate the royalty he was convinced he was part of in a previous life.

"Be right back." She slipped through the sliding glass doors into her cottage to refill her mug and grab a treat for Milly. Although she was more of a cat person, she always kept treats on hand for Pam's and Pete's dogs when they stopped by the house.

As soon as Milly spotted the treat in Lucy's hand, she sat without need for a command. Her tail wagged so hard and fast it was shaking her entire body as she tried to sit still for her treat.

"Good girl." Lucy leaned down so Milly could grab the treat from her hand. The dog ate it and then danced around in circles to show her appreciation.

"You're spoiled rotten." Pete rolled his eyes at Milly. As if he wasn't the one who was constantly spoiling her. Lucy had nearly eaten a dog treat the last time she was at their house for dinner. It was from the dog bakery downtown, but it looked exactly like a human's cupcake.

"Like father, like daughter." Lucy gave Pete a knowing smile.

"Guilty as charged." Pete held up his hand. He liked to treat himself to the finer things in life.

"What brings you by on this fine morning?" Lucy raised a hand to shield her eyes from the sun so she could see Pete better across the table.

"Well, I had an interesting conversation with Steve yester-day." Pete raised an eyebrow.

"Steve?" Lucy ran through their mutual friends before it hit her. "Oh, the server at the Waterway?"

"Yep." Pete nodded, his eyes sparkling. Having grown up in a similar small town, Pete traded gossip like the town's early settlers traded seafood and timber for spices and silk. "He overheard a conversation he wasn't meant to overhear."

Fearing Pete was about to share some sort of marital confidence Steve had overheard between Mildred and Marty, Lucy's eyebrows knitted together, her mouth pulling to one side.

"Is this something I should know?"

"It involves that Logan fellow." Pete raised an eyebrow.

Lucy's heart rate matched that of the hummingbird hovering nearby above a red hibiscus bloom. Had someone seen her with Logan at the Sand Dollar? Had they looked as if they were on a date, making them fodder for the gossip mill? She had to admit at times it had felt like a date. She remem-bered the tingling that had shot up her arm and across her chest when they'd shaken hands in agreement over playing fair with the community forums.

Pete's voice interrupted the memories of dinner replaying in Lucy's mind. "Seems he paid Mildred a visit."

She felt as if someone had dropped lead in her stomach. Lucy knew the Waterway Café was on the chopping block, but she didn't like the idea of Logan going to speak with Mildred. What was he trying to sweet-talk her into? Or, rather, out of? Hadn't they agreed to let the community forums do the work —no more going door-to-door downtown trying to sell people on his ideas without someone to present the other side?

"I had a sneaky suspicion you'd want to know." Pete wagged a finger at her.

"When was this?" Lucy silently prayed it was before they'd

had their ceasefire conversation. Hopefully Steve was just slow in sharing the information.

"Steve told me last night, but it sounded like it happened a few days ago."

It had been a few days since their ceasefire conversation. Maybe he'd hit up Mildred before then.

"Okay, spill. What did he overhear?" Her mind raced with possibilities. It was obvious the night when they'd spoken at the restaurant after the council meeting that Logan thought something had to be done about the restaurant and their below-market-value lease.

"He was bringing some takeout up to the hostess stand and overheard Mildred talking to Logan about the city buying out the lease. It sounded like a done deal." Pete tsked, crossing one leg over the other while he waited for Lucy's reaction.

"Did Steve say how Mildred reacted? Should we check on her and Marty?" Lucy looked at her watch. She could probably drop by the restaurant quickly before she headed to the shop and catch them prepping for lunch.

"He said Mildred didn't sound surprised. She just asked how much they were willing to offer."

"And?" Lucy hoped Logan had insulted Mildred with a ridiculous number.

Pete shrugged. "That's all Steve heard."

She looked out toward the ocean, as if it might offer her advice. Then she threw up her hands. "Well, what can we do? We can't just ask Mildred about it. We're not even supposed to know."

"Can you close the store for lunch? Maybe we should have lunch at the café and poke around, see if she'll mention it. I can close down around two and do a late lunch. We're slow in the afternoon this time of year, anyway, because everyone's out on the beach or playing golf."

"Sure, I can do that. Bob won't leave during the day, but

I'm sure Pam will." It was commonplace for businesses downtown to close for lunch at varying times, merely placing a sign in their windows to indicate what time they'd return. Many of the businesses were run by owners or operated with a single sales associate, so there wasn't always someone to keep things running while they stepped out.

Lucy considered calling Logan and demanding he tell her what was happening, but she didn't trust him to tell her the truth. She and Pete agreed they'd simply engage Mildred in a conversation about the waterfront project and see what happened. If nothing else, at least they'd all get a good lunch.

Lucy was surprised when they entered the restaurant and instead of finding Mildred at the hostess stand where she was essentially a permanent fixture, one of the servers greeted them.

"Is Mildred here?" Lucy asked as they were escorted to their usual table.

"No, poor thing. She broke a crown and had to go to the dentist. It's the first time she hasn't been here since I started working here last December. There must be a better way to get a day off though." The server laughed.

Lucy turned to look at Pam and Pete as they approached their table, and they exchanged defeated looks.

"Should we ask if Marty's in back?" Pam whispered after the server left.

"Mildred would have been easier. He's not as—" Pete searched for a word.

"Loose-lipped?" Lucy giggled. Mildred was an open book, but Marty could be moody and was less inclined to be chatty.

The other two smiled and Pete pointed at Lucy. "Exactly."

"Still worth a try though?" The community forum was

that evening, so Lucy didn't think it would look that suspicious for a group of downtown business owners to be checking in on the Bankses before the big meeting.

Steve appeared to take their drink order, but didn't let on in front of the group that he had anything to share, and Pete didn't bring up their conversation. Lucy knew Steve socialized with Pete and Frank outside of work. They were all part of the local artists' guild, so he probably felt more comfortable with Pete. They asked if he'd send Marty out when he went to fetch their drinks.

"So Taylor was in the store dropping off some clothes the other day, and she mentioned you've been spending a lot of time with Logan." Pam raised an eyebrow in Lucy's direction. "Keep your friends close and your enemies closer?"

"Something like that." Lucy busied herself with unrolling her silverware and laying it out at her place setting. That was how it had started. Now, though, Lucy couldn't exactly call him the enemy. He was helping her with a personal matter.

"He's been making the rounds." Pete nodded. "Missy came in to buy her dad a tie for his birthday and told me Logan tried to sell her on bringing cruise ships into port. I've been sitting around waiting for him to come visit my store, but no sign of him yet. I have a shirt set aside that would just make those gorgeous green eyes pop. Somebody better send him my way."

Lucy rolled her eyes even as she pictured Logan's and the way the gold in them had danced under the lights when they'd shared dinner at the Sand Dollar. Pete would probably roll over even faster than Missy if Logan laid on the charm, especially since Lucy herself was struggling to resist. Pete was a flirt by nature. He tested his lines on men and women alike, and they all loved him. Logan's charm made everyone feel like the most important person in the room, and Pete's made them feel like the most beautiful. She had to admit she'd seen Logan's eyes drink her in on more than one occasion lately, and it made her feel appreciated in a way she hadn't in a long while.

"I ran into him on the beach last week." Pam took her tea from Steve when he returned to the table, the silver-and-gold bangles on her slender wrist tinkling. "Ava bounded right over to him and soaked his shirt."

Pete's mouth dropped open as he took his tea from Steve. "Did he take it off? Please tell me he took it off."

Steve raised an eyebrow as he placed Lucy's tea in front of her, but he pretended not to eavesdrop on their conversation. Lucy decided not to share that she'd seen Logan with his shirt off more than once on his morning runs, and it was definitely a sight to see.

Pam turned to frown at Pete. "No, he did not take off his shirt."

"What?" Pete turned up his hands. "You said you were on the beach. People take off their shirts on the beach." He shrugged. "I was just trying to get a visual."

"Yes, I'm sure you were." Pam turned back to Lucy. "Anyway, he didn't tell me much. Just that he planned to hear everyone out and try to find something that worked for us all. He mentioned he had some ideas, but he didn't elaborate. Do you know what might come up at the meeting?"

Lucy sighed, poking her straw at an ice cube in her sweet tea. "Cruise ships. Another casino boat." She shrugged. "I wish Helen was here to lead these meetings, but she left me the number of her water expert."

"Did y'all ever do the dinner cruise on that dreadful casino boat?" Pete scowled. "I could have broken a tooth on the roll they served with my dinner, and the fish was definitely frozen. I do love me some blackjack and a spin or two on the roulette wheel though." He wiggled his eyebrows, eliciting laughter from the rest of the table.

Marty approached, interrupting Pete's commentary.

"Afternoon." Marty nodded. He was dressed in a chef's coat and black pants, both perfectly pressed and clean. Lucy knew from Mildred that Marty didn't do much of the cooking anymore, preferring instead to check orders before they went out to make sure the presentation was up to his standards. Marty was in his mid-sixties and his hair was now more salt than pepper, the deep lines in his face making him look older than he really was. He and Mildred were practically at the restaurant every waking hour, and it had taken a toll on both of them.

"Hey, Marty." Pam smiled up at him. "We heard about Mildred. Poor thing. I dread going to the dentist."

"Yeah, she wasn't real excited about it either. She'll be fine though. Hopefully she'll feel up to going to the forum tonight because at least one of us needs to be here for dinner service."

"We heard the city wants to make you an offer," Pete blurted, much to the surprise of both Lucy and Pam.

Lucy stared at him, her eyes wide.

Marty's expression darkened, the line between his eyebrows deepening. "Is that so? First I've heard of it."

Lucy looked to Pete. They'd all just assumed Marty knew.

Pete hesitated, as if deciding how much to divulge. "Oh, maybe I'm mistaken."

Marty frowned, crossing his arms over his chest. "I doubt it. I'm sure they'd love to toss us out on our keisters. I've already talked to our attorney."

Steve started to approach to take their order but did a quick U-turn when he realized they were talking to Marty.

Pam, ever the reasonable one of the group, spoke gently. "That's probably why they want to make an offer, right? They have to give you incentive to go willingly."

"Yeah, well, they'll have to pry me out of here. I'm not going to just sit back and watch them turn this into Coney Island or some nonsense." Marty's voice was getting louder and Lucy looked around to see if anyone was sitting close enough to overhear.

"I'll bring it up at the forum tonight," she said. "I'm sure everyone there will be on your side."

"Except Logan Lancaster," Pete snarked, crossing his arms as he leaned back in his chair.

"Yet another blunder by the city, hiring that guy." Marty shook his head. "Did you hear about what he did in San Diego?"

Lucy looked from Pete to Pam, but they looked as confused as she was. When Logan was first introduced as the new consultant, she'd meant to search for more about him online, but she'd been so busy she'd never gotten around to it.

"What did he do? Bulldoze the waterfront and throw up some gaudy condominiums?" Pete was leaning forward on the table again, eager to hear the gossip.

Marty raised an eyebrow, clearly surprised the group wasn't better informed. "No. He blew the whole thing. Spent over a year there working on a new waterfront project to replace their old port. Some 'live, work, play' concept. Apparently, he was dating the daughter of the biggest investor in the project and dumped her before he crossed the finish line. Her father pulled his money out of the deal and convinced every other deep pocket in town to follow suit. Logan was chased out of town with his tail between his legs."

Lucy was too stunned to speak. Had he used this man's daughter to grease the wheels of his project then let her go once he'd gotten what he needed from her? She'd heard the way he charmed Mildred that first night and then Missy in the flower shop. Maybe he was the type of guy who used his good looks and charm to weasel his way into the hearts of women who could help him achieve his professional goals. Was that why he wanted to help her buy the building? Did he think she'd be so grateful she'd just turn to putty in his hands and go along with his ideas for the waterfront?

"Lucy?"

Pam's voice startled her. She was so caught up in her thoughts, her mind racing with questions, she hadn't heard Pam's question. She stilled her bouncing foot.

"Sorry, what did you say?" Lucy looked around the group and realized all eyes were on her.

"Has Logan mentioned what happened in San Diego? You've spent the most time with him."

"No." She shook her head. "He's never said a word about San Diego."

"Isn't that alone suspicious?" Pete raised an eyebrow as he looked around at the others.

It was, and Lucy vowed to investigate it more later.

The group promised Marty they'd look out for the restaurant at the forum, even if Mildred couldn't make it. Lucy didn't have much of an appetite and only took a few bites of her burger when it came. She was too preoccupied with thoughts of Logan and whether their time together had been sincere or not. Maybe those looks he gave her that made her feel as if he could see into her soul was just something practiced, like the prosecutor on the television show she watched practicing the facial expressions and eye contact his jury consultant taught him.

As they walked through the square back toward their respective shops, Lucy told the others she was veering off to check the Little Free Library.

Pam's eyes lit up. "Ooh, is your friend still leaving you books?"

Pete stepped forward, effectively blocking their path. "Wait, what did I miss? Dish!"

Pam looked to Lucy for permission to proceed, and Lucy

nodded, shrugging a shoulder as Pam told him about Gatsby's Ghost.

"So he knows who you are, but you don't know who he is?" Pete was as intrigued by the story as he might be about a whodunit thriller.

"No, he doesn't know who I am either." Then she realized he might. She wasn't really sure. "At least, I don't think he does."

"How does he sign his notes? What kind of books is he leaving you?" Pete was in full detective mode now.

"He signs them all Gatsby's Ghost, and it's all kinds of books. It started because I left a book about Hemingway's wife, and then he left me one about F. Scott Fitzgerald. You know I love the twenties." Lucy's birthday party the previous year was *The Great Gatsby* themed.

"Hmm." Pete tapped a finger along his jawline. "Who do we know who also loves the twenties?" His mouth fell open dramatically. "Frank! Maybe my dear Frank is thinking about stepping out on me." Shaking his head, he frowned. "But he hates reading. Who else?"

Pam laughed. "Basically everyone who came to her party all dressed up last year?"

Everyone had really gotten into the spirit with their flapper costumes and tuxedos. It had been one of the best birthdays she'd ever had, which she'd desperately needed with Carter newly gone off to Chicago.

"I still have the invite list. I'll have to check it when I get back to the store." He winked and then clapped. "I love a good mystery."

After they said their goodbyes, Lucy checked the Little Free Library and was disappointed to find nothing new from Gatsby's Ghost. Back at the bookstore, she removed the "Gone to Lunch" sign from the window while silently hoping no one came in. She wanted to look into what Marty had said about Logan's project in San Diego.

The story wasn't hard to find. Every major newspaper and online outlet in San Diego had multiple articles on Logan's deal gone wrong. They hadn't spelled it out, but the insinuation was clear: Logan had used his relationship with the investor's daughter to seal the deal. His only mistake had been breaking up with her before the project was complete.

At first, Lucy couldn't reconcile what she was reading with the Logan who'd taken her on the historic tour and gazed at the gingerbread detailing like most men would a steak. Or the Logan who'd taken her to dinner and broken down some of her walls. Or the Logan who was helping her buy her building.

But then she remembered the Logan who was going door-to-door charming the downtown merchants, like Missy. The Logan who dramatically ripped up the former development plans and tried to sweet-talk the town at his first meeting. The Logan who was making offers to Mildred behind Marty's back.

Had she let Logan charm her just like he'd charmed the investor's daughter and probably countless others across the country? Hadn't she suspected all along that was how he did business?

She remembered the line Gatsby's Ghost had underlined in the Mel Robbins book. "Your feelings don't matter. The only thing that matters is what you DO."

What was she going to do?

Lucy found herself wondering what Gatsby's Ghost would say in this situation. He had solved her problem and helped her get back to writing, or at least the book he'd left her had.

She couldn't help but feel a connection to Annie through him. Annie had always given her the right advice—

or the right book—to help her navigate obstacles. She didn't tell her what to do, she just gave her the tools to build a solution. Gatsby's Ghost had done the same. If he hadn't left her the last book, she might not be working on a new manuscript. Maybe he could help her figure out her Logan problem too. She couldn't just stand by while he sweet-talked Mildred and the others into signing off on his plans, and she couldn't sit around and wait, hoping Gatsby's Ghost magically delivered another book that steered her in the right direction.

She had another idea.

Maybe they could meet.

But that was crazy. They'd been sharing book suggestions. He didn't want to be her therapist or her business coach or whatever she was asking him to be when it came to the waterfront development. It wasn't like he'd even known about her writing career being in a shambles when he suggested *The 5 Second Rule*.

But it had been the exact book she'd needed at the exact moment she needed it. And if she'd learned anything from the book, it was to push aside her hesitations and go with her gut. And her gut said it was time for them to meet.

This time, she wouldn't leave him a book. Just a note in an envelope addressed to him.

Dear Gatsby's Ghost,

I'm sorry I have no book recommendation today. I've been busy, and I have you to thank for that. Your last book suggestion was so antithetical to my nature that I questioned your wisdom. Thankfully, however, the author made a compelling argument, and I found myself doing things boldly, without hesitation. Things I never would have done just a few weeks ago. One of those things even lead to a major breakthrough for my writing career.

I'd like to thank you in person. But I have to admit I have selfish motives. It's just that you've given such good advice, and I find myself in need of more than I can ask for in a note like this.

Meet me on the benches by the marina on Thursday at 5:00 p.m.? I'll be the one holding your copy of The 5 Second Rule.

I hope you'll be there,
Island Girl

Before she could change her mind, Lucy nearly sprinted across the square to the Little Free Library. Propping up the envelope on the top shelf where it would be at eye level, she shut the door and forced herself to walk away, even while her heart pounded and a voice in her head yelled at her to take the envelope back.

No more hesitation. No more standing in her own way. It was time for her to stand in someone else's way. And that someone else was over at city hall getting ready to make his pitch to her community. There was no time to waste.

Sixteen

Logan

In an effort to keep himself from thinking about the community forum that started in just a couple hours, Logan grabbed the baseball book Island Girl had left him a few days earlier and headed to the coffee shop for an iced coffee to go. Once he had his drink in hand, he walked west toward the water, settling on the first bench he came to adjacent to the marina. Reading was the only thing that kept his brain from continually running over his talking points for the meeting. He needed the distraction—from that and to keep from obsessing about Boston and the future of his career.

The book was an easy read, a fun look at what would happen if two data-driven nerds were allowed to make all the decisions for a baseball team. The tension in his shoulders eased as he laughed at the colorful general manager and inhaled the fresh salt air.

Pausing to watch a pelican diving repeatedly into the water

in front of him, no doubt hunting its meal, Logan couldn't stop thinking about who Island Girl could be. Lucy had mentioned a friend named Taylor he hadn't met yet. What if Lucy's best friend was his pen pal? No, he did not want that. Nothing about that felt right.

He'd wondered before if it might be Lucy, since she obviously loved books, but she'd said the last book she read was a thriller. Plus, he'd seen her several times with the stack of advance reader copies she was working through, none of which were anything like the books he'd been trading with Island Girl. Besides, he was still pretty sure Island Girl was in a bad marriage based on some of her comments.

Missy, Pam, Jessica from the Parks and Rec department... None of the women he'd met fit the profile. The town was small, but he obviously hadn't met everyone, and there were the tourists who'd already started pouring in for the warmer weather. She could be anyone.

He tried to get back into the book, but thinking of Lucy only made his mind race in circles. Grabbing his phone, he decided to call his sister and take a walk. She'd always been the calm, reasonable one in his family. She'd talk him off the ledge.

"So you do remember my phone number," Carly teased him, in lieu of an actual hello when she picked up on the first ring.

"We've texted almost every day since I got here." He sipped his iced coffee, already feeling calmer just hearing her voice.

"Not the same. I can't tell what you're hiding when you text."

"Hiding? Why do you always think I'm hiding something?"

"Because you usually are. Out with it. You didn't call because you're bored. You only call when you're worried about something."

He sighed. "Tonight is the first of three community forums here. You know how much I love community forums."

"Yes, I know you hate it when people don't agree with you or defer to your expertise."

He could practically hear her rolling her eyes through the phone.

"Well, this *is* what I do for a living. Why does everyone always act like I'm the bad guy? The projects I help design provide jobs and increase tax revenue, not to mention the new housing, shopping, and dining opportunities."

"You're not a bad guy. You're just the only guy on the planet who loves change. You know normal humans resist change, right?"

"So people just want to live like cavemen? I mean, why change what was working, right? Who needs wheels or electricity?" Logan slipped off his shoes as he reached the end of the sidewalk where it sloped down to meet the sandy beach. A woman in a wheelchair was sitting at the edge, her eyes closed and head tilted toward the sun. He made a mental note that any plan for this area had to include accessibility options. Everyone should be able to enjoy the beach.

She let out an exasperated breath. "I'm sure these people will let you include electricity in your plans."

He remembered Lucy's story about the dentist downtown and repeated it to Carly. "Isn't that fascinating? I'd never thought about how dentists worked before electricity. See, innovation is good."

"You mentioned a woman told you about this dentist. Anyone I should know about?"

She was always trying to marry him off, although she'd never thought Catherine was "the one," despite never having met her. Carly said she wanted him to find someone and settle down because she loved her family so much she wanted him to have one. He wasn't sure that was in the cards for him, not with his lifestyle. There was always another city to move to. Another project to finish.

"No, it's not like that. Lucy is my competition. She owns the local bookstore and is the head of the Downtown Business Owners Council." He didn't need to mention he was helping her with something personal, knowing his sister would read too much into it.

"Is she single?"

"I have no idea, and it doesn't matter." He was fairly certain she was. He'd never heard her mention anyone. "Did you just hear me? She's my opposition."

"Okay, all right. I just think it wouldn't kill you to go on a date and remember that not every woman is a self-obsessed cheater like Catherine. Have you tried to charm her into seeing things your way? Maybe you're losing your touch." His sister loved teasing him.

"We've"—he searched for the right way to describe the situation without having to divulge too much—"reached an understanding. She's a worthy opponent, but I've gotten bigger projects than this approved."

"Please tell me you're not going to bulldoze this poor woman's bookstore."

"No, she's actually in a gorgeous historic building. You know I wouldn't touch that. The entire historic district here is beautiful. You'd love it." He watched a family laughing together on several brightly colored towels spread out in the sand about thirty yards in front of him. The kids looked to be around Alexandria and Aidan's ages, making him wonder if he should ask Carly to bring her family down like Lucy had suggested.

A gull cried out overhead.

"Are you at the beach?"

"Yeah, you basically walk right off the sidewalk downtown

onto the beach. It's a nice little town." One long-weekend visit from family wasn't going to derail his timeline here. "Hey, Carly. Why don't you and Nick and the kids come down? I'm here for at least another month or two."

"Gosh, that would be amazing. I'll have to talk to Nick though. Not sure we can swing it right now. We just had to replace the refrigerator and the water heater in the same week." Carly was a stay-at-home mom and Nick was a cop in Berlin. Logan was always trying to send them money, but they never accepted his help. Instead, he spoiled the kids on their birthdays and at Christmas.

"My treat."

She began to protest, but he cut her off.

"What is the point in me making all this money if I can't ever do anything with it? I don't need a permanent residence, and I already get to travel and eat out. The one thing I can't buy is time with my family, but I can buy you plane tickets. I'm not taking no for an answer. See if Nick can get a weekend off and, if not, you come down with the kids."

"What has gotten into you?" His sister sounded skeptical. "It's not like you ignore us or anything, but you've never pushed this hard to spend time with us. What's happening down there?"

He knew Carly worried about him after what happened in San Diego.

"Nothing bad." He assured her. "To be honest, it wasn't entirely my idea. Lucy—the woman who owns the bookstore —doesn't have any family, and she made me see the error of my ways."

"I like this Lucy woman. Maybe I'll come down just so I can meet her and ask her if she's single."

"Never mind. I'm revoking my invitation," he grumbled, feigning irritation, but he didn't really mean it.

"I'd love to see you, and the kids would love the beach, but—"

Carly was cut off by Aidan's excited voice in the background.

"Yes! Are we going to the beach to visit Uncle Logan?"

"Now you have to come. Can't disappoint the kid." Logan smiled as he finally let himself picture his family here with him. He couldn't wait to show Carly the buildings downtown. She loved historic structures almost as much as he did.

"I'll talk to Nick tonight." He could hear her relenting, and he let himself get excited about the idea.

He'd have to remember to thank Lucy later.

When Logan arrived at the council chambers, he found Lucy alone inside the small room, seated in the front row reviewing her notes. The walls were wainscoted in dark brown, a stark contrast to the colorful beauty that existed outside the doors. It was probably last decorated in the seventies and was just another example of the city's strangled budget.

"Evening." He approached her from behind. "You ready for this?"

"I don't know, am I?"

The cold edge to her voice sent a warning as he walked down the center aisle.

Walking more slowly toward her, he tried to read her face as she turned to stare him down. Gone were the warm brown eyes and the smile he'd gotten used to lately; they had been replaced with the sort of disappointed look his mother had given him when he skirted his duties on the farm as a kid. He racked his brain trying to think of what he could have done to hurt her. Whatever it was, he'd fix it. He'd thought they were, if not on the same team, at least becoming friends.

"Did I miss something? You seem upset."

"That's because I am." She put her notes on the chair next to her and stood to face him, crossing her arms over her pale-pink sundress.

"Are you going to make me guess why?" He took a few steps closer, but left plenty of room between them. He wanted to reach out and touch her arm, to assure her they could fix whatever it was, but she looked ready to recoil if he came any closer.

"Are you going behind Marty's back to coerce Mildred into some sort of buyout on the café's lease?"

Mildred. He should have known it was a bad sign she wasn't telling Marty about their conversation yet. He understood why she wanted to wait until she had a number, but he certainly hadn't asked her to keep Marty in the dark. But how had Lucy even heard about their conversation?

He put his hands in his pockets and rocked back on his heels as he decided how to respond.

"Those conversations are confidential. I would just say it's not up to me to dictate how Mildred and Marty communicate about their business."

She flung out her arms, losing her composure. "What kind of an answer is that?"

He'd never heard her raise her voice. She usually had a soft, soothing tone you'd expect out of someone who'd been a librarian. She was really upset, but she had to know it was unlikely the restaurant would survive whatever new plan they eventually agreed upon. The building was barely sound at this point, thanks to the hurricanes that had damaged the pilings underneath. If the city was going to put in money to shore it up for long-term viability, they'd need to see more of a return than the restaurant lease had been giving them.

"An honest one. Negotiations between the town and individual business owners are confidential."

"Apparently they're also confidential between you and Mildred because Marty told us today he had no idea the town was preparing to make an offer to end the restaurant lease. He's not going to give up his livelihood because you wave a check in front of his face. Is that what you do? Charm women like Mildred and Missy"—her voice broke—"and even me into going along with your plans so you can pack up and move on to the next town?"

Logan was completely baffled. He'd been doing his job. It wasn't his fault Mildred was keeping her true desire to retire from her husband. He was about to tell Lucy that when she brushed past him to where her bag sat on a nearby chair, her coconut scent passing over him like a wave.

Lucy grabbed a stack of papers from her bag and handed them to him. Printouts of newspaper articles.

"I've read all about what happened in San Diego, and suddenly it all made sense. Why you'd take a project in a place like Heron Isle and why you'd immediately cozy up to me and offer to help me buy my building. You need a quick win, and the only way you know how to win is by manipulating women with your green eyes and your dimple and your smooth talking about how much you love historic buildings." She was gesturing more wildly now, her brown eyes fiery and her blonde curls bouncing with every movement.

He was so caught off guard by her assumptions about what happened in San Diego—about him—he could hardly formulate a response. Clearing his throat to buy himself time to respond calmly and not grow defensive, he laid the papers face down on a nearby chair. Turning back to Lucy, her brown eyes demanding answers—answers he very much wanted to give her—Logan spoke quietly.

"Do you always believe everything you read?" He searched her eyes, looking for any indication he might reach her. He hadn't exactly done himself any favors in the press. He'd been so upset over Catherine and the project that he'd done a poor job of explaining himself to the few reporters who'd reached out for his side of the story.

A wrinkle appeared between her eyebrows as she gave him a questioning look. "You're telling me it's just a coincidence you dated the daughter of the biggest investor who came into the project?"

"No, it's not a coincidence." He continued before she could interject. "I met her because I was courting her father to come onto the project. In fact, *she* bought *me* at a date auction. Do you really think I'd break up with her before the project was complete if that was all I was after?" He raised an eyebrow, asking her to do a little critical thinking before she threw more accusations his way.

Before she could respond, the chamber doors opened, and the first few people started to trickle in. Lucy's expression softened slightly as she waved in their direction.

"Hey, y'all. Go ahead and take any seat you'd like. Thank you for coming tonight." Turning back to him, she said coolly, "We'll finish discussing this later. Stick to the agenda and we'll be just fine." She reached around him to grab the papers, folding them, and shoving them inside her bag before waving at more people coming in.

He watched as she walked to the door and greeted people as they entered. She was shaking hands, complimenting outfits, and asking several of them how their businesses were doing. She'd stolen the move he'd tried to use that first night after the town council meeting where he was introduced.

He could tell she was setting the stage for an evening of us versus them with him as the "them," even though the town council and mayor were due to attend as well. If she could successfully paint him as the bad guy, even the council members and the mayor would hang him out to dry to save face. After all, they had to continue to live in the community and some of them would be up for re-election soon.

The room was near capacity by the time Lucy joined him at the front to open the forum. She stood as far as she could from him, as if she might catch something. She smiled broadly anytime she addressed the crowd, but she refused to make eye contact with him.

When she turned it over to Logan, he explained they'd be using the giant white board behind them to brainstorm ideas.

"If you'd like to add an idea to the list, all you have to do is raise your hand. Lucy"—he turned toward her, but she still wouldn't meet his eyes—"I'll let you call on people since you know everyone better." Normally, he would have taken charge and tried to control the flow of the meeting to his advantage, but he thought better of it after Lucy's attack.

She locked eyes with him briefly then, her mouth a tight line. "Yes, I do." Turning back to the crowd, she smiled. "While you all are thinking on ideas, I'm going to share one Helen sent me. She sends her regrets, but she's engaged in some very important research right now. She'd like us to explore the idea of adding an aquarium experience to help our visitors learn more about the fish, water mammals, flora, and fauna in our area. I know many of us don't want to see a large building blocking the view of the water from downtown, so she said to make sure I told you that she's been researching a concept she saw in Seattle where visitors actually descend into an underwater room for viewing."

Logan considered the idea as he watched Lucy write it on the board. The city could own and operate the aquarium and charge an admission fee. Construction of that sort of attraction sounded expensive, though, especially since it probably required special care so as not to disrupt the natural underwater environment. He was all for being environmentally conscious, but it also meant the project was probably cost prohibitive.

"I also wanted to add the idea of renting out stand-up paddle boards and small two-person watercrafts, that sort of thing." Lucy directed the idea toward the crowd, not acknowledging that those had been his ideas. "We could rent them right from the marina and direct people toward the back side of the island where the water is calmer."

He let Lucy claim the idea. It wasn't important who put what up on the board. He certainly wasn't going to call her on it in front of everyone.

Hands started raising in the audience.

Lucy pointed at a weathered-looking man. "Wayne."

"What about a maritime or shrimping museum? Pay homage to all the men and women who trawled the waters before us." The heads of several similarly dressed men around him bobbed up and down.

Lucy continued to write ideas from the crowd on the board: a shrimping museum, an old-school arcade, and an open-air market, which seemed to have the most support.

The next woman Lucy called on suggested an amphitheater, which Logan had on his list. It was relatively easy and inexpensive—at least as far as development projects went—to build an amphitheater that blended in with the natural surroundings. It could be rented out to bands and acting groups, host seminars and more.

When everyone with a hand up had been heard, Logan cleared his throat. "I've got a couple more ideas I'd like to add to the board as well."

Lucy scowled at him, anticipating his additions, but waved a hand toward the board to give him the floor.

"I'll preface this by saying I know these won't necessarily be popular options, but they are potentially lucrative ones that don't require building anything new on the waterfront." He scanned the audience. Normally he did enough work before a meeting like this to curb any real opposition. He knew better than to come into a room full of potential opponents and throw a grenade into the crowd, but Lucy hadn't left him much choice after she'd gotten him to agree to the ceasefire. He took a deep breath and pulled the pin.

"I'd like us to consider allowing *small* cruise ships like the ones that go into Savannah and Charleston."

When members of the crowd started expressing their discontent, Lucy did nothing to silence them. She just stood there with her arms crossed, an eyebrow raised in his direction as if saying she didn't know why he was even bothering. Clearly, she was confident he wouldn't get the support he needed for his ideas.

Logan decided it was best to let people vent for a few moments before he tried to go on. When the din of conversation began to lull, he took the opportunity to jump back in.

"I simply ask that you all come to the next forum and listen to the representative from the cruise company. We're not talking about those big, towering ships that go to the Bahamas. These ships hold fewer than one hundred people. The rep can explain how much the downtown business owners would benefit as passengers disembark to shop and eat, and the upside is that it won't put any pressure on the infrastructure here to add hotel rooms or parking."

As he spoke, faces softened. Some people even nodded, as if now that they understood a little more, they thought it might be something they could stomach.

Lucy glared at him. "Let's not forget that we have a limit on the length of boats that come into our marina for a reason. Also, I'll have an environmental expert here at the next meeting to tell us about the fish and plant life the cruise ships would destroy. Then we can discuss the idea once we've heard both sides."

Heads bobbed as people agreed with her.

"Anything else you'd like to add?" she asked him, a challenge in her tone.

Glancing out at the crowd and back at her, he coughed to clear his throat. "I do have one more thought that we'll discuss at the next meeting while the water expert is here. I'd like you to consider bringing back the casino boat"—he held up his hand as the crowd began to murmur—"from a *different* operating company than last time. I know you weren't thrilled with the previous owners. I've spoken with people in several other cities here in Florida about the company I'm recommending, and they can vouch for them."

He'd lost the crowd. He could see it on their faces. It was going to take a lot to turn the tide at the next forum. It was his job to ensure both a profitable waterfront project and that the backlash from it didn't create problems in the voting booth when it came time to re-elect the council.

Examining the sea of unhappy faces, his eyes finally landed on Lucy. He had his work cut out for him. With the townspeople, but most of all with Lucy.

SEVENTEEN

Logan

When he woke up Thursday morning, Logan remembered the previous night. Everything about Heron Isle had been a mistake. Taking the job. Offering to help Lucy. Talking to Mildred without Marty. All of it.

He'd been so dejected after the community meeting, he hadn't even visited the Little Free Library to leave Island Girl the book he'd meant to give her earlier in the week. She might be the only person left in town who still liked him. Unless, of course, she'd been at the meeting.

The only way to get over a bad meeting was to win the next one, so he'd skipped his morning run and gone straight into work. After reviewing financial data for the whiteboard suggestions for over three hours without a break, he finally went outside for a walk to clear his head. Pacing on the docks, he pulled out his phone. His sister answered before he'd registered that he'd hit her speed-dial button.

"Two calls in a week. What is that island doing to you?"

"Don't you ever just say hello?" Logan asked.

"Hello, my darling brother. How are you doing? Why are you calling me? Again."

"Didn't you complain that I don't call you enough? Here I am. Calling you." The real reason was that he couldn't bear to be alone with his thoughts any longer. "Did you talk to Nick?"

"Yeah." Her voice was muffled as she yelled something at one of the kids. "He can't get any time off, but I think the kids and I will take you up on a visit. I can tell I need to come down there and see what's going on for myself."

He smiled for the first time all day. He hadn't realized how much he'd missed seeing his sister. "That's great. Just tell me when and I'll book your tickets."

"Is this weekend too soon? Aidan has swim camp after that, and then we're watching Nick's sister's kids while she and her husband go away for their anniversary."

He should spend the weekend preparing for the next community forum, but he'd just have to work harder this week so he could take the weekend off.

"No, that's perfect. I'll get it booked when I get back to my office." A pelican glided gracefully over the water in front of him, swooping up just before the docks to sit on top of a piling. Maybe he'd bring the kids down to the docks to feed the pelicans. He'd watched the fishermen do it when they came in for the afternoons and had bait to spare.

"Tell me what's really going on." Carly broke into his thoughts. "I can hear it in your voice. Did your community forum not go well?"

He let out a laugh. "No, it did not go well at all. Lucy and I had a little misunderstanding, and by the end of the meeting she had the whole town ready to pull out the pitchforks."

"Hmm, too soon to be having a lover's quarrel. Can you patch it up?"

He let out a hearty laugh. "I can assure you it's not like that. In fact, she dug up a bunch of articles on Catherine and me, and accused me of using women everywhere I go to get the job done."

He could hear his sister suck in air through her teeth. "Yikes. That's harsh."

"And completely untrue. You know that." He shoved his free hand in his pocket as he paced the docks.

"Did you tell her that?"

"I tried."

"Aaannd?" Carly asked.

"I don't think she cared. She's made up her mind about me."

"Why do you care so much what this one woman thinks? It's not like she has the only vote on the matter. I'm sure you've convinced tougher critics than a small-town bookstore owner." When he didn't immediately reply, Carly continued. "Or... is this not really about the project and more about the girl? I *knew* you had a thing for her!"

"I do not. This is strictly about business." He stopped pacing, dropping onto a bench and dragging his hand through his now sweaty hair. It had to be over ninety degrees today.

"Would it be so bad if you did have a thing for her? Honestly, I think you need a dating cleanse after that whole fiasco with she-who-shall-not-be-named. I'm not saying you have to find someone to marry, maybe just someone to grab coffee with. I worry that you don't stay anywhere long enough to make friends."

"Who needs friends when you have the best sister in the world?" He smiled knowing she was no doubt rolling her eyes on the other end of the phone. "Plus, if I get this job in Boston, I'll have Fuller."

"You never see either one of us," she countered. "I worry about you just sitting around at night brooding and probably drinking too much scotch."

He hesitated, debating whether to tell Carly about Island Girl.

"I haven't been brooding. I've actually been doing a lot of reading lately. They have this Little Free Library here. I'll show you when you come down this weekend. People leave notes with the books, recommending them."

"Cute," she said. "But sitting at home alone reading a book wasn't what I had in mind. I'm talking about making personal connections."

He cleared his throat, suddenly feeling embarrassed about the increasingly personal connection he was forming with Island Girl.

"Well, I have sort of connected with someone. We've been leaving books for each other." He wiped the sweat from his brow, the sun suddenly feeling like one of those interrogation lamps they shine on criminals on TV shows.

"Now we're talking! What's she like? Is she cute?"

He knew it was dangerous telling her. She watched way too many Hallmark movies, and he didn't want her getting any romantic ideas.

"I haven't actually met her. People sign the notes with monikers. We're more like pen pals." Logan proceeded to tell his sister everything about Island Girl and the books and notes they'd left for each other.

"Omigosh, I wish I was there now!" He hadn't heard his sister this excited since she'd called the last time she was pregnant to tell him it was a girl. "It's like *You've Got Mail*. Wait! The bookstore owner! What if it's her?" She was practically shrieking in his ear.

"No. It's not Lucy. I've seen what she reads, and she recommended a completely different kind of book than what

Island Girl has been leaving me. Besides, they don't really seem much alike to me, and I think Island Girl is married."

"Well, I'll be there soon, and you can show me all the letters and we'll figure out who she is." Carly sounded as excited as a kid counting down the days to Christmas. "Ooh, I can't wait! This is going to be so much fun!"

Logan had to admit her enthusiasm was rubbing off. Maybe he would try to figure out who Island Girl was, just to thank her for all the book suggestions and for helping him pass the time on Heron Isle outside of work. After all, corresponding with her was the only thing he hadn't screwed up since arriving.

After a productive afternoon, Logan decided to call it a day earlier than usual and make up the morning run he'd missed. Running always cleared his head, and he needed to wipe Lucy's disappointed look out of his mind if he was going to make any progress at the next community meeting. He just couldn't stop seeing the hurt in her brown eyes when she'd insinuated that he'd only been using her to accomplish his goals. He thought they'd moved past that, but it seemed he still hadn't managed to outrun the San Diego nightmare.

The beach was much quieter here than it had been in California on his daily runs, especially later in the day. It was that time between afternoon and evening when families returned to their houses and condos to clean up and get ready for dinner. He could count on one hand the number of people he'd passed since he left his cottage, the seagulls circling overhead far outnumbering the humans. The waves crashing on the shore were punctuated here and there by the cry of a gull, but the only other sound was the pounding of his feet on the sand and his steady, even breaths. Whoever said you couldn't outrun your problems had clearly never tried actually running.

As Logan ran around a sandcastle long since abandoned by its maker, he thought about how much he was looking forward to seeing Carly and the kids. Some familiar, smiling faces were just what he needed. Carly had been right about his lack of human connection these days. Maybe it was this lack that was hindering his progress here. Although he'd thought he'd made inroads with Lucy, only to have her so easily turn on him again.

Lucy. Why couldn't he stop thinking about Lucy? Carly was right; Lucy wasn't the sole deciding vote in this town. Heck, she didn't have a vote at all, only the commissioners did. Why did he care so much about what she thought?

Frustrated that work had crept into his thoughts again, he decided to turn around at the marina, which he was nearing. A few charter-boat captains were unloading their gear, their customers having already left for the day. People walked along the sidewalk licking ice-cream cones and stopping to take selfies with the beach as their backdrop.

And then he saw her. Lucy was sitting on a bench in a white summer dress, its edges lifting lightly on the breeze. Her face was covered by large sunglasses, but her head was moving as if she was scanning the people on the sidewalk watching for someone.

Logan slowed to a jog, studying her as he grew closer. She seemed on edge, her posture unnaturally straight, her foot bouncing on the ground. If he didn't know better, he'd say she was an anxious secret agent waiting for a hand off.

Then she turned to look in his direction and froze, her foot no longer tapping. An awkward moment passed, and he didn't know what to do but wave, raising his hand in acknowledgment that he'd seen her too.

Instead of waving back, she turned to look in the other

direction as if she hadn't seen him. Now she was just being childish. She couldn't even acknowledge his existence and be cordial? He was tired of being cast as the villain. He hadn't had time to properly defend himself last night, but he had all the time in the world right now.

"Lucy. Fancy meeting you here," he said as he approached.

She shoved a book in her bag like she might pack up and flee. She looked at him and frowned, then glanced over her shoulder as if someone might swoop in and save her at any moment.

"Hello, Logan."

He pointed to the green box sitting beside her, the same kind he'd seen people carrying all over town and had learned was the signature box from Nana's Bakery, a local institution.

"Let me guess. You seem like a lemon square kind of gal. Or maybe vanilla cupcakes with sprinkles? I'm a chocolate chip cookie guy myself." He'd been to the bakery twice in the past week for Nana Theresa's homemade chocolate chip cookies, which was why he couldn't skip his daily run.

She scooted the box closer to her as if protecting it before answering in a voice so low he could barely hear it over the soundtrack of the ocean and seagulls behind him.

"Chocolate chip cookies."

"See, we *can* agree on something!" He flashed her his best smile.

The sour look on her face remained unchanged. "What do you want?" She crossed her arms, looking back down the sidewalk.

"If you didn't constantly jump to conclusions about me and my intentions, you might find we have a lot in common." He started counting things off on his fingers. "We both grew up in small towns. We both love historic buildings. And apparently neither of us can resist Nana Theresa's chocolate chip cookies."

"Yes, well, apparently the similarities end there. I don't try to pit husbands and wives against each other or tear up other people's towns and then leave them to deal with the consequences."

He could feel her stare from behind the large sunglasses, even if he couldn't see her eyes. She wasn't going to make this easy.

"Can I sit?" He gestured toward the empty expanse of bench next to her, its brown wood weathered to the point that it looked more like driftwood. He made a mental note to add new Polywood benches to his plans.

She protectively placed a hand over the spot next to the box. "You may not. I'm expecting someone."

Undeterred and unwilling to let either of them continue festering in their confrontation from the evening before, he said, "I'll just sit with you while you wait."

She scooted down the bench as far away from him as she could, angling her body toward downtown so she could watch for whoever was coming.

"Who are you waiting for? Pam? Pete?"

She turned to scowl at him, that deep wrinkle forming between her eyes. "None of your business."

A man with a small tote bag began walking down the sidewalk in their direction, and she straightened up, sitting taller.

"Please leave," she hissed. "Haven't you done enough damage for one week?"

The man veered away from the benches and walked down into the sand in front of them, pulling a towel from his bag and putting in headphones. Logan could feel Lucy deflate next to him as she sighed. Who was she waiting for? A date perhaps? She seemed too nervous—and now that he really looked at her, more made up than usual—to just be meeting a friend. Was she dating someone? He'd never seen her around town with anyone, so he'd just assumed she was single. What kind of guy would she get all dressed up for and bring cookies? Maybe they were his favorite too. Whoever he was.

Logan batted away thoughts that were beginning to border on jealousy to focus on the task at hand. He'd have to break some confidences, but since there didn't seem to be much that stayed secret on Heron Isle for long, he decided to take his chances before Mr. Lucky arrived.

"Just so you know, Mildred came to me. She wants to spend more time with their daughter and their new grandchild. She asked if I could come up with a number high enough to convince Marty to let the restaurant go. They're both exhausted, and she wants to retire. She was going to tell him as soon as I had a final number."

Lucy's expression softened, although she still looked skeptical. "Didn't you tell me it was all confidential?"

He shrugged. "It is, but I trust you." And he did. She might not like him much right now, but she hadn't done anything wrong. She was just protective of her island. It was kind of sweet how much she loved it, how hard she'd fight for it, even if it meant fighting with him.

She looked out at the ocean, as if trying to decide whether she believed him. He followed her gaze, watching a pelican as it dive-bombed the water's glossy surface, and then flapped its wings to take itself airborne again. A slight breeze floated on the salty air, and it made her hair dance around her face and over her shoulders. He had the strongest urge to reach out and tuck a strand behind her ear, but forced his eyes back out to the sea.

She looked at her watch and then down the sidewalk toward town, a worried look creasing her forehead.

"Your friend late?"

"Maybe." She bit her lip and started to bounce her leg again. "You don't have to stay and"—she searched for the word she wanted to use—"entertain me. He'll be here soon."

"Oh, so it *is* a he." Logan kept his tone light, teasing her like he used to tease Carly about her dates in high school.

"Yes." Her tone indicated that the answer wasn't simple. "I think so." Her brows furrowed. "It's hard to explain." Her shoulders drooped as she slumped back against the bench.

She looked like the wounded fawn he and Carly had found in the back pasture as kids. They'd patiently tip-toed their way toward it with a bowl of water. He didn't want to spook Lucy, but he so badly wanted to wipe the pained look off her pretty face.

"Try me." He angled toward her, putting an arm on the back of the bench, his fingertips almost reaching her shoulder.

She studied his face, started to open her mouth, but then snapped it closed.

"Blind date? Someone set you up?"

"Sort of. Something like that." She looked around as if embarrassed to have anyone else overhear their conversation.

"And you said you'd meet him here on the benches?"

She nodded. "But I guess he's not going to show."

"Maybe something came up."

"Or he took one look at me and ran." Her voice was quiet, sad. She pushed up her sunglasses, as if she could hide more of herself behind their oversized shades.

It was completely impossible. No one could see the woman sitting here, looking as if she belonged on a swing in a Renoir painting, and not count his lucky stars. He looked out at the water to keep from making her uncomfortable before he spoke.

"No, I'm sure that's not it. He must have a good reason."

"It was silly anyway. He's probably just passing through like everyone else."

He could hear the hurt in her voice, and he thought of what the mayor had told him about her mother leaving. A long silence followed as they both gazed toward the horizon. He could only think of one thing to show he could relate.

"Remember how I told you that the newspapers didn't tell the whole story about what happened to me in San Diego?"

She turned to meet his eyes and nodded. "Yeah."

"Well, my side of the story is that I thought I'd met the perfect woman for me. I'd even bought a ring. I was waiting until we could celebrate the new project getting a green light before I asked her because I hadn't had a lot of time to spend with her as we went through the final phase of government approvals."

He paused, taking a deep breath. He hadn't told anyone except Carly what had happened next.

"Then I came home one night to find Catherine in bed with another man."

Lucy gasped, her hand flying to her mouth to cover it.

"This particular man happened to be the son of her father's arch nemesis. Your basic *Romeo and Juliet* plot, I guess. Except Catherine had worked out exactly how she could get her father to accept Joe. She'd made sure I would catch them together and be the one to break up with her. Then she ran to her father, playing the victim. She somehow convinced him that I'd driven her to Joe because I didn't pay her enough attention." He ran a hand through his hair. "Honestly, I still don't understand the mental gymnastics she went through to pull it off. All I know is that in the end her father blamed me for her being with Joe. And, well, you know the rest."

Lucy was quiet. He wasn't sure what else to say, so he watched the ocean instead of her face.

She surprised him when she broke the silence. "I was engaged once. Did I ever tell you that?"

He turned back to look at her, but now she was the one staring out at the water.

"No." He didn't feel right pressing her for more.

"Yeah. He was assigned here for work for a few years, but after we got engaged, he got a job offer in Chicago."

"Why didn't you go with him?" He was pretty sure he knew the answer, but he wasn't ready for her to stop talking yet.

She spread her arms out in front of her. "He asked me to, but Heron Isle is my home. It's where I want to be. I know it might not be much to someone like you who's lived in New York, San Diego, and St. Louis, but this town is more than just streets and houses and hotels. Do you know what the town did when my dad passed a couple years ago?" She looked at him as if he should know the answer.

"They didn't just set up one of those meal trains where everyone makes sure you at least have something to eat every night. They took shifts at the bookstore so I didn't have to work for a few weeks. Pete was measuring guys for suits in the back room between customers, and Nana Theresa actually moved a case of her baked goods into the store so she could run my register, all just to make sure I didn't lose my dad and my livelihood. That's the kind of place I want to call home."

Earlier in his career, he might have pitied her and the way calling a place home kept her tied down. He'd always thought he had the enviable life, getting to experience new places and meet new people. But who did he have that would be there for him when the chips were down? He had his sister and Fuller, but he hadn't lived near either of them in a long time and was lucky to see them once every year or two. Lucy was so much stronger than she seemed to give herself credit for, and it was because she didn't try to do everything on her own. She let other people in, and they were what made her strong.

Lucy sighed. "So Carter moved to Chicago, and I stayed here, where my best prospect is some stranger who stands me up." She laughed, shaking her head. "It's fine, though. I don't need someone else to make me complete. This place, the people here, they make me feel whole."

She had the connections Carly had pointed out he was so severely lacking. He never stayed anywhere long enough to develop those kinds of friendships, but it was probably for the best since he'd only have to leave them to move on to the next job. It even made him feel guilty for trying to befriend Lucy. He'd never be a real friend, here to pitch in during her time of need. He'd be off in Boston and then on to the next place.

But there was a nagging feeling in the pit of his stomach that he wanted to be part of it all. That he wanted to be Lucy's friend. More, even.

He was so lost in his thoughts, he didn't notice when she stood.

"I think I'm going to call it a night. Thanks for keeping me company." She smiled, and it felt genuine. Then she hesitated, searching his face before she continued. "And for telling me about Mildred."

He couldn't find any words, so he simply nodded.

"And, hey," she pushed her sunglasses on top of her head, waiting for him to look up. "You take the cookies." She motioned to the green box still sitting on the bench beside him. "You know, for keeping me company."

Gone was the icy glint in her eyes. In its place, warmth radiated from her brown eyes as she smiled at him.

"I'll see you around."

As he watched her walk away, he could only think about how he was looking forward to seeing her again soon.

EIGHTEEN

Logan

Logan sat on the bench for a while after Lucy left trying to make sense of everything that had just happened. One minute he was sitting next to her on a bench to keep her from feeling alone, and the next minute he was the one feeling alone, in every sense of the word.

He opened the green box next to him and took out a cookie the sun had kept warm and gooey, just the way he liked it. He wasn't usually an eat-your-feelings kind of guy, but it would be a shame for them to go to waste.

Tucking the box under his arm as he stood, he decided to walk downtown for a coffee to go with his dessert. Weaving his way down the sidewalk, he dodged a football being thrown between two kids while their parents sat on a nearby bench reminding them to be careful. The fading sunlight filtered through the oak trees, creating a light show on the path ahead of him as small spots of sunshine danced across the aging concrete.

Ahead, a petite woman with short brown hair was closing the door to the Little Free Library and holding the hand of a boy who looked to be around five. She wasn't anyone he recognized, at least not from the back. Could she be Island Girl? It was the first time he'd seen a woman taking or leaving anything from the library, so he couldn't help but wonder.

As she walked down the path in the opposite direction, no book in hand, he detoured around the fountain to get a better angle on her. She looked to be in her thirties. She wasn't unattractive, but nothing really stood out about her. She wore simple white shorts and a blue tank top with a small purse hanging across her body. It was too small to hold a book, so that meant she'd either left one or just been browsing. Besides, she had a kid. He hadn't thought of Island Girl as a mom, but that didn't mean she wasn't.

Her fast pace was moving her too far out of his sightline to register any other details, so he swung back around the fountain toward the library. If there was a new book there for him, it could mean he'd just spotted Island Girl.

Swatting at a fly that seemed to be joining him on his walk, Logan thought about whether he really wanted to know her identity. It had occurred to him that he should say goodbye to her somehow before leaving town for good, but he hadn't really considered trying to do so in person. That could be nice, just to tie up everything in a bow before he closed the chapter on Heron Isle.

The door to the Little Free Library creaked as he opened it, almost as if it wanted to mimic what the front door to the original house would sound like if it were still standing at the end of the square today.

The first thing he noticed on the ledge in the back next to a stack of new books was a white envelope that looked as if it had been torn and then taped back together. Two different sets of handwriting were on the envelope. One was in Island Girl's familiar loopy handwriting addressing the envelope to Gatsby's Ghost. Under it, however, was different handwriting.

So sorry! Took this home with my books accidentally and my son ripped it open. Promise we didn't read!

His heart started pounding, the sound of it in his ears drowning out the cars that passed nearby and the kids playing outside around the square.

Island Girl had written him a letter? Was she the woman he'd seen walking away from the library? Or was that the woman who had accidentally taken the envelope? He looked around, as if someone might be watching for his reaction, but he was alone.

She'd left him a letter without a book. What did it mean? And why was he so hesitant to open it? He picked it up, and it felt heavy in his hands even though it couldn't be holding more than a page or two.

Something was so important she'd written him a note instead of leaving a book. Was it her saying goodbye first? He wasn't sure why that was his immediate fear. So she was a tourist passing through. What did he care?

He cared because she was his only real connection here. The only person who got to see the real him and not the Logan he had to put on display to get the job done. His mind wandered back to Lucy. Sure, he'd opened up to her a little on the bench earlier, but that was just to show her they weren't so different. It was to get her on his side. Wasn't it?

The pained look on her face when she'd realized her date was a no-show made Logan want to track down the guy so he could punch him in the face for hurting her and pull her close to protect her from ever being hurt again. He and Lucy might not see eye to eye on the waterfront development, but who in their right mind would ever stand her up? She was beautiful and smart and witty. She was the complete package. If he lived in a place like Heron Isle, she was the kind of girl he'd want to marry.

But he wasn't staying here. And she'd never be interested in him. Not that way. Heck, he could barely get her to tolerate his efforts at friendship.

Looking down at the envelope again, he flipped it over and slid a finger under the tape to release its hold. Inside was a single piece of light-blue paper from a legal pad with Island Girl's handwriting on it.

Meet me on the benches by the marina on Thursday at 5:00 p.m.? I'll be the one holding your copy of The 5 Second Rule.

He barely registered the rest of the note, focusing on those two lines. The banging in his chest was back, and this time it felt as if it was reverberating through his entire body. Wasn't today Thursday?

He glanced at his watch. 6:07. He'd run into Lucy on a bench by the marina at what must have been shortly after five. She'd shoved a book in her bag, but she owned a bookstore: she probably took a book with her everywhere. Had there been anyone on the other benches? He'd been so focused on Lucy he hadn't noticed.

He tried to recall what Lucy had said earlier, attempting to push away the thoughts of what it would mean if she was Island Girl, but it was as if he was sweeping sand off the floor of his cottage, attempting to force it out the door even as more was blown in.

What had Lucy said about who she was meeting? He'd asked her if it was a blind date, and she'd said, "Sort of" or "Something like that." He couldn't even remember. The thoughts were racing to the beat of his heart as if each was trying to outrun the other.

Had his sister been right? Was Lucy Island Girl?

She'd mentioned a career breakthrough. Was she talking about him helping her buy the building? No. That was something he, Logan, was doing, not something he'd have any way of knowing or helping with as Gatsby's Ghost. But maybe the book he'd left as Gatsby's Ghost helped her make the decision about the building.

His brain felt as if it might explode with the what-ifs and his unsuccessful attempts to remember everything Island Girl had said in her notes and annotations.

He had to get to the bottom of this. Had to know if she was Lucy.

He ran back to his cottage on the beach as if he was sprinting in an Olympic trial. Once there, he pulled every book she'd given him from his shelf and reread the notes and then the annotations. And when he read them, it was Lucy's voice he heard.

Nineteen

Lucy

Lucy had checked the Little Free Library quickly before she'd gone down to the beach, and she hadn't seen the letter, so she assumed he'd taken it. She'd gone straight to the Little Free Library from the beach, and checked it again, but there was nothing there from Gatsby's Ghost.

Maybe he had seen it but something terrible had happened. Maybe he'd been in an accident?

Sighing as she let herself into the bookstore the following morning, Lucy locked the door behind her and plopped her purse on the worn wooden counter that had been handmade by Annie's grandfather. She leaned down to pet Alice, who was circling around her ankles. When she started leading Lucy to the back of the store by walking a few feet and then turning around to meow, Lucy knew she was ready for breakfast.

She was feeding the cats in the back of the store when she

heard someone knocking on the front door. It was still nearly an hour until she opened, so she figured it was someone she knew. Her breath caught for a moment as Logan popped into her mind, his green eyes sparkling. Maybe he'd come to check on her this morning. Just as quickly as hope had surfaced, it faded. It would be a pity visit because she'd been stood up, and she didn't want his pity.

She was relieved when she rounded the corner and spotted Taylor with her hands up against the glass door, peeking inside.

"Morning!" Taylor gave her a quick hug as she came in, then headed for one of the blue armchairs by the front window. "Sorry I didn't answer your call last night. Jack and I went to the movies."

"What'd you see?"

"Some stupid sea monster movie. It was terrible." She rolled her eyes. "Tell me about last night! Was he handsome? Are you in love?" She leaned forward, grinning as she waited for details.

Taylor was the only person Lucy had dared tell about her attempt to meet Gatsby's Ghost.

"Quite the opposite." Lucy fell into the other armchair. "He never showed up."

Taylor's mouth fell open. "What? Did he leave a note? Did something happen?"

Lucy shook her head. "Nope, no note. I checked again this morning. I waited for half an hour, and there was no sign of him. I guess he could have seen me and changed his mind and left." Lucy shrugged.

"You mean because he was so intimidated to find out his pen pal is a hottie?" Taylor wiggled her eyebrows at Lucy.

Lucy frowned. "No. You know that's not what I meant."

"Stop it. You're beautiful. I can't believe he just left you sitting there all alone."

"Well"—Lucy paused—"I wasn't exactly alone. Logan walked by while I was sitting there."

Taylor groaned. "I still can't believe what he did to poor Mildred and Marty." Taylor had missed the community forum because she was doing hair and makeup for a bride-to-be with an evening engagement photo shoot.

"He actually cleared that up. Turns out Mildred was the one keeping it from Marty. It wasn't really Logan's fault."

"I see." Taylor raised an eyebrow. "So now we're Team Logan again?"

Taylor still hadn't met Logan, so her opinions of him were informed entirely by what Lucy had told her, which included both his generosity in helping her buy the building, but also the way he seemed to be trying to manipulate everyone into doing things his way.

"No, we were never Team Logan." Lucy shook her head, trying to dislodge the voice reminding her how kind he'd been the night before and what he'd shared about his past. "We just need to get along until we come up with a viable plan for the waterfront, and then we can wave goodbye and let him go mess with some other town."

"Are you going to let him finish helping you with the building?"

"I don't know. I jumped to conclusions about the whole Waterway Café thing. I shouldn't pretend to know more about what Mildred and Marty need than they do. I'm just going to stay out of the way unless they ask me for help. So I'd probably need to apologize to Logan if I'm going to ask him to keep helping me. And, man, I hate that because I know how much he'll love it."

"I would say Jack could help you, but he's so busy with the renovation at the hotel I barely even get to see him. Our hiking trip was supposed to be a little quality time together in the midst of all the chaos, but we didn't even get that."

Lucy bit her lip. "Do you think he'll get a new assignment once the renovation is over?" It was something she'd been too scared to ask because she was afraid she wouldn't like the answer.

Taylor sighed, settling back farther into her chair. "Probably. His regional manager has been going on and on about what a great job he's done reimagining the place while staying true to its character. He already asked him to go to Nashville to look at one of their other properties and give his thoughts on what they might be able to do there."

"Would you go with him? If he asked?" Lucy stared at the floor, focusing on a swirling knot in the wood. What would she do if her closest friend and confidante left her here all alone? Sure, she had Pete and Pam and the others, but they were more like stand-in parents than the kind of best friend you share secrets with over wine and sappy Hallmark movies.

"I don't know. Maybe?" Taylor shrugged. "I already told him we'd have to at least be engaged. I'm not uprooting my life for a boyfriend."

Lucy could feel the hot tears stinging her eyes. Even her best friend was going to leave her. What would she do without Taylor on Heron Isle?

Taylor reached a hand toward her, opening and closing it to indicate she wanted to hold Lucy's hand.

"Hey, don't get upset. We're talking hypotheticals here. We haven't gone ring shopping or anything. And who knows when it would even happen. He's still in the middle of the renovation here. And even if I did move, we've got texting, emails, phone calls, even airplanes to take us back and forth to see each other. You'll always be my best friend, no matter my address."

Lucy half-heartedly squeezed Taylor's hand. She couldn't help feeling that, eventually, everyone left her. A part of her was glad now that Gatsby's Ghost hadn't shown up. One less person who could leave.

After children's story time, the bookstore quietened down for the morning. Lucy fished her notebook from her purse, opening it on the counter next to the computer so she could begin typing the synopsis of her new novel to send Leona. As she read through her outline, however, she felt something was missing. Sure, the two main characters were falling in love via the notes they were leaving in the Little Free Library, but there was no conflict. No real stakes.

She flipped to a blank page and let herself do a brain dump. *Maybe she finds out he came to town to open a competing bookstore?* No. She didn't want it to be just like *You've Got Mail*. *He could be a developer though.* They were always coming in to ruin small towns, a fact she knew all too well. She wrote down a few more ideas, crossing out each one as she tested it against her current storyline.

After staring at her messy brainstorm for a few minutes, she ripped the page from the notebook and crumpled it before tossing it in the waste basket. She couldn't send this to Leona. It wasn't good enough.

She looked around the store, and Debra Brannon's *Hydrangeas on Hill Street* caught her eye. She walked across the creaking floorboards and grabbed a copy of the book. When she returned to the counter, she propped it up next to her for motivation. Debra was right. Lucy had been standing in her own way.

Authors often mined their lives for ideas, so she thought about the people she'd dated over the years and why they hadn't worked out. There'd been a smattering of dates here and there with a few boys in high school, but nothing memorable. In college, she'd dated two different guys for about a year each, and although she'd said "I love you" to both of them, the relationships hadn't been exceptional or unique, and she wasn't sure she'd really known what love was. They'd been "safe," as Taylor had called them.

There'd been dates in Ocala when she worked in the library there, but no one who stuck around for more than a few dinners. Then she moved back to Heron Isle and met Carter. She'd thought he was the great love story of her life. He'd made her feel beautiful and interesting, but in the end he'd loved his career more than her.

There had been no one since then. The original idea for the story had come from her relationship—or whatever it was —she'd been forming with Gatsby's Ghost. Except she didn't want her book to end with the heroine getting stood up.

She was still brainstorming when she heard the front door open and looked up to see Logan entering. His now familiar scent wafted in with him and when he smiled she couldn't help but smile back. Although her smile was more from embarrassment as she remembered the night before. Hopefully he wasn't there to check on her, as if she were some wounded animal in need of tending.

He nodded. "Afternoon."

"Afternoon to you too." She put her pen down on the counter.

"Working on your business plan?" He pointed to the notebook.

Flustered, she closed it. "Oh, no. Just a little personal project."

He raised an eyebrow but didn't pry. "I was just on my way down to the coffee shop and thought I'd stop in. I know we've had our differences lately, but I'd still like to help you, if you'll let me."

She shifted from one foot to the other, avoiding his eyes.

After taking a deep breath, she said the words she'd been dreading but knew she had to say to him. "I'm sorry about the whole Marty and Mildred thing and for misjudging your intentions. That wasn't fair of me."

Lucy expected him to gloat, but he shrugged. "I understand. Water under the bridge. Now, let's get down to business. I found some good charts on my phone earlier for creating a maintenance timeline for a building like this. May I?" He pointed at the computer on the desk.

"Sure. Go for it. You said you were headed to the coffee shop. Want some? I don't have anything fancy. Just plain old coffee."

"Caffeine is caffeine. I'll take it."

He moved to the end of the counter and waited for her to step out. Their arms brushed as he stepped to go behind the counter a beat too soon, and she felt the same electric shock she'd felt when they'd first touched travel through her body. The tingling stayed in her chest all the way into the back room. It really had been too long since she'd been on a date if Logan was making her insides stir.

His professional ambitions aside, though, there was no denying he was heartbreakingly handsome. If a woman was into chiseled jawlines and dazzling green eyes, of course. Taking deep breaths, she busied herself with getting the coffee started, then poured the cats more water and reorganized a shelf while the coffee maker did its work—anything to keep her hormones from overtaking her brain. Logan Lancaster was off limits.

As she walked back to the front counter with two steaming mugs, Logan turned to look at her with a slight smile playing on his lips, his eyes squinting ever so slightly as if he was trying to figure something out.

"What? You're amazed I have the technology to make a cup of coffee?"

Logan pointed at the screen. "Are you writing a book?"

She was so surprised she nearly dropped the coffees as she tripped on the toe of her shoe. She'd completely forgotten she'd left her email to Leona on the screen. First, he'd been witness to her being stood up. Now he was going to discover her previous failures as an author. She tried to recover as she set both mugs on the counter.

"No, it's nothing. I thought you were finding me a business plan or something."

"I was, but this was up on the screen. Just natural curiosity. Are you working on your first book or have you been writing—what is it my sister calls them—bodice-rippers under a pen name no one knows about?" He was grinning ear-to-ear like a Cheshire cat.

"This would be my first." It was the truth. It could be her first to actually be published. No need to tell him she'd already written two that had tanked.

She reached across him to grab the mouse so she could close the email. He made no effort to move, and as her arm bumped up against him she could feel his strong chest, immediately starting to picture him with his shirt off.

After successfully closing the email, she stepped away to create some distance so he wouldn't hear her heart pounding.

"I didn't know you were a writer," he said.

"I'm not. Really, it's nothing."

"What's it about?"

"I'm still working on it." Her voice was quiet now. "I'm supposed to be sending my agent a synopsis, but it's not ready yet."

"You have a literary agent?" Logan's voice rose an octave, excitement permeating his features. "Lucy, that's incredible. I've heard getting an agent is difficult. You must be a good writer then."

For the first time in a long time when it came to her writing, she felt a sense of pride welling in her chest. Maybe it wouldn't be so bad to tell him.

"I had a book deal once. Almost got published." It was the first time she'd told anyone other than the author in the store recently about her agent or her publishing deal in nearly two years. Carter had known, but he'd never encouraged her writing. If she was being honest, he'd always been a little more interested in where his career might take them than where hers might.

"What do you mean you 'almost got published'? If you don't mind me asking."

Just a few days ago, Lucy would have immediately put up walls if someone had asked her that question, Logan being top of the list. But just like with Debra, the story started to spill out. She told him how excited she'd been when she landed her deal, how her friends at the library had taken her out to celebrate, how they'd picked out exactly where on the shelf her book would live, and then about the pitying looks and whispers when her publisher had gone bankrupt and her deal had died. She even told him about the second book and how Leona had shopped it around to no avail.

"I'm sorry, Lucy. That must have been really hard. I think it's incredibly brave that you're writing again."

"Brave? Or stupid? Most days I think it's the latter. I haven't written anything in a long time. It wasn't until this author"—she picked up the book she'd left propped on the counter—"came in the store last week that I started writing again." She told Logan about her conversation with Debra and how Debra had told her she was her own worst enemy.

"This Debra woman sounds like a smart lady. I think there are a lot of things you could do if you just believed in yourself as much as the rest of us do. Like buy this building." He swept an arm around the room.

Lucy's heart fluttered like the wings of the hummingbirds

that stopped by the feeders off her back deck. Did Logan just say he believed in her? He barely knew her, and yet he was going out of his way to help her buy this building, even after the terrible things she'd said to him.

A little voice in her head asked if maybe Debra and Logan only believed in her because they didn't really know her, didn't know how often she'd failed or how many people had left her behind. Then she did something she'd never done before when that little voice appeared in her head. She pictured it as one of the tiny crabs that ran across the shoreline, and then she pictured a seagull swooping down to eat it in a single, swift bite.

"You know what," Lucy said, feeling her chest visibly puff out with newfound pride. "Let's do it. Let's whip up a plan so I can buy this building."

"That's the spirit," Logan said, raising a fist in the air to signal his victory over her protests. "Grab a piece of paper, and I'll walk you through this timeline and what I have in mind for your reserve goals."

Lucy opened the drawer to her right and pulled out a blue legal pad. When she turned back toward Logan and the computer monitor, his face had gone white, his brow creased.

"Are you okay? You look like you just saw a ghost."

He cleared his throat, replacing the surprised look on his face with a tight smile. "I've just never seen a blue legal pad before."

She shrugged. "The yellow ones always remind me of lawyers." She crinkled her nose, thinking of the estate attorney she'd had to deal with after both Annie's and her father's passing.

"Hey, do you mind if I come back on Monday to help you with this?" He looked at his watch. "I forgot my sister and her kids will be here this afternoon, and I have to go grab them from the airport." He was already moving past her and around the counter toward the door.

"So you did invite them? That's great. Let me know if you need any suggestions on things to do while they're here."

"Yep, will do," he said, already halfway out the door. "Have a good weekend, Lucy."

She smiled, shaking her head as he hustled out. Maybe she'd had an impact on Logan Lancaster. Mr. Nothing But Business was going to try being a family man this weekend. Maybe Heron Isle could work its magic on him after all.

TWENTY

Logan

Lucy is Island Girl.

Island Girl is Lucy.

She'd confirmed it when she pulled out the blue legal pad the previous day. A flurry of thoughts had clouded his head like an early morning fog that refused to let up. He'd needed to get out of there, so he used Carly's arrival as an excuse.

Truth was, he'd still had hours before he needed to be at the airport. He'd gone back home and gone through the notes and annotations in the books again. Reading them this time knowing for certain they were from Lucy.

Island Girl had been a bit of a mystery, her incongruent thoughts about herself and life intriguing. He saw it all differently now he knew she was Lucy. Because Lucy was a dichotomy, at once optimistic and hopeful about the world, but also jaded because her life had been the opposite of a fairy tale.

There was obviously so much he hadn't known about Lucy, probably still didn't know. Would never know. Because the notes would stop when Lucy found out he was Gatsby's Ghost.

He'd thought about Lucy—and about Island Girl—all the way to the airport the night before, but as soon as he saw his sister with her kids in tow in the airport lobby and they ran to hug him, all his stress from work and the revelation about Lucy slipped away. When he realized how much taller the kids were than the last time he'd seen them, he was thankful Lucy had suggested they visit. Aidan had grown a foot, his face leaner and more angular than the chubby kid he'd once been, and Alex's transformation from toddler to little girl had her looking so much like her mother he was immediately transported to his childhood.

"This is the life." Carly let out a big sigh as she plopped down in the chair in the sand next to Logan on the beach. "Where could you possibly go in the future that's better than this?"

"Boston." He recognized the lack of enthusiasm in his reply. "I already submitted my resume."

"You're not even done here yet and you already know your next move? No wonder you always beat me at chess growing up."

He shrugged. "That was the whole point in coming here. I needed a quick win so I could apply for the Boston job. It'd be kind of nice to live somewhere I already have a friend." Gulls called overhead, floating above a family nearby where a toddler was throwing food in the sand and then giggling as brave birds took turns swooping down to grab it.

"Uncle Logan, watch this," Aidan yelled from the edge of

the water as he ran toward the waves with the boogie board Logan had found in the rental house.

"You always made friends so easily as a kid. Heck, you were voted Best All Around in the high-school yearbook." She shook her head. "Which is why I find this life you chose to lead so bizarre. You're never anywhere long enough to make friends or really get to know anyone outside of your work."

"Making friends *is* my work. That's why I'm so good at what I do." He pumped his fist in the air at his nephew as he successfully rode a wave in to shore. "Attaboy, Aidan!"

Carly frowned at him. "You know that's not what I mean. Just look at what's happened here. The only real friend you've made is through the Little Free Library, and you've already screwed that up because the woman had already met you in 'real life'"—she held up her hands to put air quotes around the words—"and thought you were manipulating her to ram your project through so you could get out of here."

He'd told her about his discovery the previous evening. Carly had been delighted to learn Lucy was Island Girl as they'd sat talking on the porch swing on the back deck after putting the kids to bed.

"That's not exactly true. Lucy doesn't think I'm manipulating her anymore. We're getting along just fine, in fact."

"Except she doesn't know you're her book buddy."

He sighed. "No."

Logan had no idea what to do next when it came to the Little Free Library. He knew he had to tell Lucy. If she found out he'd been keeping it from her, she'd never trust him again, and he also couldn't bear her thinking Gatsby's Ghost had stood her up. She didn't deserve that. It should have been easy to convince himself he only wanted her trust because of the waterfront development, but he knew it was more than that now. He wanted Lucy to trust Logan the way Island Girl trusted Gatsby's Ghost.

He turned to Carly. "Maybe I should just write her one final note. I can tell her Gatsby's Ghost is leaving town and enjoyed reading together while it lasted. Leave it at that. Maybe she never needs to know it was me. I think she'd be mortified to find out anyway."

Carly looked thoughtful as she cocked her head to the side and stared off into the distance. Then she leaned forward, smiling. "I think we should watch *You've Got Mail* tonight. You know, for inspiration."

"This is my real life, Carly. Not some movie. And have you ever really paid attention to that story? It's not a fairy tale. He put her out of business."

"The way I see it, if he could still win her heart despite ruining her family's legacy, then surely you can win over little Miss Bookstore here." She raised an eyebrow in his direction.

"Quit trying to make this a love story. I have a working relationship with Lucy. That's all it is. That's all it's going to be. With any luck, I'll be in Boston before the end of summer."

He remembered what Lucy had shared with him about Carter leaving her behind for an opportunity in Chicago and the mayor telling him about her mom abandoning her as well. There was no sense in letting her get any more attached to Gatsby's Ghost, because Gatsby's Ghost would eventually have to leave her for Boston or wherever he got his next job.

"Ugh," Carly grunted, leaning back in her chair. "I just want you to find your person."

"What kind of person is going to follow me around while I jump from city to city living in rental units? It's not like I have a home base, much less a home."

"Home isn't a place, Logan. It's a person. And sometimes it becomes several people." She smiled as she watched her kids splashing each other in the surf.

Lucy's brown eyes and sweet smile flashed through his

mind. Lucy had a home, and it was here. And after the story about how the town had come together for her after her dad passed, he couldn't blame her. Their lives were simply incompatible. She was a person who craved stability and, based on what he knew about what she'd been through, she deserved to have it.

The real problem was that he had begun wondering what it would feel like to be the man who could secure it for her.

When Carly suggested they all go to the bookstore after lunch, Logan didn't even attempt to argue with her, knowing it was futile. She insisted she needed to meet Lucy *and* that she needed a new book to read on the plane ride home anyway.

"Uncle Logan, can I have a book too?" Alex asked from the back seat.

"Of course, you can," he said, smiling at her in the rearview mirror. "You can have all the books you want."

"Yes!" she said, doing a little victory dance.

Carly rolled her eyes. "She acts like I've never bought her a book before."

It was a busy afternoon downtown, so they parked a few blocks away near Hill House.

"Isn't it a beauty?" Logan asked, stopping on the sidewalk in front of it.

"It looks like it's haunted," Alex whispered, as if the ghosts she imagined inside might hear her.

"It certainly looks like it's seen better days," Carly quipped.

"It has character," Logan said, before launching into a list of the repairs it needed and how it was all just cosmetic.

"Didn't you and Fuller talk about restoring historic

houses once you got your careers established?" Carly shot him a sideways look.

"There are plenty of historic houses in Boston," Logan countered, shuffling the group toward Lucy's store. Although Boston wasn't a permanent job, maybe he'd at least be there long enough that he and Fuller could buy something and get it started. After all, Fuller would be there long-term to see it through.

When they entered the bookstore, Lucy turned from the customer she was helping and surprise filled her expression. Tilting her head, she smiled at him then finished speaking with the older woman scanning the new releases.

"Uncle Logan, look at this ladder. It's just like *Beauty and the Beast*!" Alex exclaimed as she ran over to it.

"Alex, honey. It says don't climb it. You can look, but don't touch." Carly followed Alex over to the where the ladder stood at the end of the bookshelves closest to the front window.

Lucy left the woman to read the back of several books she'd pulled off the shelf for her and walked over.

"Uncle Logan, huh? Is that your sister?" She nodded in Carly's direction.

"It is." He smiled at her. "Hey, Carly. I want you to meet someone."

Carly approached and held out a hand. "Hi, Carly Simmons. It's so nice to meet you. I've heard so much about you."

As Lucy shook her hand, she glanced at Logan. "Oh, is that so? Only good things I hope." Her laughter was stiff, a little nervous.

"I did leave out the part about how you still have an answering machine." He winked at Lucy. "This is my nephew, Aidan." Logan put his hand on Aidan's shoulder and then pointed in Alex's direction, where she was bent over petting Lizzy. "And that's my niece, Alexandria, who goes by Alex."

"It's so nice to meet you all." Lucy smiled broadly. "I'm glad you decided to visit Heron Isle."

"I hear that's thanks to you." Carly nudged Logan in the arm. "I don't remember the last time my brother invited us to come visit him somewhere. My guilt trips never work on him. You'll have to tell me your secret."

Lucy blushed, looking at the ground. Her long lashes fluttered as she looked back up at Carly and then him.

Aidan, who'd been fidgeting next to Logan, broke into the silence. "Do you have the new Werewolves of Wichita book?"

"I sure do. Second shelf on the right over there." Lucy pointed to the other side of the store. When she saw Logan's confused expression, she said, "Really popular graphic novel series."

"Come on, Uncle Logan. I'll show you." Aidan motioned for him to follow.

Logan didn't love the idea of leaving his sister alone with Lucy—no telling what she might say—but it felt nice that his nephew wanted to hang out with him. He really should make a point to see Carly and the kids more often. His parents too.

By the time he and Aidan emerged from the graphic novel section, Carly and Lucy were like old friends. They were sitting in the big blue chairs at the front of the store, talking as if they'd known each other forever, with Alex sitting a few feet away petting one of the cats. He hung back for a minute before they spotted him and watched how animated Lucy was as she talked about the books she'd pulled out for Carly to read. She smiled while she spoke, looking off into the distance as she described the big family in one of the books and how nice it must be to have so many brothers and sisters.

Carly caught him watching Lucy and raised an eyebrow in

his direction. It was clear she thought Lucy was his perfect match. He could see it in her knowing stare.

She turned back to Lucy and joked, "Yeah, well having a sibling isn't all it's cracked up to be." Carly jerked her head in his direction.

"Yeah, I can imagine with one like that." Lucy laughed, but warmth filled her eyes, the warmth he'd been so attracted to that first afternoon on the sidewalk talking about archaic dental practices.

He put a hand over his heart. "Hey, why is everyone ganging up on me?"

"Easy target." Carly smiled. "Lucy, have dinner with us. I insist."

"No." Lucy shook her head. "You need time to catch up as a family. Besides, Logan has had to deal with me enough lately. He probably needs a break."

When he said nothing, Carly glared at him, her eyes widening as she tried to telepath that she expected him to jump in and back up her invitation.

"From you? Never." He locked eyes with Lucy. He didn't smile or laugh. He didn't try to play it off like a joke. He wanted her to know he meant it.

Because against all odds, and even against his better judgment, he wanted to spend more time with Lucy Sullivan.

Twenty-One

Lucy

"You made her night." Carly wrapped an arm around her daughter's shoulders as the five of them walked down the sidewalk to dinner.

After Lucy had locked up the store, she'd let Alex climb the ladder and told her to hold on as she slid her down the wall of books, just like Annie had done with her so many years ago. It made her picture having a daughter of her own someday, something she hadn't dared to let herself dream of since Carter left. What were the odds she was going to meet a man her age in Heron Isle who actually planned to stick around long enough to get married and build a life here?

"Don't tell anyone," Lucy said, placing a finger over her mouth. "I only let special little girls on the ladder."

Alex put her hand to her mouth and made a movement as if she was turning a key, and Lucy laughed. Carly's kids were terrific, and she and Carly had made an immediate connection in a way she'd never experienced with another woman. She felt as if she'd known her forever.

When they reached the end of Main Street, they turned the corner to the right along Front Street and went into the Marina Restaurant. Lucy asked if they could be seated at a table on the second-floor balcony so they could look out over the water while they ate. It was a popular place for tourists, but Lucy usually got her food to go and ate it in the bookstore for lunch. It was nice to have a group of people to sit down and eat with.

"I could get used to this view." Carly slid her sunglasses on top of her long brunette hair as she looked toward the water.

A half dozen sailboats bobbed on the water to the right of the Waterway Café, taking advantage of the calmer water on the southwestern side of the island. Farther south, they could see the outline of Amelia Island—Pete's hometown—with its fort that was still intact. Islands dotted the coastline in both directions from Heron Isle, part of the more than one hundred that made up the Sea Island chain running from South Carolina to North Florida.

"I have to admit, I take it for granted sometimes. I can't remember the last time I sat up here." Lucy turned to follow Carly's gaze, allowing herself to take it all in.

"And you want to build a bunch of crap out there?" Carly frowned as she nudged her brother and nodded toward the waterfront.

"No, he just wants to park giant cruise ships and casino boats out there so we can become the Bahamas," Lucy teased.

Carly's mouth fell open as she gave her brother a look that said she thought he was crazy.

"There you two go, ganging up on me again." He turned to his sister. "When's your flight back?" He looked at his watch.

"Not for thirty-six more hours, so strap in, baby brother."

Carly laughed before leaning over to help Alex decide what she wanted for dinner.

They ordered, each of them getting some version of shrimp, then they settled into easy conversation about everything from the history of the island to how Lucy came to own the bookstore. Carly asked her smart questions about how she chose the books to carry and didn't once make her feel like an alien just because she didn't have an online store or a Facebook page. She even admitted that she was taking a self-imposed social media break while trying to raise kids who weren't glued to their phones.

"These will keep us busy for a while." Carly lifted her bag of books from Lucy's store, two for herself and one for each of the kids.

"Did Lucy tell you she's writing a book?" Logan smiled in her direction.

If Lucy hadn't known better, she would have thought there was a hint of pride in Logan's voice.

She could feel herself blushing under his gaze, so she turned to Carly. "It's no big deal. I'm just playing around with an idea."

"Ooh, tell me about it." Carly leaned over to take a sip of her Miami Vice, a swirling pink-and-white mixture of piña colada and strawberry daiquiri with a towering crown of whipped cream complete with a cherry on top.

Lucy bit her lip, afraid Carly would ask her where she got the idea. She was a terrible liar, and she didn't want to tell Carly the story about the Little Free Library. But if she was going to send the idea to Leona, she might as well get used to talking about it.

"Well... Have you ever seen one of those Little Free Libraries that are popping up? People leave their used books and take one if they see something they like."

"Oh, yeah, we just got our first one recently. Such a fun idea."

"We got our first one not too long ago too. And I thought"—she swallowed hard, reminding herself of her no-hesitation vow—"what if two people started corresponding through the Little Free Library? You know, instead of meeting online or on social media or whatever, what if they somehow met through the Little Free Library?"

"Cute! I like it," Carly gushed, her eyes shining as she smiled at Lucy, then at Logan, and back at Lucy again. "So they write notes inside the books or something like that?"

"Yeah. We do something like that here. There are index cards and pencils in the library, and people are encouraged to leave a note telling the next person why they might like the book. We all use monikers, and it's become a bit of a game in town to try to figure out who's leaving what. Last winter we were all convinced Bob, who owns the hardware store—total guy's guy—was leaving all these romance novels in the library."

"I have to admit, sometimes living in a small town wears on me," Carly said. "But it's stuff like this that reminds me how special it is to be part of a tight-knit community. This place is a lot like where we grew up, just with an ocean instead of pastures. Right, Logan?"

"I definitely prefer the ocean version." His smile was tight, and a look passed between sister and brother that Lucy couldn't quite decipher.

"Do your parents still run the farm?" Lucy asked Carly.

Another look—a darker one—passed between Carly and Logan, and Lucy worried she'd stumbled onto a sore subject.

Carly recovered first and gave Lucy a weak smile. "No, they're retired now. Lucky for me, they live nearby and like to babysit." She patted her daughter's head. Alex was deep into reading her book about a young ballerina.

Lucy sensed she shouldn't ask more about the farm, so she changed the subject just as their food arrived, asking Carly about her husband, Nick, and how they met in high school. Lucy couldn't help but be a little jealous that Carly had found love in her small town. Unfortunately, Lucy hadn't dated much in high school, so there was no sweetheart to reunite with at a reunion. She'd just have to keep hoping she'd meet someone who came to town and fell in love with both her and Heron Isle. Was that really so much to ask?

Twenty-Two

Logan

"She is *perfect* for you." Carly sat on the porch swing and patted the seat next to her as Logan stepped out and closed the back door behind him. When he didn't immediately respond, she grabbed his shoulders and shook them. "The woman is literally writing a book about you!"

The kids had been wiped out from their day in the sun and both had fallen asleep reading their new books. Carly had wanted to go outside so they could talk without waking the kids and listen to the sound of the waves.

Logan pinched the top of his nose. "What have I told you? I cannot get involved with Lucy Sullivan." He took a drink from his water bottle. "Besides, she'd never see me like that. She thinks I'm a heartless bureaucrat here to destroy her town. Trust me, she does *not* want me to be Gatsby's Ghost."

"Nope." His sister's tone was matter-of-fact. "I saw the way she looked at you. That is not a woman who hates you."

"Well, I don't think she *hates* me anymore, but I'm definitely not her type."

"And what do you think her type is?"

"The stable kind who stays in one place. Someone who loves this island as much as she does and who wants to raise a family here."

"And you could never be that guy?" Carly raised an eyebrow, the lights from the house combining with the light of the full moon to bathe the back deck in a pale glow. "I saw the way you looked at that house today. Almost the same way you looked at her."

Logan sighed. "You know how I feel about being stagnant. I don't want to become the kind of person who gets set in my ways and resists change."

Carly raised an eyebrow. "Aren't you already that guy? You're stuck in a never-ending cycle of your own, and you're refusing to believe change for you could be good."

He'd never thought about it like that before. Just because he moved a lot didn't mean he wasn't set in his ways.

What would it be like to live somewhere like Heron Isle, restore an old house, settle down and start a family? Growing up, he'd sworn he'd never live in a small town again, but thirty-six-year-old Logan knew a lot that eighteen-year-old Logan had not. He'd thought the endless excitement of seeing new places, eating different things, and taking on new challenges would be all he'd ever need. But being here on Heron Isle had highlighted the importance of having people in his life he could count on and who really knew him. It was something he hadn't realized was missing until he came here.

He let himself lean into the swing as he used his feet to begin rocking it back and forth. He'd always planned to advise the town to hire someone to manage the city-owned real estate and businesses on the waterfront. The last manager had retired and never been replaced because they'd been waiting to see what sort of person they'd need to manage whatever project got through the town council. Logan was overqualified for the job, and they certainly couldn't afford to pay him what he could make in Boston. He'd made smart investments, though, and he'd learned money was pretty useless if he didn't have time or people to spend it on.

"You have to write her back." Carly broke the silence. "Whether you decide to tell her it's you or not, you can't just leave her hanging like that. She's too sweet. She doesn't deserve it."

She was right. Lucy had experienced enough pain in her life. He couldn't be the source of more, at least not when it came to their pen-pal relationship. It was bad enough they might not ultimately agree on what happened with the waterfront.

"Yeah, I know." He grabbed his water bottle. "I think I'm going to need something stronger."

Logan went inside and poured a scotch for himself and a glass of wine for Carly, carried them outside, then went back in to grab a pad and pen. He sat at the small glass-top table on the deck and took a sip of his drink, the amber liquid burning its way down his throat.

"Okay, so what do I say?"

Carly got up from the swing and walked over to sit across from him. Folding a leg underneath her, she leaned her forearms on the table.

"Tell her you got unexpectedly called out of town and feel terrible you left her sitting there alone. And you need an excuse for why you're not immediately setting up another time to meet. Tell her your schedule is up in the air at the moment, but that you got a new book for her while you were out of town and can't wait to hear what she thinks."

Furrowing his brows, he met his sister's eyes. "And what is this exciting new book?"

Her lips pursed as she thought, and then she bolted upright in her chair. "I know just the one! We read it in my book club earlier this year. She hates change, right? Definitely not one to take a risk? Time to change that."

She took her phone from her back pocket and punched some things in before handing it to him. "Here, put in your address. It'll be here Monday." When he gave her a skeptical look, she said, "I know, I know. We should be supporting indie bookstores and not online megastores, but just this once, the fast shipping wins out."

It wasn't where they were buying the book that had him questioning her, but the whole plan. Carly wanted him to commit to continuing the letters with Lucy. Was that really the right thing to do, or should he just tell her he had to leave town and end it now before it got any more complicated?

He picked up his scotch with his free hand and swirled it, the two ice cubes inside clinking against the glass.

"What? Why aren't you writing?"

"I just don't know if I should keep this up. Maybe I should just tell her it's time for me to leave town and that I enjoyed it while it lasted."

Carly gave him the look she always gave when she was getting ready to dole out sisterly advice. As if she could see everything clearly and didn't understand why he didn't, but she was going to walk him through step-by-step.

"Tell me this. What do you miss the most about St. Louis?"

His forehead wrinkled as he frowned. "St. Louis? Why?"

"Just answer the question." She rolled her hand in the air, indicating he should get on with it.

He shrugged one shoulder. "The baseball games, I guess. My apartment was right down the street, and the city always had extra tickets."

"And Phoenix?"

"The golf. I hear they've got some good courses here, too, but you'd have to play at dawn to keep from dying of heat stroke this time of year."

"What about San Diego? Can you think of anything good there?"

Despite the black mark it had left on his resume, he'd still liked the city. "Sure, the weather was always perfect, and nowhere does fish tacos like San Diego."

His sister leaned forward, her eyes locked on his. "And what about Heron Isle? What will you miss the most when you leave here?" She raised an eyebrow.

He didn't have to answer. She'd asked because she already knew. Lucy.

"All the cities over all the years, and how often do you ever think of a single person you met anywhere?" She paused, and when he didn't answer after a few seconds, she said, "There's your answer." Carly relaxed back into her chair and sipped her wine with the expression of a prosecutor who'd just delivered the smoking gun in front of the jury.

Like a man on death row with nothing to lose, Logan lifted the pen and began to write the letter to Island Girl.

TWENTY-THREE

Lucy

Lucy hated herself for returning to the Little Free Library every day, for holding her breath as she opened the door and searched the spines, hoping to see something new Gatsby's Ghost might have left.

It had been nearly a week since he stood her up, and a smarter woman probably would have taken the hint. Still, she couldn't help hoping the fun summer they'd been having leaving books and notes wasn't over.

Having once read a book on manifesting, she channeled what she remembered and pictured a white envelope addressed to her sitting right on the ledge. She held her breath as she swung the door open, only to exhale loudly when she walked in and saw there was no envelope. So much for manifesting.

Shoulders slumped, she began to go through the stack of

new books. She picked up each one and read through the notes, smiling at the one in the thriller that said to sleep with the lights on after reading.

The last book she picked up was *Harley and Me: Embracing Risk On the Road to a More Authentic Life*. The picture of a motorcycle on the front combined with the female author name had her intrigued. When she flipped it open, she was surprised to find a folded-up piece of paper with *Island Girl* written on it.

Her heart began pounding. He was back. She nearly dropped the book as she fumbled to open the letter.

Island Girl,

I'm sorry. Unfortunately, my work unexpectedly took me away, and I wasn't able to meet you. For that, I cannot apologize enough.

I know you took a risk. A risk you weren't rewarded for taking. Thousands of years of evolution have taught us when to trust and when to stay holed up safe in our caves, and I betrayed the trust you probably had in me. Don't let my absence prevent you from future risks, however.

It's the moments—and the people—we least expect who have the power to change our lives the most.

I hope to hear from you again.

Gatsby's Ghost

Lucy read the letter twice before sitting on the bench.

He hadn't intentionally stood her up. Even better, he hadn't taken one look at her and left. Life had simply gotten in the way.

She smiled as she leaned back and read the book's blurb. It wasn't one she was familiar with, but it certainly sounded interesting. It was about a professor and mom who, in her late forties, bought a motorcycle and learned why women don't take more risks, but should.

She remembered interviewing for the library job years ago and being asked how her friends would describe her. "Risk averse" hadn't been one of her three words—she'd chosen *loyal, friendly,* and *reliable*—but it certainly could have been. The biggest risk she'd taken in her life was probably keeping the bookstore, and someone else had chosen that path for her.

Flipping the book over in her hands, she marveled at how Gatsby's Ghost chose the perfect book for her every time. He seemed to know her better than any of her friends, except for Taylor. Lucy had always thought what a person read said a lot about them, but it was crazy just how much she'd learned about Gatsby's Ghost simply from trading books and writing a few short notes.

Who was he? Would she ever know? He didn't ask to reschedule a meeting. Maybe he didn't think she'd trust him enough to try again, and he was probably right. Or maybe he was simply meant to teach her something, to help her grow. She did believe people came into her life for a reason.

Okay, maybe she'd read one too many books, and her imagination was getting away from her. Regardless, she was content to continue trading books with Gatsby's Ghost and nothing more. It was safer this way.

A stranger leaving anonymous notes in books wasn't going to break her heart.

Lucy was getting ready to close up for the day when Jack surprised her by walking into the bookstore sans Taylor. He'd never come to shop in her store before, only tagged along with Taylor a few times.

"Jack, so nice to see you." Lucy put down the stack of books she'd been reshelving and walked to the front to greet him.

"Lucy, hey. You busy?" He looked around the store as if checking to see if they were alone.

"Not at all. I was just putting some things away. It's been a pretty quiet afternoon. I'm sure Taylor told you we have another community forum tonight. People are probably getting ready for that."

"Yeah, she mentioned it." He glanced around, shifting his weight from foot to foot and stuffing his hands in the pockets of his dress pants.

"So what can I help you with? I'm surprised to see you away from the resort. Taylor said the renovation has you working around the clock."

"It's been a real bear, but I think it's coming out nicely." He rocked back on his heels and drew in a breath. "I came by because I need your help. You know Taylor better than anyone else."

Were he and Taylor having some sort of trouble? She hadn't mentioned anything, but something felt off, and Lucy couldn't quite put her finger on it.

"Sure. What kind of help?"

"Well." He rubbed the back of his neck, not meeting

Lucy's eyes. "I want you to help me pick out an engagement ring. I want to propose to Taylor."

Lucy's mouth dropped open before she broke into a huge smile. Her best friend was getting married!

"That's wonderful." Lucy crossed the short distance between them and went up on her tiptoes to give Jack a hug. She really liked him, and she was so happy her best friend had found her person.

"So you'll help?" Jack was smiling at her now, his shoulders relaxing.

If he'd been this nervous to tell Lucy, how was he ever going to propose to Taylor?

Lucy laughed. "Yes, of course. I know exactly what she wants. We talked about it back when I got engaged—" Lucy's smile evaporated for a moment as she remembered the heart-wrenching moment she'd handed the ring back to Carter before he left for Chicago. "Anyway, yes. Of course. I'd be happy to help."

"Great. Do you have time to go shopping with me tomorrow? It's the only other day I can slip away this week. We're waiting on a big shipment of fixtures to come in, so things are a little slower."

"Wow. Once you decide to do it, you're really ready to do it, huh?" Lucy loved that he was so excited about proposing to Taylor.

"I'm sure Taylor told you I've gone up to Nashville a couple of times to consult on a renovation for the property up there. They've officially asked me to move in August, and I'm going to ask Taylor to go with me."

Lucy felt as if all the air was being sucked out of the room. That was why he was in such a hurry. She suddenly felt nauseated, and just like that the idea of her best friend getting engaged went from a joyous occasion to a bitter reminder that no one ever stayed. The person she leaned on most, who knew her best, was going to leave her behind too. Intellectually, she knew this wasn't about her, and that friends moved away from each other all the time and maintained close bonds, but she couldn't help feeling that, in the end, people always leave.

"You okay?" Jack took a step closer and held out a hand. "You look like you're about to faint."

She smoothed her hands down her skirt. "I'm fine. It's just a lot to take in. The engagement. Moving."

"I know you probably don't love the idea of her moving, but we won't be that far away. There's a direct flight out of JAX to Nashville. Only takes an hour." Jack smiled at her as if it was no big deal that instead of seeing her best friend every few days, she might only see her every few months, and that was probably best-case scenario. Taylor would get up there, her business would get busy, and their visits would get further and further apart. Long-distance relationships were never the same.

Lucy turned away so he wouldn't see the tears shining in her eyes, even though they were a mix of happy tears and sad tears.

"Yeah, of course. Tomorrow's good." She moved over to the counter and started stacking the research she'd printed about the impact of cruise ships on historic ports for the forum that night.

"Great! Maybe when you close up? I talked to Linda over at Rothchild's and she said she'd stay late if she needed to." Linda owned the jewelry store downtown just across the square.

Lucy nodded, but didn't speak. She just wanted him to leave so she could process the news in private.

"Okay." His voice was hesitant. "I'll meet you there at five?"

Keeping her back turned, she nodded. "Yep, sounds good."

She'd help him, of course. She knew Taylor wanted to marry Jack and that she'd already considered it might mean moving around with him. Lucy certainly wasn't going to try to stop her from finding her happy ending. She just wished everyone else's happy endings didn't have to come at her expense.

Twenty-Four

Logan

Logan made a beeline for the Little Free Library after he parked downtown. It was almost time to head over to city hall for the community forum, but he was anxious to see if Lucy had been by and found the book. He'd wanted to go all day, but had forced himself to sit at the dining-room table in his cottage and go over the plans from both the cruise line and the company that operated the casino boats. They'd both be in attendance tonight to give their formal presentations, and Lucy's environmental experts would be there to poke holes in the plans.

Although he'd managed to sit there all day, he wasn't sure he'd absorbed anything. His mind had drifted again and again to Lucy, to the Little Free Library, to the way she'd seamlessly fit in with his family at dinner, to how she had a habit of biting her lip and tucking her hair behind her ear when she was nervous. He couldn't get her out of his head.

The numbers for both the cruise ship and the casino boat looked good. They were solid revenue generators for the city, and the cruise line had the potential to benefit virtually all the businesses downtown. Admittedly, it was impossible to have their environmental impact be zero, but a small cruise line like the one he was proposing had minimal impact. The benefits outweighed the disadvantages by a wide margin.

Approaching the Little Free Library, Logan opened the door as he'd done so many times before and hoped to see his book gone from the ledge. His eyes scanned the books waiting to be shelved and then moved to the nonfiction shelf. It wasn't there. A small smile pulled at the corners of his mouth. He wished he'd been able to see her reaction. Had she been excited? Skeptical? He was pretty sure she wasn't angry, based on their conversations as Lucy and Logan and the fact that she'd worked the whole thing into her book proposal. Maybe he could find a way to bring up the subject later without her getting suspicious. He needed to know how she'd felt about the letter.

When he entered the council chambers, Lucy was already there along with a woman he assumed was her environmental expert. The woman was dressed in a black pencil skirt and a pale-pink cardigan set. She was testing a slide on the projection screen, but much to his disappointment, it gave nothing away.

"Evening, ladies." Logan had nearly walked all the way up to them before they noticed him.

"Oh, Logan. I didn't hear you come in. Maybe you can help us." Lucy turned to the woman. "He's much better with technology than I am."

"That's the understatement of the year," he said under his breath in a playful tone. He smiled at them both. "What seems to be the problem?"

"I can't get it to go into presentation mode." The other woman clicked the mouse a few more times to no avail.

"Here, let me." He waited for her to move aside and, with a few clicks, he had the presentation up and running.

Lucy smiled. "You do realize you just helped your opponent, right?" Her eyes sparkled. The frustration with him and his waterfront ideas was gone, replaced by a sense that she now saw him as a worthy opponent.

He smiled. "I like a fair fight." She was in a good mood. Maybe because of his letter in the Little Free Library? Forcing his eyes away from her, he turned to the other woman and offered his hand. "Logan Lancaster."

"Miranda Clark." She shook his hand firmly. "Southeastern Clean Water Foundation."

The sound of the back door opening attracted their attention. It was Mark Sandberg from the cruise line. Logan had met with him earlier in the day before he'd gone back to his hotel to change for the meeting. No sooner had he entered than one of the gentlemen from the casino boat, with whom Logan had only spoken on the phone, walked in behind him and introduced himself.

As the townspeople started filing in, they moved to sit in their usual groups. He nodded at those he recognized, like Pam, Pete, Missy, and Mildred, along with some of the men he'd met at the Freemasons' lodge. All the council members filed in and took seats in the front row, where they were joined by the mayor.

Logan and Lucy had already agreed to begin with a presentation by Logan on the ideas from the last meeting, which he'd now had time to vet and go over with the council and the mayor. They'd lay out which ones were still on the table and which had been deemed untenable. Then they'd have presentations from the cruise line and the casino boat before hearing the opposition from Ms. Monroe and opening the floor to members of the community to offer their support or opposition for any of the remaining ideas.

After detailing his plans to continue moving forward with research, vetting, and proposals on a number of ideas ranging from food kiosks to the rental of paddleboards and other watercraft, Logan prepared for the part he knew was going to be more controversial. He'd already discussed it with Lucy, and Mildred was there to speak as well.

"The one idea we feel everyone is behind is the establishment of an open-air seafood market. I'm pleased to say that we believe we've found a way to move forward with that part of the plan." He paused, clearing his throat before continuing.

"Mildred Banks, who I'm sure you all know as one of the owners of the Waterway Café, has asked to speak to the audience." He motioned to Mildred to join him.

Mildred walked tentatively toward the front of the room, not meeting anyone's eyes as she focused on the floor. Logan was nervous she and Marty had reconsidered, but she gave him a smile before she turned to the crowd.

"First, I want to say thank you to everyone here who has eaten at our restaurant over the past three decades. Your support and your friendship has meant so much to Marty and me. We've always been grateful to be a part of this community, and we intend to be so for a long time to come—" Her voice broke and she stopped. Reaching into a pocket of her dress as she smiled through her tears, she pulled out a tissue and blotted at her eyes.

Regaining her composure, she continued. "We intend to be part of this community for a long time to come, just not as restaurant owners." She paused again, but this time she smiled out at the audience.

"I know this probably comes as a shock to many of you, and I appreciate those of you who have vowed to fight to help us save the restaurant. I wanted to come here, however, and tell you that Marty and I made this decision on our own. No one pressured us. As many of you know, our daughter recently had our first grandchild and lives in Raleigh, and we'd like to spend more time with them. We always talked about buying an RV and traveling the country when we retired, but I'm not sure we ever would have retired if this opportunity hadn't been presented to us. And that's what this is. It's an opportunity for us all. I promise Marty will buy fish at that market and have a fish fry out at the house every now and then, and the whole town will be invited."

Despite the tears sliding down her face, Mildred was smiling. Heads in the crowd nodded their understanding, and the mood in the room visibly lifted.

Lucy spoke as Mildred stepped down from the podium. "Let's all give it up for Mildred and Marty, who've kept us fed and happy for so many years." She began clapping and soon everyone in the room was applauding along with her as Mildred walked back to her seat.

As the crowd quieted, Lucy spoke again. "Mildred, I think I speak for everyone when I say we hope you and Marty enjoy your retirement. You deserve it."

Logan returned to the microphone so he could explain further. "The Waterway Café has agreed to a buyout of its lease in the marina building. Our plan is to remove the exterior and interior walls, leaving only the roof and necessary supports. After some repairs to the pilings under the foundation, we'll be able to use this space as an open-air seafood market."

People were quiet as they processed the information, but they looked intrigued, not disappointed or angry as he'd feared. Logan took a deep breath. He knew his future depended on the rest of the meeting. The ideas he'd detailed so far weren't enough to bring in the revenue the town needed. If he could get a consensus on either the cruise line or the casino boat, it could be enough to seal the deal. Then he'd only need a council vote and the waterfront development would be off and running.

After introducing Mark from All-American Cruises, Logan stepped aside to let him come to the podium. His presentation was quick and efficient, highlighting the economic impact on similar towns without boring the audience with industry jargon and endless stats. Within ten minutes, Mark was launching into what Logan knew was his closing.

"According to surveys of our travelers, they spend an average of seventy-eight dollars in each port on everything from food to toiletries to souvenirs. In comparison, someone who stays here in town averages one hundred and seventy dollars per day. However, there's also a cost to that in terms of infrastructure needs like housing, roads, and parking. We think our proposal allows you all to open up to more tourists without having to tax your current infrastructure or add to it. You obviously have small-town charm here in spades, and we think this is a great alternative that allows you to further monetize your waterfront while controlling growth and commercialism."

Logan surveyed the crowd as Mark finished up. He'd seen a few people jot down notes, but it was tough to tell if they were writing down benefits or making notes for opposing comments later. Overall, the crowd looked more interested than it had in the beginning. Logan's step was a little lighter as he approached the podium to thank Mark and to invite up the president of the casino boats company, John McIntyre.

On his way back to the side of the room, Logan's eyes met Lucy's. She was frowning, clearly unimpressed with the presentation. It wasn't a look filled with hate and vitriol, but it wasn't the warm smile he yearned for either. He took a place against the wall a few feet from her, close enough that he could sense a vibration in the air, as if she was a magnet drawing him to her. He was so aware of her he couldn't concentrate on anything John was saying.

Admittedly, John's presentation wasn't exactly riveting. It also wasn't very impressive so far. Logan hadn't worked with his company before, but they'd come highly recommended by a friend who'd used them in Cape Canaveral. The economic benefits also simply weren't as good as they were with the cruise line.

Logan's jaw tensed as he sensed that John was losing the crowd. He probably should have asked to meet with him earlier in the day to go over his presentation, but he'd been distracted thinking about Lucy and the Little Free Library, and time had slipped away from him. He told himself it would be okay. The cruise line alone could probably generate enough revenue for the town to meet its goals.

They only had Lucy's expert and public comments left to go. This was the homestretch. All he needed was enough support for the cruise line for the council members to feel comfortable voting to approve his plan at their next meeting. It didn't have to be unanimous. He just needed four of the seven and he was home free.

Twenty-Five

Lucy

Lucy had to admit the presentation from the cruise line had been impressive. Mark had made such a compelling presentation that even she wavered.

But Miranda had some pretty compelling numbers too. Even the smaller ships took a toll on the environment and sea life. When they'd first met over the phone to prepare weeks ago, Lucy had told Miranda to come in guns blazing. She wanted to decimate Logan Lancaster and his ridiculous cruise ship idea. Even though she'd softened toward Logan, she still thought this particular idea was problematic.

Miranda was already off and running. She went through solid- and liquid-waste dumping by ships—complete with photos of ships dumping trash bags just offshore from their destinations—gas emissions spewed into the air while ships were in port, discharged ballast water, potential fuel spills, and more.

The next slide showed a pile of objects on a beach ranging from soda cans and candy wrappers to flip-flops and hats. Miranda held up a hand as she spoke.

"How many of you have found trash washed up on the beach?" Nearly every hand in the room went up. "Did you know cruise ships are allowed to dump sewage three miles offshore? And they can release wastewater basically anywhere they want. They're prohibited from dumping plastics or oil, but investigative reporters and interest groups have tracked ships and caught them dumping entire bags of trash overboard." She went back to the earlier photo of a crew clearly dropping bags of trash over the railings.

Lucy looked over to where Mark was sitting in the second row and saw him frantically writing notes, no doubt his rebuttal. She shifted her eyes toward Logan without turning her head. He had stiffened against the wall. He had his cell phone out and his thumbs were flying across the keyboard. His jaw was clenched, which accentuated the lines of his face.

His skin was tanner than when she'd first met him, no doubt a result of the beach runs she often caught sight of while she was on her deck journaling in the morning. With the temperature continuing its annual climb higher each day, he'd been running without his shirt. Pete had been right. He was indeed something to look at sans shirt. Even the button down he wore that night clung to him in all the right places. A warmth spread across her chest, and she forced herself to look away and focus on Miranda's presentation.

She was pointing to a photo of a woman holding a white rag nearly covered in something black.

"That's soot from cruise-ship engines being cleaned off one of the historic buildings in downtown Charleston. No landlord in the city ever reported soot like this prior to the cruise ships coming in." Miranda shot a look directly at Mark, who'd talked earlier about Charleston as a glowing case study of the economic impact cruise ships could have on a historic city.

He didn't meet her gaze, as he was still furiously writing in his notebook.

Lucy glanced at the council members. Their demeanors had shifted as Miranda finished her presentation. After Logan's experts spoke, they were relaxed, leaning back in their chairs, nodding, and whispering to each other casually. Now, they sat more erect, eyebrows furrowed and heads shaking as they exchanged hushed conversations.

She looked to Logan, who was tugging at the back of his neck with one hand and still typing on his phone with his other hand. When he realized she was looking at him, he held out a hand toward the podium, indicating she should go ahead and open up the public comment period of the meeting.

When she'd had her first call with Miranda weeks ago, she'd relished the idea of sending Logan out of town with his tail between his legs. But seeing the concern on his face now didn't feel nearly as satisfying as she'd thought it would back then. Somehow they'd become friends. She'd met his sister and his niece and nephew. He'd encouraged her to buy her building and given her some good advice.

She knew the waterfront project was important to him, and although she stood by her desire to keep the cruise line from negatively impacting the waters around Heron Isle, she regretted not working with him harder on a compromise. Were there more eco-friendly cruise lines? What about the shuttle idea? Could they shuttle in people from nearby islands and get a similar positive impact without as many environmental negatives?

Her legs felt heavy as she walked up to the podium. Miranda caught Lucy's eye as she stepped down after gathering her materials, smiling and nodding as if to say they'd been successful.

Lucy and Logan had agreed to the format beforehand, and she'd been surprised when he agreed to having his experts go first. Everyone knew it was better to go last in these scenarios in order to tailor the argument based on the other side's presentation. They also agreed there wouldn't be any rebuttals from either side lest it become an all-night debate.

Lucy could see Mark in the corner pointing to his notes and motioning at Miranda, obviously wanting to return to the podium to address the concerns raised. She felt a little guilty now that she'd insisted Logan's experts go first, but there were still more meetings to be held. She'd let Logan go last next time.

When Lucy opened the floor to allow public comments, it was confirmed. Virtually everyone was against the addition of either ship to their port.

Larry Fletcher, a charter-boat captain, detailed how a friend of his in Houston had been nearly run out of business by the oil spills in the Gulf.

"I've been fishing these waters my entire life, and my dad and granddad before me did the same. I came tonight because I want to be sure there's still fish in these waters for my kids and their kids and their kids' kids. So I say no to cruise ships and casino boats and outsiders who want to destroy our little town and our water just to make a buck."

Larry glared at Logan before stepping down and Lucy couldn't help but feel protective over Logan. He was just doing his job.

After the meeting, both Logan and Lucy were inundated with people who wanted to ask questions or express additional concerns. The council members had congregated in a back corner with the mayor. She'd caught Logan looking in their direction too, concern etched across his face. He looked exhausted, his hair mussed from where he'd run his hand through it over and over again during the opposition comments.

"Well, you turned out to be a formidable opponent, Ms. Lucy Sullivan." Logan approached her while still eyeing two council members who remained with the mayor in the back of the room, talking in hushed voices.

She grimaced. "I'm sorry. That was a little rougher than I'd imagined. I actually thought Mark made some really good points. I think we have a solid list of other ideas though." She tried to sound chipper to relay her optimism that they could still figure out something that worked for everyone.

"Yeah, unfortunately, I don't think that's going to be enough—"

The mayor and Councilman Turner were approaching them. Dan Turner had been involved in the development of both the major resorts on the island and half a dozen small shopping centers scattered outside the downtown area. He'd been a strong proponent of the town building a new development along the waterfront during previous discussions.

Mayor Jenkins wasn't making eye contact with Lucy or Logan, which was unsettling. Although he'd suggested the council hire Logan, he'd tried to remain neutral since he represented the interests of everyone in town. Now, though, he just looked weary. While Councilman Turner strode purposefully, like a man on a mission, Major Jenkins followed behind more slowly, his shoulders hunched.

"Lucy, do you mind if we have a word with Mr. Lancaster privately?" It was a question, but it was clear Councilman Turner was dismissing her.

She looked to Logan, apprehensive about leaving him alone to face the music. He gave a slight nod and forced his mouth into a tight smile that didn't reach his eyes. She'd never seen him so unsure of himself, and suddenly she was terrified that she'd succeeded in running him out of town.

Lucy waited outside city hall. She had to know what Councilman Turner and Mayor Jenkins had wanted with Logan after the meeting. She was sitting on the front steps chipping the pale-pink paint off her nails when she finally heard someone punch the door open twenty minutes later and looked up to see Logan exiting alone.

He was two steps down before he looked to his left and saw her rising to stand.

"Lucy." He sounded surprised to see her. "What are you still doing here?"

She shrugged. "Waiting for you. What did Councilman Turner and Mayor Jenkins have to say?" She looked back up at the door to see if they were following Logan out.

His mouth formed a tight line. "Where's your car? I'll walk you back."

"Over by the store." She nodded in the direction of the town square where her store sat on the other side.

They crossed the street into the square in silence. She didn't want to pry, but she was dying to know what had happened after she left.

He stopped suddenly, turning to her.

"Lucy, it's over. My time in Heron Isle is over, but I don't want you to worry. I'm still going to help you finish up the paperwork for the building."

Panic rose in her chest, the air suddenly so thick she felt as if she couldn't inhale a full breath, and it wasn't because she was worried about paperwork. Just a few short weeks ago, Lucy wanted Logan out of town so badly she would have packed his suitcase and driven him to the airport herself. She'd wanted him to fail. She'd opposed him at every turn, certain he was the person who held all the power to destroy the waterfront and with it the unique charm of the entire town.

Councilman Turner was the shark in the water no one ever saw coming. She studied Logan's eyes now. He hadn't seen it coming either.

Logan turned to keep walking, but she grabbed his arm to stop him.

"What? Why? Just because people don't want to bring in cruise ships or casino boats?"

When he looked down at her hand on his arm, she dropped it back to her side.

He sighed. "No, because Councilman Turner has made the town an offer it can't refuse. He's willing to pay fifteen percent over the appraised value to buy the waterfront and marina himself."

Her mouth fell open as she searched for words. What was he talking about? The town had never discussed selling the land, least of all to Councilman Turner. Was that even legal?

"Can he do that?" she practically shrieked. "Isn't that a conflict of interest or something?"

Logan grabbed his forehead as he looked down. "No, he's stepping down from the council to remove the conflict, effective immediately." He threw up his hands. "It's basically a breach of fiduciary duty for the town to turn it down at this point. It's their duty to balance the budget and manage the infrastructure. If they don't have another viable option, they'll be hard pressed to take another path now. Legally speaking, I think they'll have to put it on the open market and take competing bids, but he's opened the door to that land being privatized. I'm not sure the city has any other option."

In all the worst-case scenarios she'd imagined, this one had never emerged. What were they going to do? Councilman Turner and his company would throw up high-rises along the waterfront without hesitation. He'd already done it a few miles away on the north end of the island where they'd once had unspoiled, natural land, and now he was coming for the historic downtown as well. She knew the town had ordinances that provided some parameters, but she couldn't help thinking this was a doomsday scenario for the waterfront as they knew it.

And for Logan. She knew he'd needed a win. But what was making her really uncomfortable was the niggling feeling that the real loss here was hers. She didn't want to tell Logan goodbye.

She followed as he began to walk again toward her car.

"What will you do?" She didn't meet his eyes as she waited for his answer.

"I'll find another city that needs me. That's what I always do. Move on to the next town."

When she'd first met Logan, he always sounded excited when he talked about moving from city to city, but something was different now. His words sounded empty. His tone defeated.

She didn't know what else to say, so they walked in silence the rest of the short distance to her car. She hit the button to unlock it as they approached, then turned to face him, unsure what to say. How could it all be over just like that? No more hope for the waterfront. No more Logan Lancaster.

He smiled at her. Not the one-thousand-watt smile he flashed when he wanted things to go his way, just a small smile from a friend.

"Goodnight, Lucy."

"Goodnight, Logan." Before she could register what she was doing, she was reaching for a hug. The night held a finality she couldn't shake.

To her surprise, he hugged her back, his arms locking them together, her shoulders fitting perfectly under his arms, and her head tucked into his chest. As she inhaled his now familiar scent that struck the perfect balance between sweet and masculine, her eyes closed, and she wished they could stay just like that.

He leaned his head down against hers, and the moment was so raw and tender she could hardly breathe. The hug lasted longer than any normal hug between friends, and yet she knew that whenever it ended, it would be too soon.

When they finally parted, they stood there looking at each other for a long while, each trying to read the other.

His eyes shifted to her lips and her skin tingled at the idea that he might lean down to kiss her. She might have even leaned in the slightest amount before he cleared his throat and took a step back.

Embarrassed that she'd had such thoughts about Logan, she waved a quick goodbye and grabbed the handle of her car door. Starting the engine, suddenly in a hurry to get away, she put it in reverse and began backing out onto the deserted street.

Turning to where they'd been standing, she saw Logan was still there watching her leave, and she couldn't help but wonder how much time they'd have together before he was gone for good.

Twenty-Six

Logan

He'd almost told her he was Gatsby's Ghost.

Heck, he'd nearly kissed her. He hadn't been able to take his eyes off her perfect pink lips, and he could have sworn she leaned in just the slightest bit like she wanted to kiss him too.

But he couldn't kiss her, not without telling her the truth.

Could he tell her the truth? Should he? He'd been trying to play out possible scenarios in his head when she'd hugged him, but the feeling of her body practically melting into his and the smell of her coconut shampoo had clouded his head.

In the end, he'd been too scared. What if she was angry that he hadn't told her sooner? What if that was how they left things when it was time for him to go? He didn't think he could bear it. Those big brown eyes would haunt him no matter how far he went.

Logan had nearly made it back to his car when he saw

Fuller's name lighting up his phone. Clearing his throat, he answered and tried to sound more chipper than he was feeling.

"Hey, man."

"Hey, who's got the best friend a guy could ever hope for?"

Logan forced a chuckle. "I'm afraid to ask."

"Trust me when I say it's you. I got the skinny from a friend of mine who works in the planning board office. They've narrowed it down to three candidates, and you made the list."

Logan should have been excited. He should have been pumping his fist in the air and promising Fuller a big steak dinner when he got up to Boston, but he felt it was happening too fast. He wasn't ready to wash his hands of Heron Isle and skip town. He wasn't ready to say goodbye to Lucy.

"Wow, that's great. Thanks, man." Boston. It was the entire reason he'd come to Heron Isle, to set himself up for the Boston job. He tried to psych himself up, to push thoughts of Lucy and Heron Isle aside.

"Gee, I thought you'd be a little more excited than that."

Fuller was right. He should be thanking him. "Sorry, I am. It's great news. Thank you. Are they going to bring all three candidates up?"

"I'm not sure. There was talk of only bringing up the final two, but I don't have a good handle on how they're going to whittle it down. I've got some feelers out."

Timing was everything. Logan needed to sell himself to the board in Boston before one of the other candidates beat him to the punch. He couldn't just stay on Heron Isle and soak up the rays after the city terminated his contract. Boston was always the goal. He had to stay focused. If he didn't get it, he didn't have a backup plan. He'd have to wait for another opening somewhere else, which could be months.

"I need a meeting with whoever is leading the committee up there, and I need it fast."

"What's happening down there? I thought you had another month or so to go."

Logan raked a hand through his hair. "Nothing, it's fine. One of the council members made the city an offer tonight they can't refuse, so they're going to sell the land and the marina and get out of the property business. They'll make more than I could have found for them piecing together a bunch of little stuff. They can take it from here, so now I can focus on what's next. And that's Boston. I want that job, Fuller."

"Man, it would be great to have you up here. I told you I'd go to bat for you. Let me make a few calls, okay?"

"Thanks, Fuller. I owe you one."

His best friend promised to be back in touch soon and they hung up.

Logan was still parked in his spot downtown. Everything was closed up for the night, and his car was one of the only ones along the town square. From where he was parked, he could just make out the Little Free Library in the distance under a streetlight. He couldn't stop one question from repeating in his brain, and it wasn't about Boston.

What was he going to do about Lucy?

What was bound to happen with the waterfront was enough of a blow for her. She didn't need to be hit with more. She'd had enough people disappoint her. He couldn't be another to add to the list. It was time to get out of Heron Isle before he hurt her even more than he maybe already had.

As he pulled into the driveway of crushed shells in front of his beach cottage, his phone lit up in the cup holder. It was Fuller again.

"That was fast."

"Hey, it's all about who you know, right?" Fuller sounded like he had good news.

"And I take it it's a good thing I know you?"

"It is indeed." He could hear Fuller smiling through the phone. "It's possible the director of the planning board has an assistant who can't resist the old Fuller charm."

"I bet she can't." Logan smiled, remembering how Fuller had talked their way onto a bus full of women celebrating a bachelorette party the last time he'd visited him. The ladies loved Fuller, and he loved the ladies.

"9:00 a.m. Friday. You're on his calendar. Can you get here that fast?"

That was only a day away.

"I'll be there. Fuller, you are still the man."

"Time to get you out of Mayberry, Lancaster. I'll meet you for drinks after work Friday and you can tell me all about your meeting. I'll text you an address."

And just like that, Logan knew he was back in the game. He'd never been turned down for any position where he'd had an in-person meeting. However, as he took his scotch out on the back porch to celebrate, he couldn't help feeling that Heron Isle might have been his biggest failure.

And he hadn't just failed Heron Isle; he had failed Lucy. And that hurt most of all.

Logan had been looking forward to getting on a flight out of Florida headed for Boston since he'd first arrived on Heron Isle, but he couldn't escape the nagging feeling he'd been having since the previous evening. He'd tried to write it off as guilt over not finding a resolution that kept major development off the waterfront. Sure, he didn't have to live there, but he'd felt more protective of Heron Isle than other places he'd worked. It wasn't as easy to write it off as the cost of progress and move on.

And he couldn't stop seeing Lucy's face when he'd told her Councilman Turner had made the town an irresistible offer. She'd been crushed, and he knew she'd blame herself for not finding a way to save the waterfront.

He couldn't be one more person who let her down. So he'd done the only thing he'd known how. He'd stayed up most of the night writing up business plans for the bookstore and the building. They were solid plans she could implement with the right systems and support, and he was certain between the plans and the financials they'd put together she'd be able to get the loan. He might not be able to give her a happily ever after fit for the big screen, but he could give her what she needed to make buying the building a reality and maybe that would be enough.

He typed up a note so he wouldn't give away his identity as Gatsby's Ghost through his handwriting and told her he was going to Boston, but that he wanted her to have everything she needed to get her loan and that he believed in her.

On his way to the airport, he stopped and slid an envelope through the mail slot at the bookstore. As he pulled away, he couldn't help but wish he'd seen her through the window. Just one last glimpse of her before he left town. It wasn't even daylight, though, and the streets and sidewalks of downtown Heron Isle were as empty as he felt as he drove to the end of Main Street and took the left that would lead him off the island and toward his destiny in Boston.

By the time he got to his hotel in Boston, the sun was just beginning to slip behind the buildings that filled the city's skyline. He ordered room service and settled in to study every news article he could find about Boston's comprehensive plan and the types of projects they'd be pursuing. Fuller had sent him a breakdown of the power players in town and who wanted what. Logan found all the commission and planning board meeting minutes from the past two years and dissected them. He wanted to know everything he could about the situation before his meeting tomorrow so he could impress the planning board director.

After turning in well past 2:00 a.m., Logan woke at dawn and went over his notes once more. By the time he got to the director's office, he knew every discussion the city had had over its future development plans. But even with all that knowledge, he had trouble summoning his confidence as the director's assistant showed him down the hall to the man's office.

"You're a friend of Cameron's?" The pretty brunette turned back to smile at Logan.

"Yeah, we went to undergrad together at USC. Thank you for getting me on Mr. O'Connell's schedule."

"Of course. Any friend of Cameron's is a friend of mine." She reached the door and motioned for Logan to enter.

"Mr. Lancaster." Kevin O'Connell rose from his desk and extended his hand to Logan.

"Please, call me Logan. Thanks for seeing me on such short notice, Mr. O'Connell." He gave his hand a firm shake.

"Feel free to call me Kevin. Please, sit." He pointed to one of the brown leather chairs in front of his desk. Kevin O'Connell looked to be about Logan's age and had deep auburn hair and a smattering of freckles across his pale skin.

"Cameron tells me you were roommates in college. I can only imagine the kind of trouble he must have gotten in during his college days." He leaned back in his tall leather chair.

Logan laughed. "Let's just say things were never boring."

"He tells me you were in charge of the redevelopment south of the arch in St. Louis and then the warehouse district in Phoenix. Impressive resume."

He'd skipped San Diego, but surely he'd done an internet search on Logan. Or maybe he'd simply gone on Fuller's word up to this point.

"Thank you. I appreciate the kind words. I'm just finishing up a small waterfront project down south that I took on while I was waiting for the position here to open. I've heard a lot about what you're planning here, and I'd love to be part of it. I know there's a formal process, and I certainly respect that, but I never turn down the chance to get a little face time."

They talked about the various parties looking to be part of the deal, the budget, projected timeline, and the sort of resources someone like Logan would have at their disposal. It was exactly the job Logan should want next. It was the type of project that not only wiped out what had happened in San Diego, but also put him on track to becoming one of the most accomplished consultants in his field.

And absolutely nothing about it appealed to Logan as he sat and listened to Kevin talk about municipal bonds and zoning variances and infrastructure improvements. He didn't even get excited at the prospect of tying the new project into the existing historic footprint in downtown Boston and the opportunities he'd have to work alongside Fuller. His mind kept drifting to Heron Isle, his brain trying to find a solution that didn't involve the town selling the land to Councilman Turner. There was still time, they weren't due to give preliminary approval of the sale until the council meeting on Tuesday.

Logan left his meeting with the director of the planning board feeling the job was practically his by the time he walked out of the office. Turned out Kevin did know about San Diego, but Fuller had already told him Logan's side of the story, and Kevin had shrugged it off like it was nothing.

Fuller was right. It was all about who you knew.

As Logan walked along the wharf toward the bar to meet Fuller for happy hour, he slowed to look at the businesses along the waterway. Obviously, Boston was a different city than Heron Isle, but that didn't mean there might not be an idea or two they could borrow.

As he neared a line of people, he saw a big sign for Boston Cruise Company. They had ferries to the Harbor Islands, Provincetown, Salem, and more. They offered whale watching tours, sunset cruises, and eco tours.

He had an idea. He wasn't sure how the numbers would come out, but it was something.

He caught up with Fuller and listened to all the stories about his latest romantic escapades, then Logan told him about Heron Isle. From how the cruise ship idea had effectively sunk to how he couldn't stop thinking about finding a way to keep Councilman Turner from developing the waterfront. He even told Fuller about Lucy and the Little Free Library. He hadn't intended to share the latter part, but it was impossible to talk about Heron Isle without mentioning Lucy. It all just came tumbling out as they ordered a second round and then a third.

"I feel if I'd just had more time, I could have come up with something. I saw Boston Cruise Company on my way over here and was thinking maybe something like that would work. There are all these little barrier islands nearby they could ferry people to and from, and people love those sunset cruises. The town has restrictions on bigger boats, but those are small enough to meet the regulations and have minimal impact on the environment."

"Seems to me if they went ahead with that they're going to need someone to manage the marina and all these contracts going forward." Fuller raised an eyebrow.

"You mean me?" Logan was surprised to find his heart leap at the idea. He was more excited about that prospect than he'd felt all day about the Boston job. It was too late, though. The town was ready to vote at the council meeting on Tuesday to sell the land to Dan Turner.

"I've never heard you talk about any place like you just talked about this tiny little island. Don't you want to do work that excites you? Man, I love my job here. Wouldn't trade it for anything, and don't think I haven't had other offers. And that woman—Lucy?—she sounds like someone worth sticking around for. I've never had that, but if I did, I don't think I'd let it go so easily."

Logan shook his head before taking another drink. "It's too late. They're voting on the sale Tuesday. I could try to pull something together between now and then on the ferries, but I don't think that alone is enough to change their minds."

"What do you know about shell middens?" Fuller donned a mischievous grin, just like back in college when he'd convinced a professor to let them miss class for two weeks to go to Major League Baseball's spring training to "study the historic preservation efforts used to save minor league ballparks."

"Shell middens?" Logan was stumped. "Nothing. What are they?"

"They're how you're going to save your waterfront." Fuller slapped him on the back before downing the rest of his beer.

Twenty-Seven

Lucy

Lucy nearly tripped over the thick envelope when she walked in the front door of the store Thursday morning. Her name was printed in neat block letters on the front, but there was no address or postage.

After opening the metal fastener on the back, she pulled two stacks of papers from the folder, each secured with a small binder clip. A single sheet of paper slipped to the ground, sliding across the floor until Lizzy grabbed it with a paw and began attacking it.

"I think that's for me," she told the cat before running a hand down her back. Lizzy arched in reply and began to purr. As Lucy continued petting the cat, she read the neatly typed note.

Lucy,

I'm headed up to Boston, but I wanted you to have this before I left. It has everything you need to convince the bank to approve your loan for the building.

You can do this. I believe in you.

Logan

She flipped through the two sets of paperwork. They were complete business plans for both the bookstore and for the building, including timelines, maintenance schedules, reserves, and more. Everything they hadn't gotten to. He must have spent hours on this.

It wasn't until she read through the note a second time that his words sank in. *I wanted you to have this before I left.* Her heart sank. He was gone already? It hadn't even been twenty-four hours since the community forum. She'd thought it would take him a little while to figure out where he was heading next. He couldn't have lined up another job this fast, could he?

She had to sit down. She moved to one of the blue armchairs by the front window and read the note again. He believed in her. But he was also gone. Two competing thoughts fought for her attention, like a tug-of-war inside her head. He'd believed in her so much he'd spent hours finishing up the business plans and delivering them to her. But then he left. Just like everyone did eventually.

The bells on the front door jingled, drawing her attention. She wasn't open yet, but she'd forgotten to lock the door behind her. Her breath caught as she turned to see who had come in. Maybe Logan hadn't really left without saying goodbye.

But it wasn't Logan lumbering toward her. It was Mayor

Jenkins. She really wasn't in the mood to talk, but she plastered on a smile.

"Good morning."

"Mornin', Lucy. I wanted to come by and see how you're doing." He sat in the chair next to her.

Setting the paperwork on the small table between them, she sighed. "I'm fine, I guess. Obviously, I'm disappointed. Maybe the cruise ship wasn't such a bad idea. If I'd focused on compromising instead of winning, maybe we could have figured out a solution that didn't involve selling out to a developer."

"Lucy, this isn't about you doing anything wrong or not doing enough. It's just business." The mayor shrugged. "I don't love the idea of selling to Turner either, but it's not my decision. The council is prepared to approve the sale. It's the fastest way to get the money the city needs. We have to weigh the infrastructure needs against whatever disadvantages the sale might bring. Besides, we don't know exactly what Turner plans to do with the land just yet."

Lucy frowned. "I have a pretty good idea. Has he ever developed anything on this island that didn't end up being a high-density eyesore?"

The mayor didn't argue. He simply sipped the coffee he'd brought with him and petted Lizzy, who was now circling his legs.

Lucy glanced at the note and plans she'd set on the table, and she couldn't resist asking about Logan. "So the town just ends its contract with Logan, and he goes on to the next place?"

"I wouldn't worry about Logan. Sounds like he already has his next job lined up in Boston. It's probably better suited for him anyway."

Her heart sank. "Well, that's the end of that, I guess."

After studying her face, the mayor raised an eyebrow. "He

has a meeting up there tomorrow morning, but he hasn't moved out of the cottage yet. He told us he'd be back next week to pack up."

The corners of her mouth turned up before she could stop them. She didn't want the mayor to think she cared one way or the other about Logan and where he ended up, but she did care. He hadn't left without saying goodbye. And although she knew it was just postponing the inevitable, she was glad he wasn't gone for good just yet. She wanted to show him that his time spent with her hadn't been wasted, even if his time working for Heron Isle maybe had been.

As soon as Mayor Jenkins left, she grabbed her purse, locked the front door behind her and hurried to Main Street Bank. It was just like the book from Gatsby's Ghost had said. She needed to accept some risk into her life instead of running from it. It was time to embrace a new way of being.

After closing the shop on Thursday, Lucy walked the few blocks to Rothchild's to help Jack pick out the perfect ring for her best friend. Instead of letting feelings of impending doom swallow her like they would have just a few short days ago, she pictured how happy Taylor was going to be when Jack got down on one knee.

Although the proposal would likely take Taylor away to Nashville, Lucy knew it had nothing to do with her. Their getting engaged and moving wasn't a reflection on her or even Heron Isle. It was just change, and it happened. And maybe sometimes change was good. Taylor would have more opportunities—maybe she'd even get to work on the set of a country music video or something really cool that could only happen in Nashville. She would no longer be limited to destination weddings and the rare photo shoot or black-tie gala.

By the time Lucy pushed open the door to Rothchild's, she was smiling and skipping as if she was going to pick out her own ring. Jack was already there looking at one, and she was delighted to see he was headed in the right direction.

"What do you think of this one?" He held it up, and it sparkled in the light like a disco ball with two rows of tiny diamonds around the band.

Lucy took it from his hand, holding it up to the light. "It's beautiful. I think it's close, but..." She looked in the case, searching for something a little simpler. Finding what she was looking for, she pointed for the clerk—a younger woman Lucy only knew by name, Parker—to take the emerald-cut sparkler from the case. "She'd like this emerald-cut more."

Jack took it from the clerk and held it up to examine it from every angle. As he talked to the clerk about the specifics, Lucy drifted farther down the case to see if anything else caught her eye. That was when she saw the ring of her dreams. A princess-cut diamond that might not be a full carat with a row of three sapphires on each side of the center stone.

"Would you like to see that one too?" Parker walked toward Lucy.

"Oh, no. The one he has is perfect."

"But you like that one?" Parker gave her a knowing smile.

Lucy had met Parker once or twice in passing around town, but she hadn't lived on Heron Isle long and was a full decade younger. Lucy heard she'd moved to the island with her husband, who was a chef over at Jack's resort.

"I do." It was silly to think about an engagement ring when she wasn't even dating, but she couldn't help herself. It was beautiful.

"Can't hurt to try it on." Parker winked as she reached into the case and pulled it out.

Lucy looked around before she slipped it on, even though she knew they were alone in the store. She would die of embarrassment if anyone saw her trying on the ring. It was bad enough Jack was nearby, but he was consumed with examining the ring for Taylor.

Lucy looked down at the ring on her hand, which was nothing like the ostentatious one Carter had given her. She knew he'd meant well when he bought it, equating its size and price to value and wanting to show her some sign of the giant life he had planned for them. But in the end, she hadn't wanted that life, and he hadn't been happy "playing it small" on Heron Isle.

She thought of Logan then. In the beginning, she'd thought he was like Carter. Always on the search for something bigger and better. But something was different about his aspirations. He seemed less inclined to chase accomplishments and more focused on trying to prove something. She'd just never figured out what.

After seeing Logan with his sister and niece and nephew, Lucy had thought about what sort of woman Logan might settle down with one day. It had been obvious how much he loved his family when they visited, but given his career choice, she wasn't sure he even wanted to settle down.

Just as she started to imagine Logan as a husband and father, a little boy with his bright-green eyes running around on the beach, Jack interrupted her thoughts.

"I think you're right. This is the one."

He was grinning, and Lucy could tell the ring would burn a hole in his pocket until he could give it to Taylor.

"Great! I'll leave you to it then. Everything is on for tomorrow night still?"

He nodded. "Yes. I've got the photographer lined up, and then we'll meet you and the others up at the bar afterward to celebrate." Jack stopped and a shadow crossed his face. "I mean, assuming she says yes."

Lucy laughed, placing an arm on Jack's. "Don't worry. She'll say yes."

After confirming what time Jack planned to pop the question, Lucy realized she'd left the book she wanted to put in the Little Free Library for Gatsby's Ghost at the store, so she walked back. Just as she was walking to the door to lock up again, her cell phone rang. Taking it from her purse, she saw Leona's number on the screen. Leona only called with really good news… or really bad news.

Lucy answered as cheerfully as she could, but her voice cracked. "Hi, Leona."

"Lucy, my love. Are you sitting?"

"No. Should I be?"

"Yes, I do think this is sitting news." Leona paused, seeming serious about Lucy needing a chair, so she walked over to one of the blue armchairs and sat.

"Okay." Lucy spoke slowly and softly. "I'm sitting. What's wrong?"

"Nothing is wrong." Leona's voice came in a rush of words now. "Everything is glorious, my dear. I sent off your synopsis to a couple of editors who loved your work before, but just couldn't make the last one work with their list, and there's going to be an auction!"

"A-An auction? What does that mean?" Lucy's mind was racing. She didn't know Leona was going to show anyone the synopsis, she thought she would just read it and give her feedback before she started writing the book.

"It means four different publishers are interested in your book. They're positively salivating over it. It's going to be a big, wonderful fight that will drive up your advance and ensure whoever buys it puts some real marketing power behind your debut."

Lucy could hardly follow, Leona was talking so fast and

excitedly. Was she saying more than one publisher wanted her book? "You mean I'm going to get a book deal?"

"Honey, by the time I'm done you're going to have at least a two-book deal and a big fat advance!"

Leona was right. Lucy had needed to sit down for this. Her hand was shaking so much she could hardly hold the phone to her ear. Someone wanted to publish her book. Several editors at different publishing houses, in fact. When the voice nagged at the back of her mind and said she'd gotten a deal before and it had all fallen through, she shoved it mentally through a door and slammed it shut. It was like Logan had said, she needed to believe in herself as much as everyone else did.

After Leona explained how the auction would work and promised to call as soon as she'd received the offers, Lucy hung up and was enveloped by the silence of the empty store around her. She felt the overwhelming urge to tell someone. She could tell Taylor tonight so it wouldn't overshadow her engagement the following evening, but they weren't meeting for dinner for another hour. Staring at her phone, she wanted to dial Logan's number. He was the only other person who even knew she'd sent the synopsis to Leona. But he was in Boston. She felt silly interrupting his trip for his new job. Maybe she'd get the chance to tell him before he left town. To thank him.

In the meantime, she'd go drop off the book in the Little Free Library for Gatsby's Ghost. Maybe she should tell him. After all, this was definitely a risk that had paid off.

Taking the note she'd already written out of the book, she jumped up and walked over to the counter, where she scribbled a new message on the pad by the computer, ripped it off, and tucked it back between the pages. She'd drop off the book and buy a bottle of champagne on her way to meet Taylor. She deserved to celebrate.

TWENTY-EIGHT

Logan

Fuller was brilliant. Shell middens were shells and animal bones left behind by Native Americans who'd inhabited the island before European settlers. Some of the heaps often found along coastal and lake shores were ceremonial in nature, while others contained burial grounds. The Florida courts had previously ruled that developers must bring in archaeologists upon finding any sign of a historical site. Archaeologists would then document the ruins, and depending on their findings, development could be halted temporarily for relocation or permanently for preservation.

It only took a few phone calls to put plans in motion to explore Heron Isle's downtown waterfront for shell middens. Helen, the president of Heron Isle Conservancy, had just returned from presenting her latest research and offered to meet with him Saturday afternoon. He'd taken the first flight back Saturday morning, spending the entire trip researching all the different facets of his plan, from the shell middens to the smaller tour boats and even another idea that had been percolating since he'd seen the rundown Hill House on the historic tour with Lucy and Gladys.

Logan had suggested Helen meet him at the coffee shop downtown, but she wouldn't hear of it. She insisted he come out to her home, which sat on the west side of the island up against the marsh. From the moment he got out the car, he was on high alert, looking out for Sidney, Helen's "teaching" alligator. He wasn't really interested in meeting Sidney and couldn't imagine why anyone would keep an alligator for a pet, educational tool or not. As he surveyed the marsh that sat just behind Helen's house, it occurred to him that Helen might have more than one alligator lurking around this place.

Helen opened the door and he saw that she was a petite woman who couldn't weigh a hundred pounds, not the burly woman he'd pictured wrestling alligators. But she was a zoologist, not someone who lived on the swamps of the bayou trapping alligators for sport. He'd just never met anyone with her reported love of reptiles, much less a woman who'd made it her life's work. She was cheerful and welcoming, inviting him in to have iced tea on her screened-in porch overlooking the marsh.

He looked out over the water while he waited, observing the grasses standing in tall clumps along the bank and farther out into the water bending gently in the wind. The rustling of the grasses combined with the wind chimes hanging on the porch to create a beautiful melody. Oak trees towered around the house on all sides, the plentiful shade providing temperatures that felt ten degrees cooler than the deck of his beach house this morning.

Helen came up behind him, offering him a glass of sweet tea. His lips puckered as the sweet liquid hit his tongue. That was something he'd never get used to if he lived here. Might as well suck on a sugar cube. Wanting to be polite, he sipped it appreciatively and then got down to business.

They'd already spoken at length on the phone, and Helen had called an archaeologist friend, who lived just south in St. Augustine and taught at the college there, to inquire about the possibility of middens on the shoreline of Heron Isle.

"Do you think there's any chance of middens along the waterfront?" Logan asked.

Helen smiled. "I'm almost certain. I went back through some historical documentation we have on file at the conservancy, and it seems clear that the Timucuan people who lived here had a settlement along the water right where the river meets the ocean, basically in the same location as the marina we use today. Because the only current structures are the dock and the restaurant out over the water, no formal study has ever been done on the land itself along the waterfront. My friend Doug is coming up tomorrow to conduct an initial examination."

Logan clapped, startling Helen. "I'm sorry. I'm just excited. If there's any indication there might be middens, the Florida Supreme Court has already ruled in a previous case that further studies must be conducted before any development proceeds. If Turner already owned the land, we might not be able to stop him, even if there were middens. But my guess is he'll back out when he learns the costs involved with properly excavating the area and potentially fighting in court."

"And we would definitely fight it." Helen nodded. "The conservancy has access to a central fund with other conservancy organizations in the state specifically for these kinds of legal battles. It's important to protect and preserve our heritage."

They arranged to meet with Doug on the waterfront shortly after sunrise Sunday morning. They didn't want to attract too much attention in case it turned out to be nothing.

Helen had already cleared the meeting and initial exam with Mayor Jenkins. Doug's study would only require a small removal of soil in a few places along the waterfront.

"Before you leave, there was one thing Mayor Jenkins wanted me to show you. Wait right here." Helen grinned at him before exiting the porch through the door that led outside. He watched as she walked over to a barn to the right of the house. Did she have an office in there? Maybe Mayor Jenkins wanted him to review some of the historical documents she'd mentioned.

He pulled out his phone and texted Fuller to let him know how the meeting went, thanking him again for the suggestion. When he looked up, Helen was approaching the porch with something in her hands.

He nearly dropped his phone when he realized she was holding an alligator that looked about two feet long.

Helen let out a hearty laugh as she opened the door. "George told me you might wet your pants."

Thankfully, he wasn't that scared, but his heart was definitely racing as she moved closer. If he hadn't been seated, he would have backed away. He briefly considered leaping up so he could move, but Helen stopped a few feet from him.

"Logan, I'd like you to meet Sidney. He's taught many a child on the island to respect—but not fear—the alligators that live here in our fresh water. As you can see, his mouth is closed with a band. It doesn't hurt him, and he can't hurt you."

Logan held his hand up in a sort of half wave. "Hi, Sidney." He was hoping that would be the end of the meet and greet.

"Would you like to hold him?" Helen lifted the alligator in his direction.

"Oh, no. That's not necessary. I can respect him from a

distance. That's what you're supposed to do with alligators, right?"

Helen chuckled. "Yes, that's right. Maybe next time you'll feel a little braver. Sidney tends to grow on people."

Logan doubted he'd ever jump at the chance to hold a live alligator, but he nodded with a nervous smile. "Yes, maybe."

"All right, we'll let you get going. I'll see you at the marina in the morning."

Helen started talking to the alligator as Logan headed to the front door. She talked to it like people talked to dogs and cats.

"You're such a good boy, Sidney. Would you like a treat? Let's get you a little treat."

Walking slower once he was safely on the other side of the front door and heading to his car, Logan checked the time. He had one more stop to make.

He had just finished snapping photos of Hill House when Gladys arrived along with her realtor friend, Terri.

"Logan, I'd like you to meet my dear friend, Terri Neal." Gladys stood back while Logan and Terri shook hands. "I just can't tell you how delighted I was to hear from you yesterday. The foundation would love to partner with you on preserving this house."

When Logan thought about making Heron Isle his permanent address, his mind kept drifting back to the abandoned house downtown with the hand-carved gingerbread detail. He was sure if that much care had been taken on the porch, there must be more architectural surprises inside. He and Fuller had always talked about saving historic properties, and houses here were much cheaper than those in Boston.

Even if his new plan for the waterfront wasn't successful,

and his idea of becoming the full-time manager of the city's real estate holdings and marina fell through, this house was perfect for a preservation project. He was beginning to let himself feel optimistic about staying on Heron Isle.

Terri showed him through the first floor, which had a formal living room, dining room, and parlor, along with the kitchen. Upstairs there were three bedrooms. The house had already been cleaned out, nothing remained but dust and a few curtains hanging haphazardly. Most of the plaster walls showed damage, and the kitchen and bathrooms were all complete gut jobs. The floors had water damage in a few places, and large water stains bulged and bubbled in the ceiling. Even so, the house had great bones.

The floors were all heart pine, and handmade crown molding encircled the top of every room. Logan dragged a finger through the thick layer of dust on the hand-carved banister. It and the stairs appeared to be the same heart pine that had once grown abundantly in this area. Everything was stained a deep shade of brown. He was delighted to find more gingerbread detailing at the top of the doorways leading into the living room and dining room on each side of the front entry hall. Beautiful wooden panels had been added at the top of each doorway, then carved into the intricate pattern. He saw a few pieces that were cracked, but that was an easy fix with the right contractor.

He approached the ladies, who were waiting for him near the front door, and asked Gladys, "The family has already agreed to sell?" Gladys had been negotiating on behalf of the foundation in hopes they could raise the money needed to buy and preserve the house.

She nodded. "Yes, when the siblings heard we might have the funding sooner than anticipated, they all agreed it's for the best. The foundation just hadn't been able to come up with the cash to make them believe we were serious previously. That's why I was so happy when you called."

Logan smiled as he turned around in the front foyer, taking one last look at all the handmade details.

"It's perfect." He turned back to the ladies. "I need to send some photos to my business partner, but it's exactly what we were hoping to find inside."

"I bet Lucy is excited you plan to bring the library back." Gladys gave him a knowing smile.

He shook his head. "No, I haven't told her yet. Can we keep this between us for now? There's still a lot that needs to fall into place for it to happen. I don't want to get her hopes up just yet."

Terri pulled an imaginary zipper across her lips while Gladys nodded her assent.

Logan had left Fuller to make some calls to an investor they knew who was always in the market for tax credits. To maximize federal and state tax credits for historic preservation, the house had to be for commercial or nonprofit use, not residential. Luckily, it was close enough to Main Street to be in an overlay district that allowed for certain nonresidential uses, a library easily fitting within the definition. As a nonprofit, the library wouldn't need the tax credits, so they could sell them on the open market. Those funds would in turn provide the revenue the library needed to keep it solvent for at least the first few years, and during those early years they could put the infrastructure in place to apply for grants and fundraise to keep it running for years to come.

He and Fuller would split ownership of the building with the Heron Isle Historic Foundation—which was moving Gladys's office to one of the upstairs rooms—a solid real estate investment that was meaningful to all of them. He couldn't think of a more fitting way to get involved in historic preservation on a more personal level.

The look he imagined on Lucy's face when she found out was just the cherry on top.

Logan texted Fuller a dozen or more pictures of the inside and outside of the house as Terri locked it back up, promising to upload an entire album when she was back at her computer.

Riding a high as he walked back to his car, he saw the town square in the distance and decided to go check the Little Free Library. He still hadn't decided how to tell Lucy he was Gatsby's Ghost, but he was curious to see if she'd responded to his last letter.

The town square was always bustling on weekends, and Logan became hyperaware of everyone around him as he approached the library. He searched the faces, nervous Lucy would find him there. Not recognizing anyone nearby, he pulled on the handle to open the library door. Inside, he began going through the new books on the ledge. He was only a couple books in when he saw her familiar handwriting on a sticky note attached to a volume on the history of Florida's barrier islands. Opening the book, he found the index card she'd left inside.

Gatsby's Ghost,

You were right to assume I'm not much of a risk taker. The book you left was exactly what I needed. I took a chance, and guess what? It paid off! I put myself out there for something I've wanted professionally for quite some time, and I was rewarded. I can't believe I'm saying this to someone I don't even know, but I felt you should be one of the first to tell. I am going to be a published author!

Maybe one day it'll be my book you find in this library.

I wasn't sure what to leave you next, but I thought perhaps you might enjoy a book on the history of this area. I always find there's so much to appreciate around here if I take the time to open my eyes.

Thank you again for encouraging me to take a risk. I hope you finally hit that home run.

Island Girl

Logan shook his head, his mouth open wide in a smile that stretched his cheeks until they hurt. She'd done it. Lucy had sent off the synopsis she was working on and landed a book deal.

His first instinct was to run straight over to her store and congratulate her, but he knew he couldn't just burst in and tell her he was Gatsby's Ghost. As far as she knew, Logan had no idea about her book deal. They hadn't spoken since he walked her back to her car after the meeting Wednesday night.

He considered going over to the store just to say hi and see if she'd tell him about the book deal, but he knew he still had a lot of work to do before Tuesday rolled around, when he had to go confront the council to try to stop the sale to Turner. He forced his legs to walk in the opposite direction to his car. First things first. He needed to put together his presentation for the council meeting and finish the paperwork for Hill House.

Maybe after he saved the waterfront from development and announced he was bringing back the library he could convince Lucy to forgive him for the small lies he'd told since learning she was Island Girl.

She had to forgive him. He was gambling his future on it.

TWENTY-NINE

Logan

Lucy didn't know it yet, but she had helped save the waterfront. Thanks to the book she left him in the Little Free Library, Doug had found the shell middens they were looking for at a speed that would have made pirates searching for gold turn green with envy. It was like having a treasure map. The book detailed exactly where the settlement on the island had been, and it even referenced early journal entries from a European settler describing the settlement. Doug was familiar with the area, but hadn't previously had reason to look for its exact location.

Now it was Tuesday and Logan was headed to the council meeting, but first he stopped at the Little Free Library to make sure Lucy had found the note he'd left yesterday. He'd asked her to meet him—well, to meet Gatsby's Ghost—on the back deck at the Waterway Café and promised her he'd be there this time. He'd had to make the time 9:00 p.m. to account for the council meeting, so he hoped that hadn't turned her off. He'd chosen a place that was still public enough to make her feel safe, but also afforded a little privacy. And he'd asked Mildred to have champagne waiting at the table and not to seat anyone around them. She'd agreed to keep secret who'd set up the reservation. Mildred didn't know the whole story, but she was so excited about the prospect of Logan and Lucy ending up together that she said she didn't need to know anything more.

As he walked up the steps to city hall, Logan thought about how defeated he'd felt just a week ago as he stood in this same place with Lucy. Tonight, Doug and Helen were first on the agenda so they could present their evidence before the big vote. Worst-case scenario, they'd halt the sale long enough to come up with alternatives. Best-case scenario, Turner would want no part of the legal battle to develop on top of what Doug was pretty sure were the burial grounds of indigenous peoples.

Logan had also secured a spot on the agenda at the last minute so he could present his new idea for the waterfront and also ask for preliminary approval to reinstate the library at its new location at Hill House. Mayor Jenkins had already blessed everything the day before, so it was just up to the council to approve it.

He spotted Lucy sitting on a row near the front as soon as he walked in, her back to the door as she chatted with Pam and Pete. Her hunched shoulders indicated she'd come to witness what she thought was the inevitable vote to sell the waterfront property to former councilman, Dan Turner.

Pete saw him first and nudged Lucy, nodding in Logan's direction. When she turned, the wide-eyed surprise on her face quickly turned into a smile. He wanted to run across the room —jump over chairs if he had to—grab her and spin her around. They could still win this thing.

But he didn't even get the chance to walk over to her

because Helen and Doug quickly descended upon him asking for help setting up the slideshow.

As he passed Lucy's row, she whispered, "What are you doing?"

"You'll see." He gave her a big smile. He couldn't wait for her to see his presentation, to tell her about her role in it all.

By the time Logan got the slideshow set up, Mayor Jenkins was calling the meeting to order. The mayor was the only person other than Doug and Helen who knew why they were on the agenda. He'd advised that catching Turner off guard at the meeting was the best way to get a vote in their favor tonight and halt the idea of selling the marina to the developer.

Helen and Doug presented everything flawlessly. They'd decided Helen had more credibility with the town than Logan, so Logan let them lead the way. He turned in his seat from the front row several times during the presentation to gauge Lucy's reaction. At first, she'd looked confused, a tiny line appearing between her eyebrows as she tried to piece together what was happening. As Doug closed out, however, he saw the realization in her eyes. Doug was detailing how the area would have to be excavated carefully and cataloged before any development could proceed and how the Florida courts had already ruled in similar cases that development would be prohibited. Lucy burst into a smile then and looked to him and tilted her head as if she was trying to piece it all together.

Logan knew before Doug finished that Turner was out. He'd walked up to the clerk to the right of the council and whispered quickly before leaving the chambers. Logan was sitting on the far right of the front row and caught the whole exchange. Turner had taken his item off the agenda without a fight. Logan nearly pumped his fist in the air, but thought that might be a little unprofessional. He still had to give his presentation.

Mayor Jenkins flipped on his mic after Doug and Helen packed up their things and returned to their seats.

"The clerk has informed me that the next item has been stricken from the agenda."

Whispers erupted across the crowd as several council members leaned to their neighbors. The mayor banged his gavel.

"As many of you know, we expected to entertain an offer from Mr. Turner this evening, and the council was prepared to vote on the sale of the waterfront property after failing to develop our own viable plan for the land. However, with Mr. Turner's item off the agenda, we'll also remove the vote from the agenda." He motioned to the clerk to indicate she should make the necessary update in her document.

"Next, we have a presentation from Mr. Lancaster. Although he is no longer under contract with the city, he's asked to present a new plan for the waterfront"—he looked to Logan and then cleared his throat—"and other matters for consideration."

Logan appreciated that the mayor hadn't stolen his thunder on the library news. In a small town like this, it was a miracle the few people who knew had managed to keep it under wraps for even a couple days.

Fueled by Lucy's warm brown eyes and gentle smile in the audience, he gave his presentation. Along with the ideas that had had support before—the open-air seafood market, paddleboard and small watercraft rentals, and food kiosks, all of which could be set up without disturbing the area with the shell middens—he shared his new idea. He wanted the city to consider spending a little money to make even more money. He'd run the numbers and provided the council members with copies, and was suggesting they could buy a small fleet of three boats to use for ferry service to nearby islands, sunset cruises, eco tours, and more. It wouldn't take long to get up and running, and it didn't present environmental concerns like the cruise ships they'd considered. He'd also worked with Helen to design a small amphitheater along the water that would repurpose natural materials and not require any major construction, and the city could rent it for small concerts, plays, and other entertainment.

Councilwoman Gilbert asked him the question he'd been waiting for when he finished running through the particulars.

"Mr. Lancaster, as you so bluntly informed us when you were working for the town, we have a history as a city of doing a poor job acting as landlord or running extraneous business operations. What makes you think we could take all this on?"

Logan began flipping through the financial package in front of him. "If you could all please turn to page four."

As he waited for everyone to flip through their packets, he looked up at Lucy and smiled. He couldn't wait to see her reaction to this next part. It would tell him everything he needed to know.

Looking back to the council, who all seemed to have found the right page, he continued. "Line item nine is the salary for a director of external operations. I've factored that number into the budget projections because I do think you need to hire someone to run these new ventures." He cleared his throat. "And I think that person should be me."

Logan caught a satisfied smile on Mayor Jenkins's face as the council members began to confer with one another quietly. He held his breath as he turned to see Lucy's reaction. He couldn't remember wanting something so badly since he'd seen the thick USC envelope in his mailbox that signified he was leaving the farm for big-city life.

Now, he couldn't imagine anything that would make him happier than settling down in this tiny town and sailing off into the sunset with Lucy Sullivan. Her hand was covering her mouth, and tears were shining in her eyes. When she dropped her hand, a smile lit up her face and he was finally able to exhale.

But he wasn't finished yet. After the council said they'd take his proposal into consideration, he spoke again.

"I have one more proposal for the town. It's more of a formality, actually." He glanced back at Lucy, who was tilting her head again, probably trying to guess what was next. "I've entered into an agreement with the Heron Isle Historic Foundation to purchase the historic Hill House on Fifth Street. We'll be fully restoring the house to serve as the town's library and repository for the foundation's historical documents. I'm here tonight to ask that you allow us to use the name from the original library since the town technically owns the name."

No one bothered to whisper anymore. Everyone in the room seemed to be talking all at once, but he only cared about one person's reaction. Pam had an arm around Lucy's shoulders and was squeezing her while they talked excitedly. Then Lucy looked up with tears sliding down her cheeks, even as she smiled the biggest, brightest smile he'd ever seen. He thought he would burst if he didn't get to wrap his arms around her very soon.

The council agreed to consider this proposal, but Mayor Jenkins had already told him that that part of his plan would be a piece of cake. The town would gladly allow someone else to take up the library if it didn't rely on any funding from its coffers, which he'd clearly spelled out in the proposal in their hands.

The remainder of the meeting felt as if it lasted hours, but was barely more than twenty minutes. Lucy was out of her seat and at his side before the mayor had even turned off his mic.

"I don't know what to say." Her eyes were glassy. She was shaking her head so hard her earrings made a jingling sound that reminded him of the bells on her store's front door. "When did you come up with all this?"

Before he could answer, others were stopping by to slap him on the back and thank him for continuing to fight for the waterfront. Doug and Helen had made sure the crowd knew it was Logan's idea to look for the shell middens.

"Let's go outside." He put a hand on the small of her back and guided her toward the doors at the back of the room. The feel of her skin under her thin blouse made all his muscles go tight, his jaw clenching as he fought the urge to turn her around and kiss her right then and there. He dropped his hand and immediately missed the contact with her.

Once they were outside, he gave her a quick rundown of everything that had happened since the last meeting—the trip to Boston, Fuller's idea about the shell middens, calling Gladys, meeting Sidney at Helen's house—everything except how the book she'd left for Gatsby's Ghost had led him straight to what he needed to save the waterfront. He'd tell her that soon enough.

"I can't believe you did all that. So now you're staying? Here on Heron Isle?" She looked up at him through her thick lashes.

He longed to touch her again, to put a hand behind her head and pull her in close to kiss her. Swallowing hard, he remembered she still didn't know everything. One last hurdle stood between him and everything he wanted in life.

"Looks that way." He smiled, stuffing his hands in his pockets to keep from reaching out to touch her.

"But I thought you wanted to move to Boston? Isn't there some big job there?"

"There is." He shrugged. "But I don't want it. I found everything I need here." He searched her eyes, hoping she could read between the lines.

A small smile was playing on Lucy's lips when she suddenly jumped and looked at her watch.

"I'm so sorry. I have to go. I promised to meet someone. I—" She looked sheepish suddenly.

"Well, don't let me keep you." He motioned toward the street. "We'll catch up later. I need to talk to some people anyway."

She hesitated before going down the stairs, as if she was debating whether she should go.

"Hey, let me ask you something." He had to do this. "If we'd met some other way, if we hadn't been fighting on opposite sides of this waterfront thing for so long, do you think maybe... I don't know. Do you think you would have said yes if I'd asked you out for a drink?"

Looking down at her shoe as she tapped the toe against the stair above the one she was standing on, she bit her lip. Seconds felt like minutes before she looked up at him again, giving him a small smile.

"I'm sorry. I've gotta go. I'm supposed to meet him in a few minutes."

With that, she scrambled down the stairs and hurried off to meet Gatsby's Ghost.

THIRTY

Lucy

Earlier in the day she'd been excited to finally meet Gatsby's Ghost. But now as she walked the few short blocks to the Waterway Café, she couldn't stop thinking about Logan.

He'd pulled off a miracle by stopping the sale of the waterfront. Then he'd said he wanted to stay on Heron Isle. Did that have anything to do with her and the moment they'd shared before he left for Boston? And he was going to restore Hill House and open a library! It was better than any fairy tale she'd ever read, but she couldn't help thinking that in a fairy tale she would have gotten the guy too.

Maybe she still could. When she watched Taylor get engaged to Jack on the beach Friday night, it made her believe that maybe someday she'd find a great love too. Then she'd gotten Gatsby's Ghost's letter the next day and thought maybe it would be now. Maybe their letters in the Little Free Library weren't just a plot for her book that she'd fictionalized into a romcom. Maybe it would be a real story they'd tell their kids one day.

But she couldn't stop thinking about Logan, about what he'd asked her after the meeting. Had he been asking her on a date? It was hard to tell with the question all wrapped up in the what-ifs. But he said he'd found everything he needed on Heron Isle. Did that include her?

She was too curious about Gatsby's Ghost not to go to the café. Gatsby's Ghost understood her on a level she couldn't explain. He knew exactly what she needed to hear when she needed to hear it. She had to know who he was.

And yet, all she really wanted to do was run back and tell Logan yes. But there'd be tomorrow. She didn't have to figure out everything tonight.

She arrived at the restaurant, and Mildred greeted her as if she had been expecting her.

"Right this way, my dear. He asked me to seat you on the back deck. I made sure you have plenty of privacy." The older woman winked at her.

"Wait, you know who I'm meeting?" Lucy walked faster to catch up with Mildred. "Who is it? Do you know him? Do *I* know him?"

Mildred shook her head. "All I did was save the table."

True to her word, no one else was seated on the deck. This time of year, it was too humid and buggy for people to want to eat outside, but now that it was later in the evening the breeze off the water had eliminated both.

Mildred pointed to a table with a bucket of champagne and two glasses so recently filled they were still frosty. She gave her a quick smile and went back inside before Lucy could ask more.

Lucy positioned herself at the table so she could see the door into the restaurant. She wanted to see who was coming so she could prepare herself. With the restaurant situated to her left, the deck was surrounded on its other three sides by the docks that stretched out over the waterfront. This late on a weeknight, the only sounds were the lapping of the water against the boat hulls and in the distance the faint sound of waves crashing on the nearby beach. It might have lulled her to sleep if she wasn't so anxious.

After a minute of tucking and untucking her hair behind her ear, Lucy pulled out a compact from her purse and reapplied her lip gloss. She still had a few minutes before their meeting time. Surely, he was going to show up this time after he'd gone to all the trouble to set this up with Mildred.

She nearly jumped out of her skin when a familiar voice came from behind her.

"Is this seat taken?"

He stepped around her and into the glow of the light from inside the restaurant. Logan.

She looked around to see if anyone else was approaching from the other side of the deck, which was accessible from the docks.

"Did you follow me? My friend is supposed to be here any minute."

"Lucy." He paused and took in a deep breath, then he held out a hand. "I need to tell you something."

Had he come to ask her not to meet Gatsby's Ghost? To confess his feelings and explain what he was trying to tell her before on the steps? Looking around again and seeing no one else coming from the docks or from inside, she placed her hand in his and let him pull her up to stand in front of him.

An electric current shot up her arm and filled her entire body. When he didn't let go, she didn't either. Staring into his green eyes, she willed him to say the words, to say he had feelings for her.

Then she noticed his other hand behind his back. As he

moved it, she realized he was holding something. He brought it into the light, and she saw it was the last book she'd left Gatsby's Ghost, the one on the history of the area.

Why did he bring a book? And that particular book?

"I left that book—"

He placed a finger gently over her lips. "In the Little Free Library for Gatsby's Ghost. I know."

She pulled her hand from his and took a step back.

"I don't understand. Why do you have it?" She looked around again, but no one else was approaching. The restaurant was nearly empty now except for the lone bartender and one lady seated at the bar.

Logan opened the book and took out something. He dropped a pile of index cards and notebook paper on the table. As her eyes darted over it all, she recognized her handwriting. It was all the notes she'd left for Gatsby's Ghost.

She whipped her head back toward him and searched his face.

He looked serious now, afraid.

Did this mean *Logan* was Gatsby's Ghost? She replayed every book, every letter, the night on the bench when Gatsby's Ghost stood her up and Logan appeared. Had it really been him all along?

She could barely get the words out. "Y-You're Gatsby's Ghost?"

He pressed his lips together, looking more unsure of himself than she'd ever seen him, and slowly nodded.

There were so many questions running through her head, she wasn't sure which one to ask first.

"And you knew it was me? That I was Island Girl all along?" She remembered how he'd found her that day on the bench and immediately shifted from confusion to anger. "That day on the benches—you let me think I'd been stood up rather than tell me the truth?"

He reached out now, touching her arm gently.

"No. I swear to you I didn't know then. I didn't get your letter until later. Someone took it by mistake and returned it with an apology note. I swear I would never do that to you."

She was calculating days in her head as she took a small step back.

"But that still means you've known for nearly two weeks." Dinner with his sister flashed through Lucy's mind. "And you let me tell you and your sister all about my book idea." She rubbed at her temple, her mind racing to grasp the timeline. "I feel so foolish."

"I'm sorry, Lucy. If I could go back, I would have told you as soon as I found the letter. But I thought I was leaving as soon as the job here was complete. After you told me about your fiancé, I didn't want to be one more person who left you." He sighed and ran a hand through his hair. "But then I realized I couldn't leave you." His green eyes pleaded with her. "Lucy, I never want to leave you again. Or this place." He gestured around, indicating the island.

She looked back down at the letters. She thought of all the advice he'd given her all summer long, both as Logan and as Gatsby's Ghost. She thought about how much her life had changed in the course of a couple of months.

She'd gotten the call this morning that she had been preliminarily approved for the loan on the building. This week, Leona was auctioning off her book to the highest bidder. They'd won the battle for the waterfront, and even the library was coming back. And she wasn't sure any of it would have happened without Logan—the real version of him, the pen-pal version, the guy who fought to preserve the middens and historic houses.

Everywhere she looked, she saw Logan.

He'd taken a step closer, and as the wind shifted, she caught a whiff of his familiar cologne. She hadn't even realized she was crying until his hand cradled her head, his thumb sweeping across her cheekbone to wipe away a tear.

"Don't cry, Island Girl. I never want to make you cry."

A tiny voice in her head told her she should feel betrayed. That she should be angry. He'd known she was Island Girl for weeks and hadn't said. But Annie had always told her that actions spoke louder than words.

Carter had said all sorts of wonderful words, but what had he done in the end? He'd chosen a job over her.

But Logan? He'd saved the waterfront, Hill House, and the library. All for her. And it had been him—as Gatsby's Ghost—who taught her to believe in herself again and to take chances.

She let herself smile through her tears.

"They're happy tears." She nodded. "I'm so happy it's you."

Logan smiled before placing his other hand on the opposite side of her head and tilting her face up toward his. He leaned closer and gently kissed a tear falling down her cheek, his warm lips igniting something deep within her.

When his lips finally met hers, she could have sworn she heard fireworks over the water. His lips were soft at first, his hand stroking her hair, but then the kiss deepened, and he pulled her body firmly against his.

Like magnets locking together, she couldn't imagine being able to pull away as she savored every second of his mouth on hers and the tender way he held her.

Later, as they held up their glasses to toast the waterfront, her book deal, the new library, and a brand-new beginning, Lucy realized she had everything she'd ever wanted and that for the first time in her life she wasn't afraid of losing any of it.

EPILOGUE

Lucy
One Year Later

When Lucy opened the door and walked into the Little Free Library, she found an envelope addressed to *Island Girl* in Logan's now familiar handwriting. Shaking her head, she couldn't help but smile. They still enjoyed leaving books for each other with little notes in the Little Free Library. Lucy felt the same fluttering in her chest each time she opened the library as she had when it all began a year ago.

Logan had hinted that she should visit the library today after work, and the curiosity nagged at her all day through the children's reading hour and a handful of afternoon customers. Summer was just beginning, and the store was busier with each passing day. Even though she now had a fully operating online store that brought in as much revenue as the physical store, she was still excited each time the bells on the front door jingled and a potential customer walked inside. She loved helping people find the exact book they wanted, and sometimes she even helped them find the book they didn't know they needed.

Flipping over the envelope, she noticed a tag taped to the back that said, "*Open Me.*" It looked like the tags from the movie *Alice in Wonderland* that said things like "Drink Me" and "Eat Me." What was he up to?

Running a finger under the seal on the envelope, she took out the note.

Island Girl,

"Every adventure requires a first step."–Cheshire Cat

Meet me at the library.

Gatsby's Ghost

Lucy broke into a wide smile. Logan had remembered that *Alice's Adventures in Wonderland* was her favorite book.

In the nearly twelve months they'd been together, he'd proven to be incredibly thoughtful and attentive, taking note of things she said she liked and surprising her with a favorite meal or the earrings she'd seen in the jewelry store window when she least expected it.

The grand opening for the new library was still a week away, and Logan hadn't allowed her inside in weeks. He'd said he wanted the final product to be a surprise. She loved his enthusiasm for the library, and she couldn't wait to see what he'd done with the old Hill House.

Lucy practically skipped across the town square on her

way to the newly renovated building that would now be the town library, thanks to Logan and his friend Cameron. When she arrived, another tag dangling from the door handle caught her attention. "*Open Me.*"

The door creaked as she turned the handle and pushed it open. The formal living room and dining room sat on each side of the entryway, and the walls were covered in floor-to-ceiling bookshelves. A small desk sat in what had previously been the dining room to her right and would be occupied by Rosalie, a librarian Lucy had worked with in Ocala. She still couldn't believe one of her best friends from her time as a librarian had moved to Heron Isle to run the library. Rosalie had moved into her new place last week, and they'd picked up right where they left off, as if no time had passed.

Lucy was so busy taking in everything around her, she nearly missed what was sitting on the desk a few feet ahead: A single flute of champagne with a tag that read "*Drink Me.*" Picking up the glass, she looked around again.

"Logan?"

She didn't hear anything or anyone in the house. As she walked toward the back where two more rooms were filled with books, she saw a piece of paper in the shape of an arrow on the floor. "*Follow Me.*"

Following a second arrow down a hallway into what had been a bedroom, she looked back over her shoulder for Logan and called his name again. When she got no response, she wandered around the room looking at the books that filled the shelves lining all four walls. She was about to give up and go looking for Logan when she noticed a book sticking out from the others. It was a hardbound book with a tag hanging from the top of the spine that said, "*Read Me.*"

She looked around the room again. Where was Logan? Was there a camera somewhere and he was watching her reaction to the surprise? He did love his gadgets and had recently installed cameras in her bookstore. When he'd first brought them in, she told him people didn't break into stores on Heron Isle, and she was pretty sure no one had ever stolen from her. But then he said the cameras were so they could watch the cats from anywhere, and they could post the live feed on her website so visitors to the store could keep tabs on Lizzy and Alice even after they left town. He'd been right. Her customers loved the Kitty Cam feature on the new website Logan had somehow found time to build between running the city's new tour boats and other waterfront businesses and getting the library building restored and ready to open.

She set down her champagne and pulled the book off the shelf. Footsteps approached behind her just as she opened the book only to discover it wasn't a book at all. Instead, it was one of those books that held an open space inside for storage. Wedged into the navy-blue velvet that filled the opening in the center was a sparkling princess-cut diamond flanked by sapphires on either side—the ring she'd seen in Rothchild's with Jack.

Her mouth dropped open and she turned to find Logan behind her on one knee. His green eyes sparkling and his one-thousand-watt smile beaming, he asked the question she'd dreamed of hearing since he moved the last of his things into his rental house on Heron Isle.

"Lucy Sullivan, will you marry me?"

Tears spilled down her cheek as he took the book from her hands and plucked out the ring. He reached for her left hand, and she placed it in his, trembling as she put her right hand over her mouth. He'd barely gotten the ring on her finger before she pulled him up to wrap both arms around his neck.

"Yes. A million times yes."

"Good, because I've already decided on our honeymoon." He laughed as he wrapped his arms around her waist.

She scrunched her eyebrows together. "We don't even have a wedding date yet, and you're planning the honeymoon?"

"I think it's time someone finally made it to Paris."

She squealed with joy, jumping up and down in his arms. He had just lowered his lips to hers when she heard the front door open and voices started spilling inside. She pulled away, curious who had arrived.

"Mm, one more." His voice was low and deep, his desire for her turning her insides to mush. He pulled her back in for a longer kiss, ignoring the familiar voices calling out their names up front.

She'd never felt happier or safer in her entire life.

Leaning back, he looked down at her, his green eyes locked on hers in a way that said he wished they were alone.

"Okay, so I'm rethinking inviting everyone."

Someone called her name from up front, and he laughed.

"Your public awaits." Motioning toward the front of the house, he took her hand in his and pulled her into the hall.

The front entryway was filled with their friends. Pete held Milly, who barked when she saw Lucy, Frank by his side beaming. Pam, Bob, Mildred, Marty—her friends clapped and cheered as she and Logan walked down the hall toward them, yelling out their congratulations.

"Show us the ring!" Pam exclaimed as she stepped forward from the group to hug Lucy.

Lucy had barely looked at the ring herself, so she admired it as she held out her hand and everyone surrounded her. She'd completely forgotten she had ever mentioned to Logan that sapphires were her favorite stone, but of course he remembered. He was always surprising her like that.

As she looked around at the group, she couldn't help wishing Taylor could be here too. It was moments like this when she missed her the most, but Lucy had just seen her in Nashville a few weekends prior when she and Logan went for a weekend getaway before the busy season. She couldn't wait to call and tell her she was engaged.

No sooner had she thought it than Taylor rushed through the front door with Jack on her heels. Seeing the look of surprise on Lucy's face, Taylor stopped in front of her and put her hands on her hips.

"You didn't think I was going to miss this, did you?"

Bursting into a smile, Lucy hugged her best friend. Taylor had promised that moving to Nashville wouldn't change their friendship, and she'd kept her word. Lucy had visited a couple times—Logan had convinced her to hire someone to help at the store—and Taylor was back frequently for brides who flew her in to do hair and makeup for them and their bridesmaids.

Looking around the room, Lucy couldn't believe how much her life had changed in a year.

Even more, she couldn't believe how much all the change had improved her life. Her store was doing better than ever, and she was officially the owner of a historic building down-town. She was engaged to the man who'd saved the Heron Isle waterfront from development. And in just a few months, she'd be a published author. Leona had secured her a two-book deal and a very healthy advance at the auction—which, thankfully, her former editor, Sarah, had won for the new publishing house where she'd been hired.

Standing at her side, Logan squeezed her hand. As she looked around at all the people who'd come to celebrate their engagement, she vowed never again to say she had no family. Friends were the family a person chose, and she'd chosen well. She was surrounded by people who had believed in her until she'd figured out how to believe in herself.

She had always been enough. They'd always known it, and now she did too.

A Letter from Savannah

Hello!

Thank you so much for choosing my novel, *The Library of Second Chances*. I hope this book sent you on a mental vacation to beautiful Heron Isle for a little Vitamin Sea.

If you'd like to know when my next book is out, you can **sign up for new Harpeth Road release alerts for my novels here:**

www.harpethroad.com/savannah-carlisle-newsletter-signup

I won't share your information with anyone else, and I'll only email you a quick message whenever new books come out or go on sale.

If you did enjoy *The Library of Second Chances*, I'd be so thankful if you'd write a review online. Getting feedback from readers helps to persuade others to pick up my book for the first time. It's one of the biggest gifts you could give me.

Until next time,
Savannah

Acknowledgments

Wow! If you made it here, that means you've read my book. So, first and foremost, I'm so thankful to you, dear reader! Thank you for taking a chance on my debut.

This book would not have been possible if not for many years of guidance and support from Jenny Hale. When I found out she was starting her own publishing company, I knew I wanted to publish a book with her. I wrote the first draft of this novel with Harpeth Road in mind, but it's still surreal to actually be publishing it with Jenny and Harpeth Road. Jenny, I will never forget your advice and kindness over the years. I hope this is the first book of many together!

Many thanks also to the incredible editors I worked with at Harpeth Road—Elizabeth Mazer, Nicky Lovick, Lauren Finger and Liz Hurst—who took my unpolished manuscript and worked their magic to make it the book it is today. It is no doubt better thanks to your keen eyes and wonderful ideas.

And to my fabulous cover designer, Kristen Ingebretson. They say people judge books by their cover, so thank you for a gorgeous cover that has no doubt attracted more than one reader.

To my husband Chadd, thank you for listening to everything from my story ideas to my editing rants. I'm lucky to have someone who understands keeping unconventional working hours, writing and editing on vacation, the stress of deadlines and more. Thank you for always supporting all my crazy ambitions!

A huge debt of gratitude goes to one of my best friends,

Maggie Norris. She has read drafts of more than one manuscript over the years, sometimes multiple versions. I can always count on her to give honest feedback, and I know my stories are better because of her. Who knew talking her into becoming a cheerleader with me in college would lead to so many years of her being *my* cheerleader.

To Stephanie, my Twinny, your unwavering encouragement for my dream of becoming a novelist is appreciated more than you know. Thank you for brainstorming titles with me and encouraging me every step of the way.

I am incredibly lucky to have found so many wonderful friends who have supported my writing ambitions for so many years. Teresa, Michelle, Starlett, and Allyse: thank you for believing I could do this and always asking for updates. I couldn't ask for better friends!

This book wouldn't be what it is without the advice of fellow author Jessica Lepe. Jessica chose my manuscript during Kiss Pitch in 2022 and helped make it the best book it could be before I went out on submission. She has her own *Shop Around the Corner/You've Got Mail*-inspired story out this year, so don't miss *Flirty Little Secret*!

Kiss Pitch mentees of 2022, thank you for all the love and support! Getting mentored was only half the prize of being selected. You ladies were the other half!

Speaking of other authors who've helped me along the way, a big shout out to several who have answered my questions and showed me kindness over the years: Debbie Cromack, Wendy Wax, Alys Murray, Allison Winn Scotch and Meredith Schorr. Thank you, ladies!

Savannah Gilbo and Linda Camacho both gave me invaluable feedback on my submission package. Then Linda and Bryn Donovan helped me make some big decisions when I had agent and publisher offers on the table with this one. The ability to get advice from two people who are so experienced and well respected in this industry is not something I take for granted. I appreciate you ladies so much!

To my brother, the *The Care Bears Adventures in Wonderland* reference is for you. Mom and dad, you already got the dedication!

For those who don't know me, I won the mother-in-law lottery. Jane, thank you for all your encouragement and support. I know this isn't going to be your kind of book (because no one has been kidnapped or murdered), but that you'll read it anyway because you're the best. I started this book on one of our ski trips, so you've been part of it from the very beginning!

I also have some amazing aunts who've cheered me along on this journey and are always asking for updates. Thank you Shug, Luder Belle, Nank, Mary Ann and Judy! Also Gail—I'm adopting you as an aunt too! And to my cousin Peanut, thank you for cheering me along.

www.ingramcontent.com/pod-product-compliance
Lightning Source LLC
Chambersburg PA
CBHW022021310726
48972CB00006B/1751